Olympus, Indiana

Mike Ball

Olympus, Indiana
Copyright © 2015 by Michael Ball
All rights reserved.

Visit our Web site at
http://learnedsofar.com
for more information.

ISBN: 978-0-914303-23-7 (paperback)
ISBN: 978-0-914303-22-0 (eBook)

Cover and Layout by Stark Artisan Design
Published by Glendower Media

This book is dedicated to everyone who ever wondered what it would be like to hang out with the Greek Gods. You know who you are...

Also to my family, who have had to spend most of their lives listening to me talk about stuff like what it would be like to hang out with the Greek Gods.

Acknowledgements

I would like to take a few minutes to thank some of the people who have helped me bring this book into the world:

My wife Nancy, my son Patrick, his beautiful wife Shannon, who put up with it when they show up as characters in my work. And our incredibly wonderful granddaughter Caelyn, who seems to love her Papa and all the silly things I come up with.

Scott Lorenz, my publicist, my most trusted colleague, my dear friend, and my indoor skydiving buddy. Don't ask.

My hard-working Editors, Yvonne Lorenz and Tom Saunders, along with my advance readers and advisors, Pam, Xanthe, Jennie, Nancy, Leslie, Other Pam, and Anna. You guys are the only reason this book is not riddled with chain link mustard seed carport sandbox, as well as typos.

Leslie Banks, my graphic designer, who not only made all this look good, but who even pays attention to my cover ideas.

Jennie's daughter Chloe, who grabbed her sword and became my Angie for the book cover.

And all my readers, who always seem to understand the fun in all of it.

Foreword

First off, if you are one of those people who goes running off at the drop of a hat to check with Google to see if something's real or not, you probably already know that there is a place in Southern Indiana called Mount Olympus. To quote the source of all human knowledge – Wikipedia – "Mount Olympus is an unincorporated community in Washington Township, Gibson County, Indiana. It was formerly called Ennes. A post office called Ennes operated from 1879 until 1883."

I'm sure that Mount Olympus, formerly Ennes, is very nice, in that it has its own Denny's, along with a bar called the Log Inn. Nevertheless, this book is not about that particular place.

The Olympus, Indiana in this book is a town consisting of 9,314 people, located west of Indianapolis, a little bit north of Terre Haute. It has one bank, two filling stations, one barber shop, three beauty parlors, one funeral home, a second-run theater, five craft boutiques, a small drug store with a non-functioning soda fountain, a real estate office, and a hotel.

The town also shares an elementary school, a middle school, a high school, a Walmart, a Home Depot, a McDonalds, a Starbucks, and seven CVS pharmacies with the neighboring and slightly smaller town of Sparta.

By far the most interesting thing about Olympus, Indiana is the hotel, called the Delphi. It is a very old building which occupies nearly half a block in the center of town on a Main Street widened for diagonal parking by order of the Planning Commission and Olympus City Council.

The hotel has 30 rooms on three floors, a small lobby, and a combination bar and restaurant, also called the Delphi. On the particular day when this story began, the hotel had six guests, all Hoosier senior citizens who generally paid the very modest rent on their very modest rooms each month immediately after cashing their very modest Social Security checks. Nine more rooms were occupied by the owners of the hotel. This left fifteen empty rooms to accommodate any travelers who might, for some reason, happen to want to spend a night a little bit west of Indianapolis and north of Terre Haute.

For the purposes of this story, my Olympus has one huge advantage over that other town, a little further south, Mount Olympus – it's not real. Since I made up the town and all the people in it, I can do pretty much anything I want to with it, and with them. Luckily for everybody concerned, it turns out that I'm a fairly nice guy.

Now, this story has a lot of Greek Gods in it. If you for some reason happen to be familiar with Greek mythology, you shouldn't have any trouble sorting them all out.

If not, I apologize in advance; just about everybody's name starts with "A," except for Zeus, whose name obviously starts with "Z," and Hephaestus, whose name nobody can pronounce, or spell, or even remember, so I say the hell with him, and a couple of others.

If you happen to be one of those mythology-challenged folks, you will find a handy Appendix at the back of the book that lists all the Gods and some basic facts about each of them. Although to be fair, some of that material also came from Wikipedia, and the rest I just made up, so I really wouldn't rely on it too much to resolve arguments with your carpool buddy who happens to be a scholar of antiquities.

In any case, welcome to Olympus, Indiana.

One

Are they awake?

Yes. For nearly a year.

Where are they?

They're in an Olympus located in a very rural part of a place called Indiana.

What is Indiana?

It's a place where the major industries are raising hogs and drinking beer.

I understand.

You do?

No. Does what they're doing in this Indiana place involve hogs or beer?

You know what they're doing. They are becoming.

Becoming what?

Right. What.

Will they?

1

Will they what?

What?

Seriously?

Yes. Possibly.

Really?

Maybe not.

Still, it should be entertaining to watch them try.

Morning in the Delphi

Zeus sat on a stool at the bar in the Delphi, leaning on one elbow. A large ceiling fan turned slowly above his head, barely moving the molasses-thick July air. Morning sunlight streamed through the windows across the room behind him, throwing the hard shadows of the empty tables onto the ancient hardwood floor. At that moment the only occupants of the bar were Zeus and a fair-sized cockroach.

Zeus rubbed the stubble of salt-and-pepper beard on his chin and watched the cockroach scamper past his coffee mug, across the top of the bar, and behind the sugar bowl. *If I can just concentrate hard enough...* A wave of the hand, and Blammo! Smoking cockroach-sized pile of ashes.

Zeus was not a young man, but he didn't really look like a guy who had been around for more than seven thousand years. He was tall, and a little bit broader across the shoulders than the shots of grey in his hair and the crinkles around the eyes might suggest. He was, however, beginning to develop a very un-Godlike paunch.

Zeus waved his hand experimentally and felt a familiar surge of electricity flicker across his fingertips. He raised his eyebrows, tilted his head, and flipped his fingers at the roach. With a sharp *crack,* a tiny blue spark shot sideways and hit the fork next to the scrambled eggs on his plate.

The cockroach, mildly interested, looked up from the bit of bacon grease it was exploring, wiggled its antennae, then got back to business. Zeus kept his fingers trained on the target, panning with every scurrying move and trying to work up another spark.

The street door opened and a blast of hot morning air washed through the room. A musical and slightly alcohol-tinged voice said, "Maybe you should shuffle your feet on the carpet, Z."

Zeus sighed, picked up the ketchup bottle, and slammed it down on the cockroach. "Good morning, Aphrodite," he said, picking up his fork. "Are you having a nice Walk of Shame? And there's no carpet in here."

Aphrodite limped gingerly to the bar, barely wearing a very short blood-red dress, carrying a pair of very high-heeled shoes, and shielding her very pale blue eyes from the morning light streaming in the front window. Golden ringlets of blonde hair surrounded and mostly obscured her face. A sort of golden glow radiated from her, penetrating the grey haze generated around her by dust from the street and a night of hard partying.

"You're a nasty old shit," she said, and kissed Zeus on the cheek. "How do you know I wasn't out all night looking for the Amulet?"

Zeus raised his eyebrows with interest. The Amulet was a bracelet that he had worn on his left wrist for thousands of years. It served as a sort of antenna that seemed to focus the Power of the Gods. It had not only kept him on the Throne of Olympus, the Amulet was the primary reason there even was a Throne of Olympus.

But then, right around the time Nero was lopping the heads off his first batch of Christians, Zeus lost the Amulet. He had been engaged in an aerial skirmish with Ares, the God of War, and thirty Stymphalian birds, fighting high in the air over what would a couple of millennia later become Southern Indiana. Ares was attempting to defeat Zeus and seize the Throne of Olympus – a fairly common pastime in those days.

Those scuffles always turned out pretty much the same; Zeus would blast his opponents with thunderbolts, then sentence them to a couple centuries of some sort of creative punishment. But while the battle itself had not been all that serious, losing the Amulet turned out to be. It fell into a thick forest, and no matter how long and hard Zeus and the other Gods searched, they never saw it again.

"So, were you out all night looking for the Amulet?" asked Zeus.

"No."

"Right." He pushed his plate in her direction. "Care for a greasy slice of bacon?"

"Not unless you'd care to see it come right back up again." She settled on the bar stool to his right, picked up his coffee mug and took a shuddering gulp.

"Rough night?"

"So-so. Did you know that guys these days wear clothing when they wrestle?"

"Yes, I did know that. Frankly, it's one of the things in this modern world for which I am profoundly grateful."

"Not me. And also, I found out that if you slip a little tequila into the Jäger Bombs, you can get a hog farmer to try ballet dancing."

"OK, so I didn't know that." He took the cup from her, grabbed a sip, and handed it back.

The door to the kitchen swung open and another woman backed through, every bit as radiant as Aphrodite, only her hair was dark brown. And she was a lot less hung-over. She was also less provocatively dressed, in jeans, a plain black t-shirt, and sneakers. She carried a coffee cup in one hand and a half-eaten bagel in the other. "Hi you two," she said. "So, how was the Walk of Shame this morning?"

"We've already covered that," said Zeus.

"Hi Athena," said Aphrodite. "Yeah, you know the guys around here. They like to get up early to sleep with their hogs."

"Slop," said Athena.

"What?"

"Slop. They don't "sleep with" the hogs, they "slop" the hogs."

"Is there a difference?" asked Aphrodite.

"I'm willing to bet some of them sleep with the hogs," said Zeus. "Last week I saw a pig playing a banjo."

"Ew," said Athena.

"I know, right?" said Aphrodite. "Banjos are gross. So, Z, when are we getting out of here? I want to live where I can enjoy some sea breeze."

"You want to live where you can enjoy some sea men," said Athena.

"That too. How about it, Z? Maybe Malibu? In fact, I hear there's a naval base in San Diego..."

"You know as well as I do that we're stuck here in Indiana until we can find that Amulet and cook up some Power."

"I still say we might want to whip up a few worshippers." Athena picked up the pitcher of coffee creamer, sniffed it, wrinkled her nose, then dropped it into a bus tray next to the sink behind the bar. "Some good old-fashioned praise and devotion might draw at least some Power back to us. I can't really say that I miss the entrails and burning goat meat all that much, but still..."

"I've been thinking about all that. Something must have happened to kick the Amulet back into gear – at least partly – or we'd still be whiling away centuries in Club Dream," Zeus waved a strip of bacon in the air, "instead of being Masters of this joint. But you have a point, Athena. If we could just get a few of the yokels around here to throw together a temple and grovel at the feet of our statues..."

"Yeah, talk like that and the people will surely arise and sing us hymns of adoration." Athena peeked under the ketchup bottle, shook her head, and tossed it and the last of her bagel into the bus tray. "You have to be nice to worshippers." She retrieved a rag and a spray bottle of disinfectant from behind the bar and went to work de-roaching the counter top.

Aphrodite, her head cradled in her arms, began to snore softly.

"Anyway, I've never been sure that worshippers are the answer," said Zeus. "We've been spinning our wheels here for ten months. If I can just find that damned Amulet, we'd be back like that..." He snapped his fingers in the air.

A bolt of blue flame shot up from his index finger to the ceiling fan, blasting the entire fixture into a cloud of dust.

"Well all right then,"said Athena, using her hand to shield her coffee from the falling debris. "I wasn't expecting that. What do you suppose that's all about?"

Zeus stared at his fingers. "I'm not sure. It could be it means that the Gods will once again ascend onto the heights of Olympus, and that I shall regain my seat on the supreme throne of the Cosmos! See, just a little while ago there was this bug by my coffee cup..."

"It means you better get Hephaestus to put up a new fan," said Aphrodite without opening her eyes. "And call the exterminator."

"Maybe you're right about those worshippers," said Zeus.

"I'm not so sure, Z," said Athena. "I mean, do you really think a Zeus cult would have popped up in the last ten minutes? In Indiana?"

Zeus rubbed his hands together and grinned up at the wires hanging from the hole in the scorched ceiling. "Well, wherever that came from, I have to admit, it felt good. Have you guys noticed any of your Power coming back?"

"I'm the Goddess of wisdom." Athena pursed her lips and followed Zeus' gaze up to the smoking hole. "So, based on the average intelligence in this room, I guess I am riding pretty high."

Aphrodite waved her hand weakly. "I got the great legs thing covered."

"Love," said Athena. "You're the Goddess of love. And beauty."

"Yeah, that too. Love and beauty. You gotta love these legs."

"Watch this!" Zeus pointed at a chair in the center of the room and snapped his fingers again. A faint puff of smoke rose from his hand with a tiny pop. "Damn," he said.

"You better not be trying to vaporize any of Hera's chairs," said Athena. Those things cost like twelve dollars each."

Zeus hopped off the bar stool. "I can't take it. I'm going out for a walk."

Athena stood up and began to clear the dishes off the bar. "Would you see if you can find Hermes and Hephaestus? We need to open this place for lunch in a couple of hours, and I could really use a bartender and a new ceiling fan."

Zeus grunted and walked out into the blistering southern Indiana morning.

Hephaestus

A shower of sparks exploded into the air, cascading over the stout, dark man in the oil-stained wife-beater tank top and leather apron. He didn't seem to notice that quite a few of the sparks were landing on his bare arms and shoulders. When Hephaestus was working, he didn't seem to notice much of anything.

He turned off the torch, took off his welding mask and stepped back, absentmindedly patting out a small fire smoldering in his dreadlocks. He wrinkled his mouth and squinted at the brand-new iron outhouse in front of him, its freshly-cut half moon still glowing from the torch. A haze of smoke hung in the air of the old stable in the alley behind the hotel.

"Is this what I think it is?" asked Zeus, standing in the open stable door.

"If you think it's a metal crapper, then yep, it is exactly what you think it is."

"And why are you making a metal crapper?"

"Well, when I looked at this pile of iron, it just kind of spoke to me. It said, 'Metal Crapper.'"

"Of course it did. Does it work?"

"I guess it would work if I was to put some plumbing in it. Or even just dig a hole." Hephaestus poked thoughtfully at the dirt floor with the toe of his boot.

"So, what's the point of making a... never mind. Anyway, if you can break away from your work of art here, would you please go over to the bar and put up a new ceiling fan? I accidentally blasted the old one with some lightning."

"No kidding? Where did you get lightning?"

"What do you mean, where did I get it? Since you didn't forge me a decently functional lightning bolt, I must have manifested it myself."

"Right. And I'll 'manifest' us a new ceiling fan, over at Home Depot."

Zeus sighed. "I was your king once," he said, "undisputed Lord of all Gods and men. There was a time when no one would dare mock me."

"You're still my king, Z. And I'm real happy about your lightning." Hephaestus grinned and gave Zeus an encouraging little chuck on the arm.

Zeus sighed again. "Thanks. So, do you need some cash to pick up the fan?"

"No, I'll just manifest the credit card." He noticed the look on Zeus' face "OK, sorry, that was uncalled for."

"Forget it. When you get to the bar, just tell the girls that I'll be back later this afternoon. Have you seen Hermes?"

"Not today."

"Well if you see him, chase him in to work. If he doesn't show up and Hera has to tend bar again today, she will not be fun to be around."

"When was my mother ever fun to be around?"

"OK, good point." Zeus took a last look at the iron outhouse, then shook his head and walked out of the stable, muttering to himself.

Hephaestus tossed his welding mask and gloves on the workbench behind him. So the Old Man conjured up some lightning on his own, he thought to himself. Interesting.

He scanned around the stable to make certain he was alone. Then he picked up a gnarled burl cane lying across the back of the workbench, turned back and tapped once on the outhouse door. A bell tone, pure, sweet, and deep filled the air. He tapped it again and a second tone, just as pure and exactly one octave higher, rang out.

He tapped it once more, and this time the sound was a dull thud, followed by a rasping sound as a door appeared in the side and creaked open to reveal a bronze staircase spiraling down into the earth. Hephaestus looked around one more time, then began to limp heavily down the stairs as the door creaked shut behind him.

At the bottom, the staircase emptied into a small cavern, lit by a softly glowing polished bronze door on the far wall. To the right of the door a tiny waterfall fell endlessly into a small pool lined with muddy clay, then trickled off in a miniature stream through a rat-sized hole carved by aeons of erosion through the stone wall.

The door was featureless except for an embossed imprint in the shape of Hephaestus' cane. He lifted the cane up to the impression, where it snapped into place, then silently rotated itself 90 degrees clockwise. The door swung inward with a hiss and a faint puff of golden smoke.

Hephaestus retrieved his cane, then hobbled through the door and into an enormous bronze-walled room filled with a dizzying collection of partially-completed clay sculptures, machines of every size and description, loose gears, piles of tangled cables and wires, tools, and heaps of scrap.

A golden light with no apparent source filtered down from above, through a cloud of dust that hovered in the air around Hephaestus' head. The far end of the room disappeared from sight in the haze and the distance.

He inhaled deeply, breathing in the rich blend of ancient grease, oil, burnt wood, ozone and metal dust that hung in the air.

Daddy's home!

Not too far from the door stood a vaguely person-shaped pillar of clay. Hephaestus stood silently and gazed at the pillar for a few moments, then went to work, his rough hands flying over the clay with surprising precision and tenderness.

As a face began to take shape, Hephaestus hummed in a deep baritone, seasoned with just a touch of the sound of gravel being crushed to sand. Then he began to sing:

Your eyes are crystal blue, my love
They're bluer than the sea,
And your hair, the color of the sun,
Lights up the world for me...

After nearly 30 minutes he stepped back to admire the cold, grey, but fairly accurate version of Aphrodite's face that looked back at him.

Lights up the world for me.

Hephaestus gave the statue a little pat in the vicinity of its eventual rear end, gave his cane a twirl, and said, "See you later, sweetheart."

On his way back toward the spiral staircase he remembered the ceiling fan for the bar. He stopped near a small pile of wood and metal and began to stir it with the tip of his cane, softly humming a new tune.

The shape of a fan blade began to emerge; then another; then two more. Eventually an entire ceiling fan unit rose from the pile and hovered about a foot above the floor. Hephaestus reached into a pocket on the front of his leather apron, fished out a small hammer and a screwdriver, and, still humming, bent over his creation to make a few final adjustments.

Satisfied, he dropped the tools back into his apron and found a scrap of wood in another pocket. He pressed it between his hands, then pulled it through his fingers, so that it emerged as a long strip of paper with a Home Depot logo at the top and the purchase details of one ceiling fan spelled out on the front.

Hephaestus smiled and used the toe of his boot to nudge the floating fan through the door, following along behind it. *Better put it on a dolly when I get it upstairs,* he thought. *Don't want to get anybody excited. Not just yet.*

Hermes

"Keep your eye on the cup with the pea. Which one has the pea? Now you see it, now you don't. Where's that darned pea?" Hermes shuffled the three cups with blinding speed, weaving them around the low coffee table in a baffling complex pattern.

A little girl with ginger hair sat in an over-stuffed beige leather chair across the table from Hermes in the hotel lobby, her face screwed up in concentration. "It's in your hand," she said.

"Um, no, Angie, I put the pea under one of these cups."

The little girl shook her head firmly. "Hermes, I saw you pick it up. You tried to fool me, but I saw you."

"Really? What are you, like a cop?"

She giggled. "It was easy."

"You little creep. Why aren't you in school?"

"It's summer."

"So why aren't you in some kind of day care? Or kid prison, or something. Don't they have kid prisons any more?"

"We can't afford day care since we had to buy a new furnace for the house last winter, and anyway, my mom says I'm getting old enough to take care of myself. Besides, she works right across the street. And besides besides, I saw you pick up the pea, Hermes. It's in your right hand."

"Really? Darn it, I guess I'm just not very good at this." He opened his right hand and handed her the pea. Then he lifted the middle cup, and hundreds of peas cascaded from it, across the table and onto the floor. Hermes set the cup upright, and the peas kept coming, overflowing the cup.

Angie giggled again and clapped her hands. "How are you doing that?" she squealed.

Hermes scratched his head and lifted the other two cups, releasing two more green avalanches of peas. "I'm not real sure," he said, "but it looks like we have our lunch here. If you like peas."

"Nobody likes peas," said Zeus, walking up. He caught a few peas as they fell from the table and examined them. "Not really, no matter what they tell you."

"Hey Z," said Hermes.

"Hi Mr. Z," said Angie. "Look at what Hermes can do!"

"Yes, I'm seeing it," said Zeus. "Believe me, I'm as impressed as you are. When did you pick up this little trick?"

"It's pretty simple," said Hermes. "I didn't actually create them, I just set up a simple trans-dimensional conduit from the bulk bin out at Walmart..." He spread his fingers and waved his hands above the table and the flow of peas came to a stop.

"It's magic," said Angie.

"Trans-dimensional conduit. Magic," said Hermes."Same thing."

"How long?"

"A few days. Maybe a week. I just started being able to add a little bit of zip to the sleight-of-hand I've been using on the drunks in the bar."

"I got some lightning this morning."

"Really? Cool! Smite anybody?"

"The ceiling fan in the bar."

"I never liked that ceiling fan. No respect for the Old Ways. I'd say it totally deserved a good smiting."

"It was an accident."

"Yeah, or that."

"Listen, I need you to get over to the bar. Ares is running the kitchen, Aphrodite is pretty used up from last night..."

"For once."

"... and Hera is going to pop a vein and go all wrathful if she doesn't have a bartender for the lunch crowd."

"What about the twins?"

"As far as I know, Artemis and Apollo are helping Ares with lunch prep."

"Can I help you in the bar?" asked Angie.

"Sure, you could help me mix the drinks," said Hermes "And you can pour shots. You're like 22 or 23, right?"

"I'm ten and two thirds, and you know it."

"Oh. In that case, it probably wouldn't work out. I'll see if we can whip you up some lunch, though. If it's all right with your mom. Or maybe you'd rather I just cook us up a couple plates full of these peas..."

"I'll go ask my mom if I can have lunch," she said, and scampered away.

"Ask your mom if she'd like to join us," Hermes called after her.

"Would her mom happen to be the attractive woman with the red hair who works at the bank?"

"That would be the one. Sarah Cashen, our loan officer."

"Widely known among our bar patrons as, 'Smokin' Hot Sarah.' So that explains the Mother Hermes Goose routine with the kid."

"Not at all! Well yeah, partly. But also I actually do enjoy the little squirt hanging around. Kids can be fun."

"Yeah, I'm going to take your word for that. So, getting back to the whole regaining our Godly abilities thing, have you noticed any other energy coming back?"

"Nothing I can think of. Just that I can whip up the occasional trans-dimensional portal."

"Well, let me know if you notice anything."

"You'll be the first to know. Actually, you'll be the second, because if I notice it then I'll be the first to know, and then..."

"Just clean up this mess and get over to the bar. Please?" Zeus turned to leave.

"Right. Want me to send the peas back?"

Zeus stopped. "It's really that easy for you?"

"It's just a little trans-dimensional..."

"A month ago you were palming cards and pretending to pull quarters out of customers' ears. Now you can port these back?"

Hermes flicked the fingers of his left hand at the peas. They rose into the air and began to swirl, forming a green vortex that danced playfully over the table. A black hole, not much larger than one of the peas, appeared in the air and seemed to draw the vortex into it, sucking the peas through with a series of staccato little pops. When the last one had vanished the hole faded away.

"Yep, apparently I can."

"And you sent them all back into the original container?" asked Zeus.

"Um, yeah. Sure. If by 'container' you mean the building."

"So all those peas just now dropped out of the air in Walmart and onto the floor?"

"I'd be willing to bet that's not the strangest thing they've seen over there today."

"Good point." Zeus turned back to the door. "Let me know if you get any more."

"Peas?"

"Power."

Lunch at the Delphi

A large copper sauce pan spiraled through the air in a lazy arc and crashed into the wall next to the dishwasher. "If I'd wanted a bleedin' dirty pot, I'd have asked for a bleedin' dirty pot," grumbled Ares, his hands clutched into fists of rage.

"Dirty and dented," said Athena, stepping over the fallen pan and setting a bus tray full of dishes on the cart by the dishwasher. "And when did you become a Cockney?"

"Who washed the pots last night?" asked Artemis, flipping two hamburger patties on the grill. "Oh, wait, was it, I don't know, Ares... you?"

Ares kept his eyes on the sauce pan, as if daring it to try to get up. "Somebody flippin' used it since I washed it last night."

"Nobody used your stupid sauce pan," said Athena. "Now, I need two gyros and a chef's salad, plus two cups of chowder."

"The bloody chowder would be ready if I had a bloody clean sauce pan."

"Seriously? The chowder's not ready? Damn, so I'm going to have to go back out there and talk the Wilsons into switching to chili."

"Bloody chili would be ready if I had..."

Athena grabbed a large iron skillet from an overhead hook and swung it in a looping upward arc, hard, connecting with Ares under the chin and nearly lifting him off his feet. He staggered back against the wall, his head bouncing off the tiles, then his legs buckled and he slid to the floor. He looked up at Athena with his eyebrows raised. "Whoa, nice one, Luv," he said, rubbing his jaw.

"Do I have your attention now?" She tossed the skillet on the counter.

"Right. I'll get some bleedin' soup started." He struggled to his feet, picked up his dented sauce pan and headed over to the sink to give it a quick wash-out. "I was thinking of using just a bit more coriander in the chowder this time."

"You really are a great cook. If only you weren't such a titanic jerk."

"Titanic, I get it. Like our Gramps. He was a bleedin' Titan." He grinned at Athena then stopped, reached into his mouth, pulled out a loose molar, tossed it into the trash can, and resumed his grin.

"From what I hear," said Artemis, "you actually are quite a bit like our grandfather. Except he wasn't a total idiot."

"Yeah, well, he did love a good scrap, didn't he," said Ares, chopping chowder ingredients in a blur of flashing steel and flying food. "Only he couldn't have been all that bleedin' smart, or our old man wouldn't have been able to do him in like he done."

"Cronus was plenty smart" said Athena. "It took everything Zeus could come up with to defeat him and set the others free. And then you had to screw around and lose the stupid Amulet."

"It weren't my fault," said Ares. "I were just helping me Mum take control of the Cosmos."

"Gods, that accent is annoying," said Athena, looking thoughtfully at the skillet on the counter.

"I heard about the thunderbolt this morning," said Artemis. "What do you think it means?"

"Zeus seems to think it might mean that there are some people worshipping us again, and that might be channelling some of the Power from the Amulet - wherever it is."

"I kind of miss having all them bloody little humans worshippin' me," said Ares. "But not as much as I miss seeing them slice each other up in all of them smashing great ground wars we used to have. There was this one time, at Troy it might of been, when these two blokes basically cut each other in half with their swords, right at the exact same time. Boy, did them fellas look surprised..."

"What do you think?" asked Artemis.

"I'm not sure," said Athena. "Where would worshippers even be coming from? We're slinging beers and baklava here. Not a lot of opportunities to inspire fear and adoration among the masses."

"Mostly fear," said Ares. "And don't forget the mindless, groveling obeisance. I really loved me some of that!"

"For now I guess I'll just have to settle for a decent tip, rather than groveling obeisance," said Athena. "If you'll excuse me, I have to go make some customers forget about having soup for lunch."

"That's what you're good at," said Ares. He fired the burner under his chowder. "Or maybe them Wilsons would like some of the beef barley soup I made up this morning."

Athena stopped in the doorway, shook her head, and headed out of the kitchen.

The combination bar-dining room at the Delphi was a fairly popular lunch spot in Olympus, Indiana. More than half of the tables were filled with Hoosiers, some wearing t-shirts and jeans or overalls, some wearing shorts, and one advertising specialty salesman from Indianapolis wearing his summer-weight Hoosier business attire; khaki dockers, a short-sleeved dress shirt, and a navy blue clip-on necktie.

Hermes was behind the bar doing card tricks, performing for three farmers cradling half-full glasses of beer, along with little Angie, who was eating French fries and sipping a cherry Coke. A very attractive and larger version of Angie, known among the locals as "Smokin' Hot Sarah," sat next to her daughter, studying Hermes' face and nibbling on a Greek salad.

Hera patrolled the room like a hawk orbiting a meadow stocked with field mice. She stopped at a table where four middle-aged men in bib overalls were just about to bite into their hamburgers, and asked if everything was tasting good.

Hephaestus sat at a table near the kitchen, eating a giant steak, drinking a mug of beer, and watching his new ceiling fan rotating lazily over the room.

Karen and Bill Wilson sat at their favorite table near the front window enjoying their usual rum-and-coke appetizers. They were both retired from their jobs as teachers at Olympus High School, and they came to lunch at the Delphi every day. Bill liked to sit at that particular table because it gave him a panoramic view of the room, handy in case Aphrodite should happen to pass through. Karen also liked to sit at that particular table because it gave her the opportunity to complain about sitting so close to the front window.

"I have bad news, folks," said Athena. "We're all out of chowder. How about a nice cup of beef barley soup?"

"Oh," said Karen Wilson, "I had my heart set on chowder."

"Really?" said Bill Wilson. "Karen, you hate chowder."

"The last time I had it I got a migraine."

"You got that migraine two days after you ate the chowder."

"I think I should know what causes my migraines."

"So you're lucky there's no chowder. Have the beef barley."

"But I had my heart set on chowder."

Bill Wilson sighed, drained his rum and coke, and handed the glass to Athena. "We'll have beef barley, and I'll have another one of these."

"I'll have another one too... Minnie," said Karen Wilson with a sly grin and an exaggerated wink. Karen had been a Latin teacher, and thought it was a great joke to call Athena "Min-nie," for Minerva, the name Athena had been called by the Romans.

Athena gave her a tolerant smile. "Ha. Good one. I'll bring your drinks."

As Athena disappeared back into the kitchen, the outside door swung open and a small man strode into the bar. He was dressed in a carefully tailored beige suit, with expensive-looking brown shoes and a brown leather necktie. A sunburned pate of bald head rose above a ring of suspiciously dark brown hair. He wore designer sunglasses and pinkie rings on both hands. He hooked his thumbs in his belt and walked over to Hera.

"Good afternoon," he said.

"Sit anywhere, Mr. Smith. Would you like to see the lunch specials?"

Smith took off his sunglasses with a flour-ish and a wry smile. "No thanks. I'm here on official business. And I wish you would call me, 'Big Will.' We're all friends here." Wilfred Smith owned nearly all the commercial property in downtown Olympus, Indiana. All of it, in fact, except for the Delphi, and he was making it his life's work to correct that situation.

He was also the town's Mayor.

"Oh?" said Hera. "What kind of 'official busi-ness' are we talking about here, Mr. Smith?"

Smith smiled and said, "I'm afraid I have some bad news for you. It seems that in a special meeting of the Planning Commission, it was determined that the sidewalk in front of the Delphi is in a dangerous state of disrepair. They also decided to cede ownership of the sidewalks in front of all the businesses in this block to the businesses themselves, which means that you have 48 hours to effect repairs. At your own expense." He handed Hera a manila envelope. "All the pertinent information is right here."

She took the envelope and tossed it on an empty table. "And if we are not able to comply ahead of your deadline?"

"There is some sort of penalty. A fine, I think. Something like $10,000 a day."

"$10,000? A day? You are aware, of course, that the Delphi is the only business in this block."

"Really? Why, now that you mention it, I suppose that's true."

"Meaning that we are the only ones affected by your new ordinance." Hera moved closer to tower over Smith. "And what did a certain Planning Commission member named Athena have to say about all this?"

Smith took a step back toward the door. "She, um... Commissioner Athena seems to have been absent from the meeting."

"Her invitation must have got lost in the mail."

"It was publicly posted."

"In the break room at your office, like the last time?"

"That is a public place. It's all perfectly legal."

"Right, just ask your brother, the judge."

"Perfectly legal." He backed closer to the door, backing right into Hephaestus, who had hobbled quietly up behind him.

"What's up?" asked Hephaestus.

"Mr. Smith here was just giving me a civics lesson. It seems that we have two days to make some repairs, or we have to pay a fine that could potentially force us to sell the hotel."

"Is that a fact? What sort of repairs?"

"We have to replace the sidewalk out front," said Hera. "It seems to suddenly be dangerous, and it has even more suddenly become our responsibility."

"No problem. I'll take care of it tonight."

"I'm afraid you don't understand," said Smith. "The entire sidewalk must be replaced. The fine starts the day after tomorrow, and continues until the repairs are complete."

"I understand perfectly, Smith, and I said I would take care of it." Hephaestus stepped closer. "Now, would you like me to help you out of here and across that rickety old sidewalk? Wouldn't want you to fall down without a good reason."

Smith looked from Hera to Hephaestus. "You do not seem to take the laws of our community seriously," he said. "And threatening a public official is a very serious breach of those laws."

"And you do not seem to understand the difference between a threat and a friendly invitation to leave," said Hera.

Smith drew himself up until his eyes nearly reached Hera's chin. "Our inspectors will be around tomorrow morning to assess the status of the repairs." He shoved his sunglasses back onto his face and retreated from the Delphi.

Two

How will we know when they are ready for the Test?

You know as much about it as I do.

But I don't really know anything.

You know everything.

My point exactly.

Will the king be first?

It would be logical to assume that, but it seems like it might be the lame one.

Or the Queen?

Possibly.

Is there any danger?

There is always danger.

Wow. You really do know everything.

Thank you.

And nothing.

Again, thank you.

There is no need.

My point exactly.

Hephaestus

Your eyes are crystal blue, my love
They're bluer than the sea,
And your hair, the color of the sun,
Lights up the world for me...

"Are my eyes really blue?"

"Really, really blue." Hephaestus was sitting on a low stool, nimbly sculpting the delicate knee-cap of a perfect-to-the-knees copy of Aphrodite. "I'll get you a mirror in a second. I'm just about finished. Although feet can be a little bit tricky."

"How about getting me a decent gown, too. What is this I'm wearing?"

Hephaestus smiled and kept working. "It's some rags I had here in the shop, just to cover you up. You were getting sort of distracting. Besides, how would you even know anything about what it means to wear something?"

"I'm new. I'm not stupid."

Hephaestus answered with a deep chuckle. His hands continued to fly over the clay, sculpting two perfect calves, then two perfect ankles, and, finally, two perfect feet. Then he went to fetch a tall mirror while the statue lifted her feet off the floor, one at a time, and flexed them experimentally. He propped the mirror against a pile of iron pipes, then moved to stand beside his creation. The two of them examined the reflection approvingly.

"Wow. I'm obviously not the first woman you ever made."

"No, I made a woman before, a very lovely one. Her name was Pandora."

"Do I have a name?"

"Yes. Your name is Aphrodite. There does happen to be another Aphrodite running around, so you would be Aphrodite II. Maybe I should call you, 'Dyo.' That means 'Two' in Greek. But to everyone else you will be Aphrodite."

"Wow, clever. Will I meet Pandora?"

"No, she's not around anymore. She didn't really work out all that well."

"Oh. So what happens if I don't work out?"

"You will."

"So how about that gown?"

"Oh yes, of course. Although really, you look

just fine as you are."

"Um, no I don't. I'm wearing some rags from around the shop."

"Ah, so you are." As he spoke he looked around the workshop, finally spotting a good-sized cobweb in a corner. "It seems, my dear, I've made you in the exact image of my wife in more ways than one."

"You're married to someone who looks like this?" She turned a bit to the side, still looking in the mirror. "Seriously?"

Hephaestus just grumbled in reply. He limped over, snatched the cobweb with the tip of his cane, and began to twirl it in the air above his head. As he did, the cobweb transformed into a bolt of pure white silk, growing and waving like a long, shimmering flag from his cane. Then he tossed the cane into the air. As it fell, his hands flew over the fabric and a gown took shape.

She watched, fascinated. "You're making me a dress out of a spider web?"

"It's called 'gossamer.'"

She slipped the gown over her head, then looked in the mirror again. "I believe I like gossa-mer. So, seriously. This is what your wife looks like?"

"Yes, this is exactly what she looks like. Is that so hard to imagine?"

She studied Hephaestus, then herself in the mirror. "Yes, it is."

"Well, it's not exactly a conventional marriage. You see, a very long time ago, I sort of trapped my mother, Hera. I locked her to a trick throne that I made for her. The other Gods gave me Aphrodite to be my wife in return for letting Hera go."

"That's an interesting basis for a relationship. And does the first Aphrodite care for you?"

Hephaestus smiled at himself in the mirror. "About as much as you might expect. Let's just say no, not really."

She continued to gaze at herself in the mirror for a few moments, then her eyes widened. "So did you make me to... care for you?"

He laughed. "As tempting as that may seem to be, no. I have other plans for you."

"I see."

"You don't have to look so relieved."

"Sorry. So how does this work? Do I have to do everything you want me to do?"

"Pretty much, yes."

"What if I don't?"

"Well, for one thing, I could arrange to have you go back to being a big lump of clay."

"Is it that easy?"

"It is for me. But I'm sure it won't come to that. Besides, I think you'll enjoy doing what I need you to do."

"And what would that be?"

He took her by the arm and walked her over to a pair of overstuffed chairs near a large machine that looked like a cross between a tractor and a giant food blender. A low, simple wooden coffee table sat between the chairs. "I just want you to follow your nature." He gestured toward one chair and sat in the other. "You simply need to be Aphrodite."

She sat, gracefully arranging her gossamer gown. "How will I know how to be Aphrodite?"

"Like I said, you will simply follow your nature. The nature I molded into you. Aphrodite's nature." He reached over and tapped the center of the coffee table with an index finger. A door swung open to reveal a deep chamber, invisible from the outside, lined with frost. He pulled out a bottle of wine and two glasses, poured one glass and handed it to her, then poured another for himself. "The nature of a totally craven, soulless harlot."

"You molded whatever that is into me?" She sipped her wine.

"I certainly hope so. It seems like you already share her desire for the finer things."

"Why wouldn't she want to wear nice things? That seems only natural."

"Yes, I suppose it is. But it goes beyond that. Aphrodite is what you might call obsessed with her appearance."

Dyo thought about that for a few seconds. "I guess it wasn't wearing rags that made me uncomfortable as much as it was being nearly naked in front of you."

Hephaestus laughed. "OK, so you are a lot like Aphrodite Senior in that respect."

"Maybe it's because you created me. You're like a father to me. Sort of"

He laughed harder. "Built-in clichés! Look, I just created you. I didn't teach you how to drive or help you pick out your prom dress."

"Apparently I don't understand this whole 'father' thing."

"Don't worry. Neither does any father." He refilled his wine glass. "So what we're going to do here is have you take Aphrodite Senior's place for a while."

"And what happens to her?"

"I have some experiments I want to do." He reached over and patted the tractor part of the blender-tractor next to his chair. "There is a source of Power near here that we have not been able to locate. This machine lets me extract some of it remotely and plant it in my fellow Olympian Gods. Then this…" he tapped the blender part with his cane, "captures most of it back, so I can transfer it over to me."

"Why don't you just bring all this Power directly to yourself?"

"I tried that. There is apparently a problem if I am close enough to operate the machine. It knocked me out cold for nearly two days."

"Exactly what kind of experiments do you have in mind?"

"For one thing, I want to know if I can get better results with a Goddess…"

"Aphrodite."

"The very one. Right here, close by. In fact, strapped to the machine."

"And this power is really important to you?"

"Power is what makes a God a God. All of us have 'talents,' things we're good at doing. The more Power we have, the more of that stuff we can do, and the better we can do it."

"How does this thing work?"

Hephaestus reached over to the tractor part of the machine and tapped a large brass dial. Arrayed around the outside of the dial were ten symbols. "Each one of these symbols represents one of the Gods. This one, for instance," he turned the pointer of the dial to point to a picture of an owl, "represents Athena. When the machine is set to her symbol and I do this..." He spun a large wheel on the side of the machine, "Little Miss Smart-ass gets a burst of Power."

The wheel spun, picking up speed on its own, and the sides of the machine began to glow with heat. Then, from a small smokestack near where Dyo sat, a ball of green light shot up and disappeared into the haze overhead. "That fire went to Little Miss Smart-ass?" she asked.

"Yep. But as far as I know, she might not particularly notice it. It will just give her a little energy boost that will last..." He stood up and began to furiously turn a crank just beneath a glass carafe on the food blender part of the machine. "...until I do this." As he cranked, a glowing green mist appeared in the carafe, then condensed into a glowing green liquid.

When the liquid stopped accumulating, Hephaestus stopped cranking and took the carafe down from the machine. He dumped his wine onto the floor and filled his glass with the green stuff. "Yeah, that really looks yummy," said Dyo.

"It's actually not too bad." He drained the glass, then threw his head back, closed his eyes, and shuddered. When he opened them again, there was a green glow from deep in his pupils. He straightened up and seemed to grow larger.

Dyo gulped down the rest of her wine. "No offense, but that was really creepy," she said.

This time Hephaestus didn't laugh. Instead, he reached his hand in her direction, palm down, and slowly clenched his fist in the air. As he did, her wine glass burst into a puff of dust. "No offense taken," he said in a voice, deeper than before, and with just a hint of echo.

"OK, yeah, I was totally finished with that," she said.

Hephaestus stood motionless for a few seconds, his fist outstretched. Then the glow faded from his eyes and a smile spread over his face. "Sorry about that." He scooped a handful of sand from the floor and rubbed it between his hands. A new wine glass emerged. "Here, let me pour you another glass."

"That's all right, I'll pass. When you get a free minute, maybe you could whip up a dishwasher for those dirt glasses of yours. So, how exactly does this thing collect the Power?"

"That's a really good question; I don't actually know. It just does."

"And what will happen to Aphrodite when you try this on her?"

"I'm not really sure."

"That doesn't sound good."

"Don't worry. She's immortal, like me. I can't really hurt her."

"So how did your leg get messed up? Were you born with that limp?"

This time his laugh was a little bit forced. "Wow, I'm not sure even Aphrodite Senior is quite that blunt. No, I displeased Zeus, so he tossed me off a mountain. A really big one."

"So it seems that immortals really can hurt each other."

"Hmm, fair point. Yes, I suppose we can." He poured himself another glass of wine and raised it in a toast. "At least I hope so."

Hera

"Where in Tartarus have you been?" Hera was bent over a table in the corner of the empty bar, scrubbing at a speck of intolerable corruption on the table top.

"In a sense, my dear, I have been trapped in my own personal Tartarus." Zeus entertained an urge to give his wife a playful slap on the rump. That urge passed quickly, though – Hera was many things, but "playful" was not one of them.

She straightened up and turned to face Zeus. Her eyes, the color of storm clouds, looked every bit as dangerous. "And the rest of us are here in the Delphi, luxuriating in this Elysium of the hospitality industry."

Zeus studied Hera with a faint smile. She had her black hair piled on top of her head, like a billowing thundercloud roiling over those turbulent eyes. "So how was the lunch crowd today?" he asked.

"As if you care about the lunch crowd. Mr. Lord of all the Gods, Mr. too good to carry a plate of spanakopita out of the kitchen."

"I was just out taking a long walk. I have some ideas I need to work out."

"I heard how you worked out the ceiling fan. It's a good thing my son is available to come along behind you and clean up your messes."

"Look, I do recall that Hephaestus is your son and not mine. I thought we got over all that stuff 3,500 years ago."

"After you crippled him."

"He did bind you to your throne."

"A simple misunderstanding. We worked it all out."

"My point exactly. We worked it all out – a long time ago."

"You made him marry that little skank."

"That 'little skank' is the Goddess of love and beauty, and it was the settlement he asked for. He seemed to think that it was a pretty good deal at the time."

Hera sniffed. "And now Hermes has a new carrot-topped little tramp of his own."

"If you're talking about Smo... um, Sarah, she is not a tramp. She approved the bank loan for all the new kitchen equipment. And she is the mother of what, as near as I can tell, seems to be a very nice little girl."

"Future tramp." She picked up Wilfred Smith's manila envelope and tossed it to Zeus. "That twerp Smith stopped by. He's taking another run at us."

Zeus opened the envelope and shuffled through the papers, reading rapidly. "Really, the sidewalk? It's like he's completely out of ideas."

"Hephaestus says he can take care of it and replace the sidewalk tonight."

Zeus raised his eyebrows and nodded. "Wow, really? I don't see how, but if he says it he usually does it. At least for now, we still need this place."

Hera's face softened almost imperceptibly. "Is there really a chance for us ever to return to Olympus? Our Olympus?"

"I don't know. It does look like we're getting at least some of our abilities back."

She sighed. "I do miss it."

"Olympus?"

"Yes. And even more, the Power. I miss the ability to reshape civilizations. I miss having everything I desire just for desiring it. I miss crushing bugs like Smith as if they were... well, bugs." She locked her eyes with Zeus' and the storm clouds parted slightly. "I miss being the queen of the most powerful being in the universe."

Zeus laughed. "It is possible that I am still the most powerful being in the universe," he said. "It's just that at the moment, this does not happen to involve much in the way of reshaping of civilizations. Now when it comes to bugs and ceiling fans..."

Athena came out of the kitchen. "Hey, Z. I have some news for you."

Hera's clouds closed back in around her. "Wonderful. An update from the Goddess of 'I'm Smarter Than You Are.'"

Zeus ignored Hera. "What's up?"

"About ten minutes ago I got a Power surge."

"Really? What happened?"

"I was in the kitchen trying to explain to Ares why humans are not, as a rule, real crazy about being disemboweled with rusty swords, and I sort of... grew."

"How do you mean?"

"I was getting a little bit short-tempered with his stupidity..."

"Imagine that."

"And all of a sudden, I found myself towering over him. In fact, I picked him up in one hand."

"Ares? You picked Ares up?"

"In one hand. It was like he was a little rag doll. Do you remember that feeling?"

"I do," said Hera wistfully.

"Of course," said Zeus. "So then what happened? Did you do any smiting?"

"No, then it was like it just ended, and I realized what was happening. I dropped him and shrank back down, and it was like nothing had happened. Except... well, now I feel just a little bit more like me. Real me. Old me. Does that make any sense?"

"Not really. Although that does pretty well describe how I felt this morning after I blasted the fan. And it may have something to do with why Hephaestus says he can fix the sidewalk overnight. Hera have you experienced anything like this?"

Hera turned back to cleaning her table. "No, My Lord. All of this power must be for the more important Gods, not the mere Queen of Heaven."

Zeus tried not to roll his eyes. "What about Ares?" he asked Athena.

"I think he kind of got a kick out of it."

"I meant, have you seen any bursts of power from him?"

"Well, he hasn't exploded into a bloodthirsty frenzy of destruction and massacred all the members of his beer league softball team, so I'd have to say no, not really. You know Ares - when he has power it doesn't always end well."

"Good point."

Without looking up Hera said, "You are maligning our son."

"Yes, he is our son. And our son happens to be a meat-headed, murderous lout. He's a damn fine cook, though."

"All that he does is in your service, My Lord," said Hera.

"Oh, for pity sake," said Athena.

Hera swung around to face her. "You have always served yourself, bitch, and no one else."

Athena stood her ground. "Look, you pathetic cow – we are stuck here, and for that reason we have to work together. You don't like it, and I don't like it, and you and I certainly don't like each other. We never have, and we never will. But that's how it is. So get over it."

Hera clenched her fists and began to tremble. "Cow? You... I can't... You..." A deep rumble came from the ground, the walls, and even the air. She rose several inches from the floor and hovered there, visibly shaking with rage.

Zeus raised his eyebrows and whistled. "Now that's what I'm talking about."

"Boy, if that doesn't bring back old times," said Athena.

Hera froze, then looked down. "Oh my," she said as she settled gently to the floor. "Where did that come from?"

Zeus rubbed his chin thoughtfully. "That's exactly what I intend to find out."

Aphrodite Meets Herself

When she tried to roll over in her bed, Aphrodite woke up and discovered that her hands had been tied to her ankles.

Her first reaction to being trussed up like a rodeo calf was a mild curiosity mixed with a faint tinge of pleasure. "Whufs ghnmg onm?" she asked, learning with some interest that her mouth had been gagged tightly.

"What's going on, my love, is that you are now my captive."

She craned her head up to see Hephaestus standing at the head of her bed. Next to him was an incredibly beautiful blonde woman. "Onm. Iftps mnou. Mmoos mnur fnmenmd?"

"Yes, it is me. And my friend here is you. I made her. Say hello to Aphrodite II. I like to call her 'Dyo.'"

"I nget it. Nreek hor 'two.' Mnello, Mnyo."
She studied Dyo and narrowed her eyes. "nyu hab
her tmoo mbig mnon top."

Hephaestus studied Dyo's chest and smiled.
"Yes, I suppose I might have overshot just a tad in
the décolletage department. I don't foresee anybody complaining, though."

"No, Imn gmness nmot. Smno, whnmat hm-
napmns nmow?"

"What happens now is that I take you away,
while Dyo becomes you." He raised his right hand
over Aphrodite and her body rose a foot above the
bed. Then he turned and gave Dyo a kiss on the
cheek. "You understand your job? Party, drink,
dance, and shamelessly enjoy yourself. And just
for grins, brutally crush the heart of any man who
cares for you."

"Bnmoy, tmalmk amnboumnt mna
trmansparmnent mnomntive mnreveal!"

"What?"

"She said, 'Boy, talk about a transparent motive reveal,'" said Dyo. "And I agree. Do you really
need to have her gagged?"

"I guess not." He reached over and pulled the
gag away from Aphrodite's mouth.

"Ew, is that my teal sports bra?"

"It was the only thing I could find in your

underwear drawer that would make a halfway decent gag."

"And you had to get the gag from my underwear drawer?"

"That's what I told him, too," said Dyo. "What a waste!"

"If you're not careful, I'll find another sports bra and gag you both. And, as to my motive in all this, you could not be further from the truth. For one thing, I am not a man, I am a God, and therefore I do not even have a heart for you to crush."

The two Aphrodites gave each other a knowing look and said nothing.

After an awkward few seconds, Hephaestus cleared his throat and said, "Alright then, let's get on with it." He motioned in the direction of the wall, where a dresser swung out to reveal a low door leading to a bronze spiral staircase.

As Aphrodite drifted slowly toward the portal she smiled at her double. "OK then, Dyo, have fun. Watch out for Carl Darnell; he keeps trying to use his homemade roofies on me. You. Us. Oh, and if you run out of underwear, you'll have to do the load of laundry on the floor of the closet."

"Thank you," said Dyo. "I've never had any underwear, so I'll just have to improvise."

"Oh, really?" Aphrodite gave Hephaestus a disapproving look. "You didn't make this woman any underwear?"

"She's about four hours old! Besides, what about this whole 'prisoner' thing do you not understand?" He whipped his hand toward the portal, and Aphrodite sailed through, bounced off the far wall and ricocheted down the staircase.

Aphrodite's voice echoed up from the bottom of the stairs; "Ow. That was totally uncalled for."

"Geeze," said Hephaestus, "See why I gagged her?" He limped through the portal and pulled the door shut behind him.

At the bottom of the staircase Aphrodite was floating in the air, face down, just outside the bronze workshop door. Hephaestus unlocked the door with his cane and nudged her into the room with a tap from the toe of his boot.

A few minutes later Hephaestus had Aphrodite securely shackled to a seat on the front of the Power Generator. "Do you recognize your restraints?" he asked.

"Um, I guess I'm not really that much of a fan of Famous Shackles."

"I used these very chains to bind Hera to her throne - the day I won your... you."

"Ah, sweet memories. How could I forget? So

what's the deal here?"

"This machine generates Power. Our Power. Godly Power. I intend to see how much of it you can take."

"You want to make me powerful?"

"Hardly. I want to make me powerful. Besides, at your very best you were never much more dangerous than a Wood Nymph." He paused. "A really, really hot Wood Nymph. No, my sweet, just think of yourself as a sort of short-term storage battery."

"Should I have any idea at all what you're talking about?"

"No, not really." Hephaestus turned the dial on the machine to point at a picture of a sea shell, then spun the crank.

Aphrodite bit her lip and watched as the sides of the machine began to glow. "Something tells me," she said, "that this is really going to hurt." Before Hephaestus could answer, a fireball shot out of the smokestack, performed a tight loop in the air, and hit Aphrodite directly in the chest.

A blinding explosion rocked the workshop, blasting Hephaestus through the air and onto a pile of copper tubing. He lay there stunned and spread-eagled, as bits of metal and glass rained down on him and the report of the explosion echoed from the far ends of the room.

After a few minutes the ringing in his ears subsided and he was able to test his arms and legs, and discovered that they were all still functioning. As the smoke began to clear he struggled into a sitting position, picking some of the larger chunks of shrapnel out of his hair and beard. Where the power generator had sat there was now a shallow crater, its bottom glass-smooth. A small mushroom cloud still hung in the air. There was no sign of Aphrodite.

Hephaestus struggled to his feet and scratched his dreadlocks, dislodging a large carriage bolt and a couple of small toothed gears, and said,

"Oops."

Hermes and Some Ladies

Hermes' timing was perfect. He caught Sarah coming out the front door of the bank on her way home. "Oh, Hi!" He flashed her the most persuasive smile he had in his inventory of smiles. "What a coincidence running into you here! Can I give you a ride home?"

"I only live three blocks away," said Sarah, "and you don't have a car."

"Oh, right. Well, I was on the way to the barber shop, and just happened be passing by the bank..."

"You don't need a haircut. In fact, your hair is perfect. It's always perfect."

"I was just going in for an appraisal."

"Right. So, are you stalking me, or what?"

"What. Mostly what. No, wait, totally what.

No stalking involved. Just what."

Sarah started walking, and Hermes fell in step beside her. "Look, Hermes, I appreciate that you bought lunch for Angie and me, and I appreciate the fact that you are nice to her..."

"She's a great kid."

"... but I'm really not looking to get any kind of relationship started right now."

"Who said anything about a relationship? How do you know I wasn't going for something superficial and purely physical?"

"And you're trying to engineer that by making friends with my daughter?"

"OK, I'll admit that there are a few parts of the plan that I haven't completely worked out..."

"You seem like a nice guy..."

"And you appreciate lunch and all the niceness, got it."

"Right. It's just..."

"Too much niceness? Alright then, I can be a jerk. Let me have your credit card for a couple of minutes..."

"It's just that we live in a real small town here. Anything we do will be blown all out of proportion in no time. The most innocent date..."

"Who said anything about innocent? Like I

said, I was going for something a long way beyond innocent..."

"The *most innocent date* would have everybody in town talking."

"OK, look, I'm not trying to get a date. I just wanted to invite you and Angie to drop by the bar tonight. Apollo and I are going to take a shot at doing some live music."

"I didn't know you played music."

"Are you kidding? I invented music."

"And you're modest about it too. What instrument do you play?"

"Guitar, and Apollo plays a little harp."

"Oh, I love blues harmonica."

"No, I mean a small harp. It's called a lyre."

"That should be interesting. What kind of music do you guys do?"

"A guitar and a lyre – isn't it obvious? We're a Pink Floyd tribute band."

She stopped at the corner. "Alright, I live a block down this way, and I don't want any of my neighbors to see you walking me home. If I say we'll come tonight will you leave me alone?"

"You won't even need a court order. Probably. Almost for sure, no court order."

"What time?"

"We start at 7."

"And how long will you play?"

"It shouldn't be a real long show. We only know two songs."

She laughed. "OK, it's a date. Deal. It's just a deal. Nothing more."

"Not a date. See you at 7."

– λατερ –

When Hermes got back to the Delphi, he found Dyo sitting at the bar doodling on a napkin with a pencil from the rack of Keno tickets. "Hi, Aphrodite. What are you doing awake before dark?"

She looked up at him. "Are you the bartender here? There doesn't seem to be a bartender, and I'm pretty sure that I could really use a martini. And maybe a couple of beers. Please."

"Am I... Wow, you must have had a rough one last night." He walked around behind the bar. "A martini and a couple of beers, eh? That's unique even for you."

"Is it? What would be less unique for me?"

He wrinkled his forehead and studied her face. "Are you all right? There's something different about you."

"As far as I know, I'm fine."

As she spoke a muffled explosion shook the

floor of the bar.

"What was that?" asked Hermes.

"I'll bet it was Hephaestus. He's conducting an experiment."

Hermes stared at her for a few more seconds, then shook his head. "So how about if I make you a pitcher of apple martinis, and we go from there."

She smiled at him. "That sounds like a good idea... um... ah... Mr..."

"You've forgotten that I'm Hermes?"

"No, that's not it. Oh, wait, yes. You are Hermes! Yes, that would be a great idea." She gave him a radiant smile. "Hermes."

While Hermes was making the drinks Athena came out of the kitchen. "Hi Aphrodite. Holy crap, are you wearing gossamer?"

"Do you like it? Hephaestus made it for me."

"Hephaestus? Since when does Hephaestus make your clothes?"

"Since... earlier today."

"Why would you let him... Wait, what have you done to yourself?"

"Um, what do you mean?"

"I mean either you're doing some false advertising, in the spirit of Wonder Bra, or you've done something to the girls. And it's pretty obvious you're not wearing anything under that gown, so what's going on?" She paused and her mouth dropped open. "Oh my Gods, Aphrodite, have you figured out a way to get pregnant?"

"Nothing like that, um... ah..."

"Lucy," said Hermes."

"Of course. Nothing like that, Lucy."

Hermes and Athena looked at each other. "All right, girl, what's going on?" asked Athena.

"Yeah," said Hermes, "You can tell your old pal, Lucy."

"I... Well..."

Before she could finish, the door swung open and Aphrodite stormed in, wearing the remains of a smoldering nightgown and a furious expression. She muscled up to the bar between an empty stool and Dyo, grabbed Dyo's apple martini and tossed it down in one gulp. "Keep these coming," she said, handing the glass to Hermes. "Hi, Athena. Hi, Dyo. Gods, I am going to kill that nasty little gimp."

Hermes looked from Aphrodite to Dyo and back. "Wow, this explains a lot. At least it sure seems like it should." He looked at the two Aphrodites again. "OK, could somebody please explain this?"

Athena laughed. "Ah, this smells like a Hephaestus project. So what exactly is the nasty little gimp up to now?"

Aphrodite tossed down another apple martini and gestured toward Dyo with the empty glass. "Well, he made this copy of me," she said. She reached over and brushed a wisp of hair away from Dyo's eye. "This absolutely, totally gorgeous copy of me." She took a deep breath and gently ran her tongue over her upper lip.

"Thank you." said Dyo, gazing into Aphrodite's eyes.

"You're welcome, Dyo," Aphrodite said, picking up Dyo's hand. "Athena, do you think I should do something like this with my breasts? I kind of like the way..."

"Aphrodite, focus. Why did Hephaestus make a copy of you?"

"Oh yeah." She dropped Dyo's hand. "So he could kidnap me. He said something about Godly Power and storage batteries. Then he strapped me to some kind of machine and blew me all the way over to Boggus County."

"That must have been the explosion we heard a few minutes ago," said Hermes.

"Boggus County is nearly 40 miles away. How did you get back here so fast?" asked Athena.

"Oh, yeah. I can do this now." Aphrodite rose

three feet straight up from the floor, rocketed in a tight circle around the perimeter of the room, then settled back to the floor at the bar and handed her empty martini glass back to Hermes. "Fill 'er up, my good man."

"Whoa, it's been a long time since any of us could do that," chuckled Hermes, filling Aphrodite's glass and another one for Dyo. "So, any idea what's going on here? Anyone?"

"I think I can fill in some of the blanks for you," said Dyo, sipping her martini. "Ooh, this is good!"

"Thanks," said Hermes. "You should try the peach too."

"I prefer apple," said Aphrodite, "but peach martinis are nice too."

"Blanks?" said Athena. "Filling them in?"

"Yes, of course," said Dyo. "But to be real honest, I'm kind of worried that Hephaestus might show up and see us all here together. He said that if I messed up he could make me back into a lump of clay."

Athena stood up. "I promise you, we are not going to let that happen. OK, here's the plan – why don't both of you Aphrodites come up to my room with me and sort this whole thing out. Hermes, I'll bring you up to speed later. In the meantime, if Hephaestus shows up, just play dumb."

"It's the role I was born to play."

"And for the time being, let's keep this whole thing completely to ourselves."

"You don't even want to bring Zeus in on it?" asked Hermes.

"Not just yet. Not until I get a better grip on what's happening around here."

Three

There is some bad intent by the lame one.

There is always intent. Good or bad seems to be a matter of perspective.

There is a potential for harm.

There is always that potential.

And there is usually harm.

As we have seen.

As we have always seen.

As we always will see.

Why do we talk this way?

It depends on who is talking.

And what we are saying?

Exactly.

Oh. Right.

Music Night at the Delphi

Apollo and Hermes had moved tables around to make themselves a small stage in the corner of the bar, and set up a PA system with a couple of microphones. They sat side-by-side on bar stools, Hermes tuning an acoustic guitar and Apollo flexing the strings on a golden lyre that glowed with its own light.

The concert crowd consisted of Sarah and Angie sharing an order of onion rings and a pitcher of Coke, the Wilsons gazing fondly at two double-sized Long Island Iced Teas, Athena and Dyo huddled in conversation and sharing a pitcher of peach martinis, and two young beer-drinking, burger-eating Hoosier guys wearing khaki shorts, white Titleist golf shirts, and white Titleist caps turned around backward. Ares was banging around in the kitchen, and Artemis was behind the bar mixing up another round of martinis and Long Island Iced Teas.

At precisely 7:00 PM Apollo strummed a slow arpeggio on his lyre, sending a full, sweet, beautiful tone swirling around the room.

As the chord hung shimmering in the air, Hermes began to play the guitar, with a deliberate, throbbing bass line, pulsing like a heartbeat. After a few bars he added the bare thread of a sweet, sad, haunting tune on the higher strings, whispering at first, then gaining volume as the song began to gain strength.

Apollo rejoined on his lyre, weaving an intricate counterpoint with Hermes' guitar, a cascade of golden notes wandering from low to high and back again, dancing with the melody Hermes was chasing, and punctuated by exquisite full chords that served to blend it all into a pure silk tapestry of sound.

The tempo of the song began to accelerate, the melody lines whirling, diving, soaring in a perfect storm, now chaotic, now perfectly synchronized, now angry, now clashing, now in total harmony. Faster and faster the two Gods played, their song growing in volume and majesty and importance, until it seemed to consume the room, to devour the air, to dominate existence itself.

And then, suddenly and on cue, it stopped.

The silence exploded through the room for four slow beats, then Apollo strummed that original arpeggio on his lyre, slower than before, providing the perfect punctuation and bringing the song to its only possible conclusion.

Sarah, Angie, Athena, Dyo, and the Wilsons all sat frozen, their mouths hanging open, too stunned to applaud, or even to breathe.

After a few seconds, one of the golfers broke the silence, clapped his hands together three times, and said, "Yeah, great, terrific. Real nice. Woo-hoo. Now would you please turn the TV back on? They're showing highlights of the Tournament Players Golf Championship from last month at Sawgrass."

Hermes smiled, raised the index finger of his right hand, and drew a small circle in the air. The instant the circle was complete, a golf ball crashed through the front window. It shot across the room and struck the golfer on the forehead, squarely between the eyes, knocking him over the back of his chair. "Now there's a bit of irony," said Hermes. "I'll bet that thing came all the way from Walmart, and nobody even hollered, 'fore.'" He smiled at the other golfer. "You might want to take your friend to the emergency room and get that looked at. Your tab is on me."

As the door swung closed behind the golfers,

Hermes looked over at Sarah and Angie's table. "So, would anybody like to hear a song called 'Carlson the Pissed-off Angel?'"

Between sets, Hermes stopped on his way to join Sarah and Angie, to whisper in Athena's ear, "Where's Aphrodite?"

"We decided that she should make herself scarce, and let Hephaestus stew for a while. Now that she's a little bit more mobile, she decided to go check out San Diego."

"Have you seen Hephaestus?"

"Nope. We figured that if Dyo and I hang out here he'll show up eventually. I want to make sure he thinks we're fooled by his handiwork."

"So what is all this about?"

"Hephaestus was trying some kind of power-making scheme using Aphrodite as a Guinea pig, and his contraption blew up. He probably thinks he destroyed her. Or at least temporarily vaporized her."

"That must be upsetting for him. Do you think he's working with someone else?"

"No idea. I doubt he's working with Zeus, though, because it's hard to imagine Zeus letting him do anything that might hurt Aphrodite."

"Where is Zeus?"

"Believe it or not, he took Hera to a movie."

"Really? They're having a 'Date Night?'"

"I know, right? Strange doings are afoot."

Hermes shook his head and whistled. "I'm not sure 'strange' even comes close to covering it." He looked over to where Sarah was playing tic-tac-toe on a napkin with Angie. "Well, keep me posted. In the meantime, I have some schmoozing to do."

"So that's what they call it these days."

"Grow up."

During the second set Hephaestus came in, a sledge hammer slung over one shoulder. He stopped and eyed the broken window, sighed heavily, then scanned the room. By this time the Wilsons were both dozing in their chairs, with six empty Long Island Iced Tea mugs on their table. Angie and Sarah were still hanging in, Angie trying to persuade her mother to stay for the end of the show so Hermes could walk them home.

His gaze lingered for a few seconds on Athena and Dyo, who were well into a project of working their way through every martini variation Artemis could come up with. Then he made his way to the bar, had Artemis draw him a beer and sat on a stool to drink it.

Between songs Hephaestus carried his beer over to Hermes and Apollo. "You two sound real good. How late are you playing?"

"A couple more songs," said Apollo.

"No rush, but I have to bust up the sidewalk and replace it tonight. Plus, apparently, a window. What happened there?"

"Heckler," said Hermes.

"Wow, remind me never to talk while you guys are on stage!"

"Damn right."

– λατερ –

A half hour later Hermes was walking through downtown Olympus with Sarah and Angie, past darkened stores, past the bank, past empty offices, and past the unmoving candy-cane pole in front of the barber shop. Angie held Hermes' hand in a warm and slightly sticky grip, skipping along and swinging his arm with all her might.

"How are you still awake?" he asked.

"She's pretty motivated," said Sarah. "I told her that after begging me to let her stay for the end of the show, if she wanted to make it to puberty she better be ready to step up and party hearty afterward."

"Really?"

"Not really," said Angie. "She just said I better stay awake, because she wasn't going to carry my dead little butt all the way home."

"Same thing," said Sarah.

"Hermes, how did you do that thing with the golf ball?"

"What makes you think I had anything to do with that?"

"Herrrrrrrmes..."

"Annnnnnngie..."

"You wanna know what I think?" asked Angie.

"Not really," said Hermes.

"Good decision," said Sarah.

"I think you're really Hermes," said Angie.

"Who else would I be?"

"I mean Hermes, Hermes. We've been reading about the Greek Gods in a book I got from the library. I think you're really Hermes..."

"Angie..." said Sarah.

"... and Apollo is Apollo, and Athena is Athena, and Mr. Z is Zeus, and..."

"Honey. That's just their names."

"Mom, think about it. Did you know that Hermes invented music?"

"So he told me."

"According to my book, Apollo is the actual God of music, but the God Hermes invented it."

Sarah smiled at Hermes. "The way you and

Apollo play, I can almost believe that."

Hermes returned her smile. "Thanks. But why not go ahead and believe it?"

"You expect me to believe that you are an actual Greek God?"

Hermes shrugged. "You should believe it if it's true."

She paused. "Sometimes it's hard to tell when you're joking."

"I'm always joking," said Hermes, "but there can be truth in jokes." He stopped and held his Angie-free hand out in front of them, palm up, clenched the fingers into a fist, then with a flick, flattened them out again. A small blue flame popped into existence above his palm and danced there.

"So you're a really good magician, too. Look, I'll admit it, some of your tricks are as amazing as your music."

"It's real, Mom. If it's not magic, how are you doing that, Hermes?"

"Honey, don't ask him. Magicians aren't allowed to tell anybody how they do their tricks."

"Oh, I don't mind, because it's not a trick," said Hermes. "In this case I've created a sort of tube through a parallel universe, and back into this universe, starting in the middle of the propane tank behind the Shell station over there on the corner and ending up here above my hand. I borrowed a little spark from the streetlight over there by the re-sale shop to ignite it, and there you go."

"A tube? Though a parallel universe?"

"Well, it's like a tube. To be more accurate, it's really more of a trans-dimensional energy vortex, stretched out through a dimension that connects to the other universe, then it kind of doubles back on itself."

"Trans-dimensional bull crap. It's a trick. A good one, I'll admit, but it has to be a trick."

"The tricky part is getting the parts that are in this universe exactly where you want them, like inside that propane tank and over my hand, but with a little practice..."

"And you expect me to just believe all this?"

"It would save us both a whole lot of dialog if you did."

"Right. So how do you do all that energy vortex stuff?"

"I'm not sure I can explain it. How do you snap your fingers? Or blink?" He paused, and they all watched the flame grow to nearly three feet high then shrink back down to a few inches tall. "You just know what you want to do, and you do it."

"And you can just... move things around?"

"Pretty much." He closed his hand and the

flame disappeared. He kept his hand closed for a few seconds, and when he opened it a small gold-colored badge with the name "Sarah" on it lay on his palm.

"Wait," said Sarah, "That's my name badge from work."

"Yeah, it was in the top right-hand drawer of your desk at the bank." He handed it to her.

"All right, this is getting creepy." She examined the badge closely then dropped it into her purse. "And when, exactly, did you get into my desk drawer at work?"

"Just now."

"Right. Well, from now on I want you to keep your hands off my stuff."

"Will do. Look in your purse."

She opened her purse and poked around. "OK, where did it go?"

"You'll find it on your desk when you go in tomorrow. Or somewhere near your desk. I'm a little bit rusty at sending things back."

"How did you do that? You're really good! I didn't feel you touch anything."

"That's because I didn't touch anything. You told me to keep my hands..."

"But how..."

"I told you," said Angie, "it's real magic. And Hermes is really Hermes."

"Oh, God," said Sarah.

"Gods," said Hermes.

A Chat With Sarah

"Look, there are a lot of questions that I need answered," said Sarah. She and Hermes were sipping Merlot in the living room of Sarah's house. Angie was curled up on the couch next to Sarah, her shoulders rising and falling in the slow rhythm of total, blissful kid-sleep. Hermes was parked across the coffee table from them in a slightly worn overstuffed chair.

"No problem," said Hermes. "Shoot."

"First off, why are you telling me all this? Why aren't you keeping all this stuff a secret? I mean, isn't that what superheroes do, hide your super powers from us poor dumb mortals?"

"We're not superheroes, and we don't have super powers," said Hermes. "We're Gods. We have always interacted with mortals like... well, like Gods."

"Yeah, that explains everything."

"Look, we are just a different species from you. We don't get old, and we don't die - at least not very often, and never in the way you think of dying. We have the ability to interact with the universe in ways that wouldn't even make sense to you, which to you would look like magic or super powers."

"And you want to use your super powers to rule the world?"

"Not really. The fact is, mortals have never really posed any real concern for us one way or the other. Some of us really like you guys, and others have always been pretty much indifferent to you. I happen to like mortals a lot..." He smiled and sat back in the chair. "Especially the ones with red hair."

Sarah blushed and caught her breath and tried to steady herself. "So are you from another planet or something?"

"All of us were created on this planet, and we've never traveled anyplace else. For all we know, our species evolved here, just like yours did."

"Don't you ever wonder about things like that?

"Sort of, but it's never been real high priority. Since we're around pretty much indefinitely, we aren't as desperately curious about stuff like that as you humans are. It's like, we have forever to work it all out, so why worry about it."

"So why aren't you zooming around and living in a perfect golden palace on top of some mountain? Why would you be hanging out in this crappy little town?"

"Now that's a good question. The short answer is that we got tired. We simply ran out of Power."

"Tired? Are you telling me you're slinging mojitos in Indiana instead of standing astride the world as a deity because you're all just a little bit worn out?"

"Something like that. Back in the old days, when we did the whole standing astride the world thing, there was a Power that we could just sort of draw on. All the things I can do now, I could do a lot better."

"And where did this Power come from?"

"Another good question. Zeus had an Amulet, a sort of bracelet, that he took from Cronus in the Great War. It seemed to draw Power to it, especially to Zeus. It also seemed like it was more effective when mortals threw a little worship at us."

"Worship created Power? Seriously?"

"OK, I'll admit it sounds pretty stupid sitting here and talking about it, but the people used to build us temples and statues. They held festivals in our honor. They gave us burnt offerings and did some other pretty crazy things. And it always seemed like the more they did all that stuff, the more Power we had."

"I know about the temples and all that. We had a unit on mythology in high school, so I kind of get it. But you're telling me that people actually prayed to you, and you could hear them?"

"Yes, we could hear them if we wanted to. Sometimes we liked to do them favors, and other times we just wanted to mess with their heads. You wouldn't believe how needy some people can get."

"So what happened to all that?"

"Well, first off, in the course of a little aerial combat with Ares, Zeus lost the Amulet. It popped off his wrist and fell to earth somewhere in this general area."

"They were dogfighting without planes? In the skies over Indiana?"

"Yes, or what would later become Indiana. Remember, we pretty much had the run of anyplace we wanted to go in the world."

"And then you lost all your Power?"

"Not totally, not right away. We did notice some loss, and Zeus was pretty upset. He had us all searching this area for about three hundred years. It was a really nice forest around here, back in the day. Then, as the centuries went by, the Power just faded away. We sort of lost our interest in humans and started keeping more to ourselves. And when we quit paying attention to mortals, they quit paying attention to us."

"Which made you lose even more Power?"

"That's pretty much it. After a while we couldn't whip up enough mayhem among the humans to inspire anybody to so much as torch up a roadkill for us."

"Now you're telling me that they had roadkill in ancient times?"

"We called it 'chariot chum.'"

"Ew. So how did you get here, to twenty-first century Indiana?"

"We're not real sure about that. As the Power faded we were spending more and more time here, searching for the Amulet. Then one day, we realized that none of us had enough Power left to get back to Olympus..."

"The one in Greece."

"Yep, that one. Eventually we all just sort of dozed off and spent about seventeen centuries in a long, deep sleep."

"And why are you not still sleeping?"

"About a year ago this guy named Phil woke us up and gave us a crash course introduction to the 21st century - mostly about what coffee is and how handy it is when you first wake up. Then he gave us the deed to the hotel and signed over a bank account with a whole lot of money in it. After that he just walked away."

"Phillip Theos was a pretty memorable man around here."

"Of course, you would have known him."

"Probably as well as anybody did. He just came into town one day, back when I was pregnant with Angie. I was a brand new cashier at the bank then, and I was the one who opened the bank accounts to deposit his sixty suitcases full of one hundred dollar bills."

"Sounds like Phil."

"We actually called the Secret Service in from Indianapolis to make sure all that cash was legitimate. After I opened his accounts, he thanked me, kissed my hand, and looked into my eyes in a way that I can't forget, and I can't describe. Then he told me that my little girl would be Angelica. I had never even considered that name until that moment, and from then on I could never think of her as anything else. The next week I delivered Angie, so I was on maternity leave when Mr. Theos came into the bank with old Ralph Smith and bought the Delphi from him."

"Ralph's kid, Wilfred, wants it back."

"Yes, I know. The whole thing created quite a stir from the start. Mr. Theos hired a small staff to run the bar and the hotel for the long-time guests. From then on, the only time we saw him was if he had to come to the bank to sign papers or move money around. Then last year you, Zeus, and the others showed up out of nowhere, and we never saw Phillip Theos again. Zeus once told me that Mr. Theos was his uncle."

"We all use the last name Theos when we need a last name, because it's what was on the paper-work – the birth certificates and Social Security cards and stuff – that Phil had made up for us."

"So who is Phil Theos? Is he a God that Homer forgot to mention?"

"We really have no idea. Like I said, he only stuck around for a few days to get us squared away, then he took off. And since we can all change our appearance if we want to, issues like who's who can get sort of complicated with us."

"You can look any way you want to?"

"Well, we can when we can come up with enough Power."

"So this is what you really look like?"

Hermes looked at his hands. "Yes, I guess so."

Sarah sat back and sipped her wine, studying Hermes with narrowed eyes. "When you say all this stuff, its like it kind of starts to makes sense. Then when I stop and think about what you're really saying, I can see how totally ridiculous it is."

Hermes put down his wine glass. "OK, I'll show you some more ridiculous. Name something you have upstairs in your room."

"Alright. In my jewelry box there's a silver and turquoise ring I bought last year when I took Angie to the Grand Canyon..."

Hermes held out his hand, and a small black hole appeared in the air above it. A little silver ring popped through the hole and dropped into his hand.

Sarah looked at the ring. "That's malachite. I got it on the same trip..."

"Sorry," said Hermes, tossing the ring up into the air, where it disappeared into the little hole. Another ring fell back into his hand. "Is this the right one?"

She reached over and took the ring. "Wow. Vortex thingie through another universe, blah, blah, blah?"

"Pretty much."

She turned the ring over in her hand for a few seconds. "How did you find it? Do you have X-ray vision or something?"

"Nothing like that. We have senses you don't have, so there is no language to really describe how it works. "I can... perceive things."

"And that's not the same as seeing?"

"Nope."

"So what's it like?"

"Like I said, I have no way to describe it, any more than you could describe 'red' to a blind person. You can't, because the experience of 'red' is basic to how you interact with the world."

She considered that for a few seconds, then her eyes widened. "Can you... perceive me whenever I want to? Like when I'm in the bath tub?"

He raised his eyebrows and lifted his wine glass in an appreciative toast. "Wow, now that is a great idea!"

Sarah grabbed a pillow from the couch and threw it at Hermes. He held up his hand, and the pillow vanished, reappearing just behind Sarah so that it hit her, bounced over her head, and landed on the coffee table. "Hey, that's not fair," she said.

"What's not?"

"None of it."

"No, I suppose it isn't."

"Can you hurt people? Could you hurt me?"

"I wouldn't."

"That's not the question. Could you? Like, could you zap me through one of your vortex thingies and into a cauldron of boiling oil?"

"Well, to start with, I have no idea where I would find a cauldron of boiling oil. I mean, it seems like hardly anyone these days even keeps a whole cauldron of oil laying around. And then to find somebody who keeps his cauldron of oil boiling... for that matter, where do you people even buy your cauldrons?"

"You know what I mean."

"OK, there was a time when I could have zapped you through a vortex, and do it without hurting you. As things are now, I can't move anything that large."

"How exactly do you mean, large?"

"Now you're just fishing for compliments."

"Busted. But I guess what I really want to know is, do you Gods have ways of crushing humans like worthless ants?"

"You are not worthless. We may not always take humans all that seriously, but then we don't take anything all that seriously. Not even ourselves. But as we see it, humans, and ants, and goldfish, and zebras all belong to this world. Yes, we can hurt and even destroy humans, just like humans can destroy each other. The only one among us who seems to really enjoy death and destruction is Ares, and even he doesn't do it randomly. Well, not totally randomly…"

"So we're not in any danger from you?"

He thought about that. "On the whole, we tend to be more indifferent or even protective than destructive. Like I said, we are fond of humans."

"Lucky for us."

"True. We have had some… squabbles among ourselves from time to time, and there has been collateral damage. I'd say that even if something like that were to happen now, we would have to get our energy levels up quite a bit higher than they are before there would be much risk to you and Angie. Besides, I'll be looking out for you."

She looked down at Angie's sleeping face. "For her sake, I hope so."

Angie rolled over, smacked her lips, and favored them with a long, wheezing fart.

"Preserve the perfect little angel at all costs," said Hermes. "You can count on me."

"You bought her the nachos." Sarah opened the window behind the couch to ventilate the room and poured them each another glass of wine. "OK, here's a dumb question; why don't you all have Greek accents? You sound like you're from Chicago."

"You know, I've never really understood why

anybody would even have an accent. We're pretty good at languages, probably because we invented the idea of turning patterns of sound into a method of communication in the first place. And if you know a word, you can choose how you want to pronounce it. So why wouldn't you pronounce it like the people you're talking to? Except for Ares, who puts on those stupid accents..."

"How many languages do you speak?"

Hermes thought it over. "Thirteen thousand, five hundred, and ninety-seven. Give or take a few. Of course, nearly half of those aren't really used much any more."

She blinked. "That's pretty good at languages, all right. All I can do is curse a little in French. Merde."

"Not familiar with it."

"So, maybe Thirteen thousand, five hundred, and ninety-six. Anyway, are there a lot of Gods running around? I mean, if you guys never die, it seems like I would find myself up to my keister in immortals."

"No, there are not all that many of us, because we don't reproduce very much. At least not with each other."

"Oh, right." She drew back a little. "If I recall my mythology class, you Gods did spend a fair amount of time 'reproducing' with humans."

"Well, I'll admit that it did happen, but it was a lot less common than those stories would have you believe. Plus, if you think about it, any time a little 'Oops' comes along, it's pretty convenient to send out a press release claiming that 'a God did it.'"

"I guess that makes sense. What about the Roman Gods, or the ones from the Vikings? Are they all relatives of yours?"

"No, that was all us. We kind of got around. I was called 'Mercury' in Rome, 'Thoth' in Egypt, 'Loki' in Scandinavia, 'Quetzalcoatl' in South America, and 'Murray' by the Indians in what would become the Upper East Side of Manhattan."

"This is a lot to wrap my head around."

"I know. While you're wrapping, I have a question for you."

"Fair enough."

"Where is Angie's father?"

Sarah slouched back on the couch and stared at her wine glass. "Angie's father was a very...unusual man. I only met him once, and I can't say that I really even knew him."

Hermes shook his head and groaned. "Oh man, I'm really sorry. That was a stupid thing to ask. Completely uncalled for."

She looked up, sat up, and smiled. "No, don't worry about it. I got over being shamed and scorned years ago."

"I just wanted to know if I was going to get my butt kicked by a jealous ex."

Sarah's eyes explored Hermes' eyes, then wandered over his body for a few seconds. "Um, no I'm pretty sure that even without being a God, you wouldn't have much of a problem with that sort of thing. At least not from anybody I've ever seen around here. Besides, so far there is nothing for an ex to be jealous about."

Hermes leaned back in his chair. "Well, we could arrange for there to be."

"What were you thinking, right here on the couch next to Angie?"

"Well, that wouldn't actually be my first choice, no. In fact, that wouldn't even make into the top twenty choices."

Sarah chuckled. "Hermes, I can't say that I'm not tempted to put her to bed and run upstairs with you…"

"That's a good start…"

"…but I have a lot to process here. I just discovered that the guy I'm getting involved with, after being alone for my kid's entire life, is the

God of…what are you the God of again?"

"Basically, thieves, literature, poetry, sports, standup comedy, practical jokes, and commerce. Oh yeah, and I'm Zeus' messenger. You remember, winged shoes and all that stuff."

"So here I am, falling for a comical Fedex guy with a CEO's morals and light fingers. Like I said, it's a lot to process."

"But you did say you were getting involved with me. And falling for me. Cool!"

Sarah stood up. "A lot to process. How about helping me get this little fart pot tucked in, then you head home on those winged shoes while I lay awake and try to figure out the pros and cons of having a literal Greek God for a boyfriend."

Hephaestus Fixes a Sidewalk

Hephaestus stood under the tent he had erected along the entire front of the Delphi, leaning on his sledge hammer, and examined the sidewalk. Aside from a couple of old cracks and slightly uneven spots, it was fine. He shook his head. *It's 4:00 AM, my generator is slag, I still don't know what has become of Aphrodite, and I'm wasting my time on this nonsense.*

He tapped the sidewalk with the hammer, and the entire length of it crumbled to a layer of fine gravel. Another tap, and the gravel popped into the air, along with the soil beneath the sidewalk. He waved his cane and a small whirlwind swept down the length of the sidewalk, thoroughly mixing the gravel and soil, which then settled back into a perfectly level layer.

Hephaestus carefully aimed his cane and sprayed a stream of concrete, twitching the tip of the cane at intervals to form grooves. In less than ten minutes he was looking with satisfaction at a perfect new sidewalk of wet cement.

He shook the last few drops of concrete from the end of his cane, then rolled it over and pointed it at the wet cement at his feet. A blast of hot air roared out, instantly hardening and curing the concrete in its path.

Hephaestus had worked his way about halfway down the new sidewalk when something tore through the tent behind him and hit him squarely in the center of the back, knocking him face-first into the still-wet cement ahead of him.

He rolled over, angrily wiping concrete from his eyes, to see Aphrodite standing over him, on the dry part of the sidewalk, feet apart and her hands on her hips. She held a nearly empty Tequila bottle in her left hand. "Oh," he said, "There you are."

"Yes, here I am," she said. "And here you go." She opened her right palm toward Hephaestus, and a blast of compressed air drove his head back into the cement. He reached for his cane, but she waved her hand and sent it to the far end of the tent.

"It seems like you're a little bit angry," he said, "and I can't say that I blame you. Let me just state, for the record, that I didn't know the explosion was going to happen."

"Did you know that this was going to happen?" She turned her hand palm up and Hephaestus rose ten feet in the air. When she flipped her hand over, Hephaestus also flipped over, and when she gestured toward the ground he splattered, hard, again face-first, back into the sidewalk.

He struggled to his hands and knees, facing away from her. "That's great," he said, spitting out wet cement. "It looks to me like I've given you quite a bit of power."

"Really? Is that what it looks like to you?" She gestured again, driving him back down onto his face and ten feet forward. "So this is just my way of saying, 'Thanks.'" She lifted him again and slammed him back down.

Hephaestus rolled over onto his back. "You're welcome," he gasped.

"So what do you have to say for yourself?"

He lifted himself up onto his elbows. "Well," he said, "have you ever wondered why I put those grooves in the sidewalk?"

"What?"

"The sidewalk. The grooves. Don't you ever get curious about stuff like that?"

"What?"

"Sidewalks have grooves in them. In most cases this is to capture any cracks that may form as the cement cures." He shook his hair, sending a spray of wet cement in all directions. "Mine serve a slightly different purpose."

"What are you talking about?"

"This." He crooked a finger, and shimmering walls of energy rose up from the grooves on all four sides of where Aphrodite stood.

"Oh, shit," she said, and shot straight up, crashing against a lid of energy across the top of her new prison. She crumpled back down onto the sidewalk.

"My sentiments exactly," he said, climbing to his feet. "Oh, I wouldn't do that..."

She raised the palm of her hand and sent a blast toward Hephaestus, only to have it bounce back and crush her into the pavement. "You are really starting to piss me off," she groaned.

"I know it, and I am sorry."

"No you're not."

"No, I suppose you're right about that. In a way, though, I am a tiny bit relieved that my experiment didn't completely destroy you."

"Yeah, I'll bet you are. So what now, you stumpy little coward? I suppose you're going to strap me to another bomb."

"I'm not sure what I'm going to do with you. I'm all out of bombs at the moment. And, to be frank, that last one didn't really work out the way I had hoped. I guess I'll just have to keep you safe while I consider all the options."

"Safe? As in locked up in this box?"

"Well, nothing can get at you or harm you while you're in there. And your double is doing her job, so it's hard to see a downside here."

She stood up and clenched her fists. "You mangy little dwarf, you are so dead. I am going to kill you, and since you won't die, I will then get to kill you again. And I am going to keep on killing you..."

"OK, retribution is my fate, vengeance will be yours, yada, yada, yada... Got it. In the meantime, why don't you be a good little girl and shut up." He clapped his hands, and the walls of Aphrodite's prison momentarily clapped in on her. As the walls returned to their original size, she slumped over, unconscious.

Hephaestus considered Aphrodite for a few seconds, then held out his hand and swept it downward. Aphrodite, her cage, and the chunk of sidewalk she lay on sank down and out of sight, headed off to Hephaestus' underground workshop.

"Just look at this mess," he said, limping over to retrieve his cane. "It's going to take me minutes to clean up all the damage you've done, bitch. Whole minutes."

Athena and Dyo

"I'm getting kind of worried about Aphrodite," said Athena, pacing past the window of her room in the hotel. "She was supposed to check in with us first thing this morning."

"Do you think we could dig up another bottle of this?" asked Dyo, shaking an empty Absinthe bottle over her tongue.

"There's a fifth of vodka in the freezer compartment of my mini-fridge." She stopped pacing and looked out the window to the street below, where Wilfred Smith and three men in navy blue suits were minutely inspecting Hephaestus' perfect new sidewalk. "It just doesn't add up, Dyo. She's not answering her cell phone."

"She said she was going to have some serious fun in San Diego. They probably have lots of Absinthe there." Dyo tossed the bottle on the bed and pulled the door of the mini-fridge open. "The way she dresses, where does Aphrodite even carry a cell phone?"

"I really don't want to know," said Athena. "Hermes can't even locate her, and he has a lot of his senses back."

"Maybe she came back and went after Hephaestus," said Dyo, cracking the seal on the Grey Goose bottle and taking a long swig. "Oh yeah, this is nice."

"Do you think?"

"Oh, sure." Dyo took another drink. "It doesn't have the kick of the Absinthe, but it definitely does the job."

"No, I mean, do you think she might have gone after Hephaestus? That could be really bad."

"She was pretty upset with him. Remember yesterday, when she told us that she was going to feed him his own…"

"…I know, I was here," said Athena. She watched Smith take a geologist's hammer from one of his assistants and swing it hard at the sidewalk. When the hammer hit the new cement it rebounded violently, flying out of Smith's hand and across the street. Smith fell backward, grasping his wrist in pain. "Hephaestus has regained some serious Power. Even as strong as she is now, if Aphrodite did take him on, I'm afraid she might have some trouble with him."

"So maybe he has her back in his workshop?"

"The workshop is really well shielded, which would explain why Hermes can't sense her. If Hephaestus does have her, she might be a little bit harder to hold onto this time. Unless he can find a way to really hurt her."

"We have to go after her, then. We can't just sit around and let him harm Aphrodite. Wow, this vodka is wonderful! Have some." She handed the bottle to Athena.

"We aren't going to do anything. If you cross Hephaestus, he could kill you." She poured a double shot of vodka into a small tumbler and handed the bottle back. "Of course, all this booze might just take care of that for him." Outside, Smith's assistants helped him to his feet and into a large white Escalade, then they drove away. "Truthfully, I doubt if any of us could take Hephaestus on directly right now. We have to figure out another way."

"Maybe if we can find a way to draw him away, I can help us get into his workshop."

"Hephaestus has always made it really hard for anybody to get into his workshop, with hidden portals, and barriers, and trick locks. How could you help?"

"I was created down there, and he brought me up through a portal into Aphrodite's room. I just feel like I can go back there."

Athena studied Dyo for a few seconds then nodded. "You need to pay attention to those feelings. I wonder..."

"Speaking of feelings, can you fill me in on guys? I think I might like guys almost as much as I like Grey Goose."

Athena laughed. "It just happens that I am the last person you should ask about that. Well, second to last – Artemis is not only as indifferent to men as I am, she is the actual Goddess of chastity and virginity."

"Wow. For some reason I find that so sad." She took a long pull on the bottle. "So, are you and Artemis more interested in women? It seems like I could find a way to relate to that, too..."

"I'll tell you what, for right now why don't we just concentrate on rescuing Aphrodite, then you can get the very best information on all of these topics straight from her. It's her specialty."

"That makes sense. So what's the next step?"

"I think it's time to bring Zeus in on this. I can't picture him letting Hephaestus harm Aphrodite, and I don't think we stand much of a chance without his help."

"You trust him."

"He's my father. He hasn't always been perfect, but yes, I trust him."

"Your father? Did he help you pick out your prom dress?"

"Prom dress? Why no, I never…What?"

"Oh, right. No guys."

Athena laughed. "He did let me throw his thunderbolts now and then. I was the only one he would let anywhere near them."

"OK, thunderbolts are just as good as a prom dress. I guess."

They found Zeus in the hotel office behind the front desk, going over some paperwork. "Morning, Athena. Hi, Aphrodite." He glanced up at Dyo. "Aphrodite, there's something different about you. What is it?"

"The girls are too big," said Dyo.

"What?"

"Boobs. I've got bigger boobs."

"Excuse me?"

"Z, I'd like you to meet Dyo. Hephaestus made her to stand in for Aphrodite so he could kidnap her without us knowing."

"Dyo? Two? Girls? Hephaestus made her so… Would you mind starting over?"

"I get that a lot," said Dyo.

It took a few minutes for Athena to fill Zeus in on all the details. "… so, we're thinking that Hephaestus might have her again, and this time he might really hurt her."

Zeus sat back and scratched his head. "Green liquid? This whole thing explains why we've been getting little bursts of energy that don't really last. But what would that green liquid be? I would love to get a look at that machine of his."

"Aphrodite thought the machine blew up when she did."

"That doesn't mean he won't rebuild it, or something like it. You know Hephaestus." He turned to Dyo. "And you say you feel some connection to the workshop since he created you there. Are you completely human?"

"I'm not sure I understand the question," said Dyo. "Do you have any Grey Goose?"

"This girl can drink like Dionysus," said Athena. Then a slow smile spread over her face. "Or, for that matter, like Aphrodite."

"Hmmm. Hephaestus was trying to capture as much of Aphrodite in her as possible. I'm thinking that it's possible that he passed on a little bit more of her than he planned."

"Mind filling me in?" said Dyo.

"Let's try a little experiment first," said Zeus. "Dyo, close your eyes and think of Hermes."

She closed her eyes, and almost immediately smiled, pulled her knees together, and pushed her hands down into her lap.

"Don't think of him like that," said Athena. "Just picture his face."

"Oh, sorry," said Dyo. She moved her hands back to the arms of her chair and closed her eyes again.

"Good," said Zeus. "Now, just think about Hermes and tell me where he is."

She tilted her head to one side. "He's in the park, pushing that little girl with the red hair on the swing, and scanning for Aphrodite. He's pretty worried about her. Also, he really cares for the child, and for her mother." She moved her hands back to her lap. "Wow, he really, really cares for the mother."

Zeus and Athena looked at each other. "How do you know all that?" asked Athena.

"I just... I don't know. I just know it."

"Her senses are sharper than mine," said Athena. "I can just barely sense where Hermes is."

"She's got me beat too," said Zeus.

Without warning, Zeus snatched the stapler off his desk and threw it at Dyo. It struck her in the middle of the forehead and fell to the floor.

"Ow," she said, "What was that for?"

"OK, so she doesn't have much in the way of reflexes."

"Or she just doesn't know how to use them," said Athena. "But look, there is not even a scratch. That thing would have at least bruised a mortal."

"What are you guys talking about?"

"Baby doll," said Athena, "You may not be quite as vulnerable as we've been thinking. And that may be a really valuable asset for us, since I'm pretty sure Hephaestus doesn't realize it."

"OK," said Zeus, "why don't you take Dyo somewhere private, find out what kind of talent she has, and start teaching her how to use it. I'm going to expand the circle a little and bring Apollo and Artemis in on what's going on."

"What about Ares and Hera?"

"Ares is an idiot. For the time being it's still important for Hephaestus to think we have no idea what he's up to, and that moron would blow it immediately."

"Assuming that Aphrodite has not told Hephaestus that we know."

"She's too smart for that. Besides, if she had, he would have made some sort of move on us by now."

"And Hera? Come on, Z, you guys went to the movie together last night."

"I know. How can you trust anybody who doesn't like Iron Man? Tell her nothing."

Goddess in a Cage

"Oh good, you're awake." Hephaestus reached out with his cane and gave Aphrodite's portable prison, suspended like a birdcage on the end of a golden chain emerging from the overhead mist in the workshop, a shove. Aphrodite, who had been trying to climb to her feet, lost her balance and fell back to the floor of the cage.

"So you are making another bomb."

Hephaestus glanced down at the half-built machine at his feet. "What, this? Let's hope not, for your sake."

"I don't get it."

"No, I don't suppose you would. But as you guessed, I am making another generator – hopefully one that will do what it's supposed to do without making as much noise as the last one."

"What makes you think this one will work any better?"

Hephaestus scratched his head. "Well, I sort of made the last one by accident. I was throwing together a regular old backup electric generator for the hotel, and I happened to make the coil from some copper I got from an old Titan shield. I think it belonged to Hyperion."

"You melted down the shield of Hyperion?"

"I got quite a bit of good wire out of it. So, when I got it all put together and went to test it, I happened to lean my hammer against the casing. The hammer, as you know, was one of my symbols as a God."

"Not an orthopedic shoe?"

"Ha, you are so very funny. Anyway, when I fired up the generator, instead of turning out 120 volts AC, it blasted me senseless with a dose of pure power. Our Power. When I woke up, I had some of my old energy back." He pushed the dreadlocks back from his face and looked into Aphrodite's eyes. "Aphrodite, I feel more like me than I have in millennia."

She leaned back against the wall of her cage. "I know what you mean," she said. "I'm pretty charged up, and it does feel good."

He cleared his throat. "I realized that I couldn't use the machine on myself at close range without spending a lot of time out cold, so I modified the generator. I used symbols to direct the energy burst at each one of you, then I whipped up a sort of condenser deal to suck as much of it back as I could."

"Why didn't you just stick with doing that?"

"It wasn't very efficient. I could only get little doses of Power at a time, and it was leaving behind more than I wanted with whoever I was harvesting it from."

"What's wrong with that? Wouldn't it be nice if all of us got our Power back?"

Hephaestus clenched his teeth. "Oh yeah, that would be fantastic. Zeus would be back on the Throne of the Heavens, and the rest of you would go back to being Lords of the world. And I could go back to making everyone's swords and lightning bolts, and fixing the celestial toilets."

"That was just the one time. How was I supposed to know you couldn't flush…"

"*ENOUGH!* No, my love, that is not how this is going to work out. The only God who will be sitting on the Throne of the Heavens from now on will be Hephaestus, the cripple, Old Step-and-a-Half, the former one-man DPW of Olympus."

Aphrodite couldn't stop herself from laughing. "You? Ruler of the Gods? Exactly how do you figure that will work?"

"It will work because I will have the power to make it work. And the rest of you will have just enough power to do my bidding."

"Your bidding? Really? Who do you think you are, Voldemort?"

"Shut UP!" Hephaestus whacked the cage with his cane, sending it spinning up into the mist, then back down, to pendulum back and forth with Aphrodite holding desperately onto the side walls. "And you, my love, will be at my side. My Queen, my helpmate, bound forever to your throne with unbreakable chains of Olympian Bronze." He grabbed the cage and stopped the rocking. "Of course that whole scenario assumes that you are going to survive the next few days."

Aphrodite sat back and folded both arms across her stomach. "Do you remember those celestial toilets we were just talking about?"

Hephaestus turned his attention back to his machine. "You see, with you confined to your impenetrable energy field, there is no telling what would happen if we were to have another explosion. I do know that the entire force of the blast would be contained in that space."

"Sounds bad, all right. As I was saying…"

"Bad does not begin to describe what you could suffer. Without any way to release the energy, you might be reduced to a kind of molecular goo and splattered all over the cage…"

"Ooh yeah, wow, that would suck for sure. Um, so, about that toilet…"

"You are not really taking any of this seriously, are you?"

"Yes, I am. Totally. Chance of goo, very serious, indescribable suffering, check. But also, I seriously have to pee, and that little ride you gave me a few minutes ago sent me over the edge. And if we don't deal with that situation real soon, there is a one-hundred percent chance that it is going to be getting seriously ugly in here."

Hephaestus heaved a sigh, then straightened up and prodded the nearest wall of the cage with the tip of his cane. The wall began to indent, forming into the shape of a toilet.

Aphrodite watched and nodded with approval. "You are clever, I'll give you that. So where is this thing going to empty into when I flush it?"

"Where all celestial toilets are emptied, into the most remote depths of Tartarus."

"You know, I never knew that. It does make sense, though – Tartarus would be the best septic field ever." She stood up. "So, are you going to just stand there and watch?"

Hephaestus tapped the wall with his cane and the entire cage went opaque.

– λατερ –

"OK, I get how you generate the Power. Kind of." Aphrodite was sitting back in her cage watching Hephaestus work on his generator. This one actually looked a little bit like a generator. "What I don't understand is how you intend to get it back from me."

"I'm working on a couple of ideas. Frankly, it depends on what happens to you when I turn this thing on."

"That whole molecular goo thing again?"

"In that case I think it would be pretty easy. Kind of like straining the pulp out of orange juice."

"Nice simile."

"Believe me, I'd rather see you spend the next ten thousand years chained to a throne. Next to me."

"Yeah, that's a way better alternative for everybody concerned."

"If you survive intact, I will have to be a little bit more creative. My old method involved sucking energy through a trans-dimensional portal from the subject into a capacitor/condenser unit. Like I said, it left too much power behind for my taste." He tapped on a small brass fitting, which snapped off and clattered to the floor. "Damn."

"Yeah, I can see that this one is way better than the one that blew up."

"So if you survive receiving the charge, I'll have you dangling right here to experiment with. Then, once I come up with the best method, I'll be able to drain power from anybody, any time."

"Wow. What could possibly go wrong with a great plan like that?"

Four

Does the lame one believe he is creating energy?

He is creating it.

Of course he is. Only not really.

Not in any way that he can understand.

True.

I begin to doubt this group.

We doubted their parents.

For good reason.

True.

How many times will this repeat itself?

As many times as it takes.

A Goddess in Training

"Show me another trick," said Angie, skipping along next to Hermes. "Make Lindsay Martin into a toad."

"Why does Lindsay Martin deserve to be a toad?" Angie and Hermes were heading back from the park to the Delphi, to meet Sarah for lunch.

"I don't just want her to be a toad," said Angie. "I want her to be a toad that gets eaten by a big ugly bird. Then the bird poops her out onto King's dog food – King is Mr. Turner's dog. You know, Mr. Turner, he's the kind of creepy guy who lives next door to us and has a telescope in his bedroom window, so we have to make sure to keep the curtains closed on that side of the house? So anyway, King eats it, poop and all, because his eating habits are really disgusting, him being a dog, then King poops her out and Mr. Turner throws her in a garbage bag, even though he's not supposed to put animal waste in there, and then the whole thing goes to the landfill and it turns into fertilizer that they put on a corn field so everybody can eat the corn with Lindsay Martin in it at their Fourth of July picnic. Then they all poop her out the next day."

"Wow. That's pretty harsh. What did she do?"

"She didn't invite me to her birthday party."

"OK, I can see giving her the triple poop treatment for that. But I can't just go around turning people into toads. For one thing, I don't know how. Besides, right now I have to work on finding Aphrodite."

"Are you trying to find her right now?"

"Yes. But I'm not having much luck."

"She'll be OK, Hermes. She's a Goddess, so nothing can hurt her."

"I'm not so sure about that. I've known those two for a real long time. Every time she and Hephaestus get together it always turns out pretty bad."

"She's hanging up in the air, and she's not very happy, but I'm pretty sure she's still all right."

Hermes stopped walking. "What?"

"Look, there's Mr. Z!" She ran toward Zeus at the front door of the Delphi.

"Angie, wait. What was that you said?"

"I don't know. Hi, Mr. Z!"

"Hi Angie. Go on inside, your mom is here. Hermes, we need to talk." said Zeus. "Athena told me about Hephaestus and Aphrodite, and I've met Dyo. Apollo and Artemis also know everything."

"Good," said Hermes, "I'm beginning to think that this thing might shape up to be more than just a little skirmish."

"There's a good chance of it. Athena said you were out doing some scanning. Any luck?"

"Not a bit. But Angie just said something really strange, like she could sense Aphrodite."

"Really? When none of us can?" Zeus shook his head. "Not likely."

"So we need a plan. While we're working on that, what if Hephaestus shows up here?"

"Good question. Why do you ask?"

"Because he's headed this way. And I have a lunch date with Angie's mom. Good luck!" Hermes ducked through the door into the bar.

Zeus turned around to face Hephaestus, who was limping down the block from the direction of his barn. "Um, the sidewalk looks great." ... *OK, just exactly what are you up to?*

Hephaestus paused a second to look at his work. "Oh. Thanks. I used some special reinforced concrete." ... *Is it possible you still have no idea what I'm doing?*

"Looks great." ... *You hide your treachery well.*

"Thank you." ... *Oh, if you only had any idea how hard it is to keep a straight face.*

"So, what have you been doing?" ...*besides kidnapping and maybe torturing the Goddess of love and beauty?*

"Still working on that backup power generator for the hotel." ... *along with kidnapping and torturing the Goddess of love and beauty.*

"So, how's it coming?" ... *I'd like to strike you down where you stand and force you to release her.*

"Not bad. I'm having trouble getting the unit to output enough juice to keep the refrigerators in the restaurant running." ...*What's going on, Old Man? Small talk is not your style.*

"Do you think you might have it ready by tomorrow? They're predicting some nasty weather later in the week." ... *or maybe I should just cast you into Tartarus with your grandfather.*

"I'll try. I might just pick one up at Home Depot, soup it up, and convert it to run on natural gas." ...*That's more like it, ordering me around as if you were still in charge.*

"Good idea. If we get another tornado in the neighborhood we'll be throwing away all the food in the walk-in again." ... *so how do I deal with you? I have no idea how powerful you are. Or even how powerful I am. Damn.*

Hephaestus smiled. "I'm on it, Chief." ...*Screw the food in the walk-in, and screw this dump, and especially screw all of you. ...With luck, by this time next week you and the rest of the world will be trembling at my feet.* "Right after I grab some lunch."

"Thanks." ...*With luck, by this time next week I'll have you chained to a forge somewhere pounding out hairpins for Hera.* "Keep me posted." Zeus headed for the hotel, to Athena's room, to check in on Dyo's training.

– λατερ –

"OK, try it again," said Athena.

Dyo, sitting on the edge of Athena's bed, frowned and narrowed her eyes at the glass of water on the bedside table. "It doesn't work," she said. "I can't do it."

Athena sat in a chair facing Dyo, who was leaning forward in her own chair like a baseball fan in the eighth inning. "Just relax and concentrate. Picture the glass rising from the table. Believe it, and it will."

Dyo closed her eyes and clenched her fists. Her forehead creased with concentration and her hands began to tremble. The water in the glass began to vibrate, forming perfect concentric rings on the surface.

"That's it," said Athena. "Now see the glass floating up into the air."

Dyo clenched her eyes tighter and the vibration in the glass increased. A low hum filled the room, and the walls seemed to breathe, drawing in and expanding like a gigantic lung congested with Swedish Modern hotel room furniture. Her mouth puckered in concentration, and a drop of perspiration rolled down her left cheek.

The glass rose a few inches into the air and seemed to swell to twice its size. Then retracted, rapidly shrinking until it was a tiny dot, then with a loud "POP!" it disappeared entirely.

Dyo opened her eyes and looked at Athena. "What happened?"

Athena raised her eyebrows and shrugged her shoulders. "I have no idea. Why did you make the whole glass disappear?"

"Is that what I did? Where did it go?"

"You tell me. What's the last thing that ran through your mind before the glass disappeared?"

"OK, I was concentrating on seeing it in the air, just like you told me. Then my mind kind of wandered and... oh!" Dyo put her hand to her mouth and looked sheepish.

"What?

"Zeus."

"What about him?"

"Well, like I said, my mind kind of wandered, and Zeus' face just sort of popped into my head. Like that old uncle who is pretty cool, so you've always kind of wanted to... you know, but you never really got the chance. Know what I mean?"

Athena tried to conceal her shudder. "Not really. So you were picturing Zeus when you transported the water?"

"I guess so."

As she spoke, Zeus rapped on the door and let himself into the room, soaking wet and wiping water from his eyes. "Do you have a towel handy?" he asked, handing the empty glass Athena.

"In the bathroom. Help yourself," said Athena.

"It seems like you two are making good progress," he shouted from the bathroom.

"Yes, we are. She was able to transport that glass of water, and she was only trying to levitate it. We still need to do some work on maintaining focus, though."

Zeus came out of the bathroom with a towel wrapped around his neck. "So I wasn't an intended target? That's reassuring." He dabbed at his eyes with a corner of the towel.

"I'm really sorry," said Dyo.

Zeus held up his hand. "Think nothing of it. It was actually kind of refreshing."

"You see, it just popped into my head that you were kind of like that uncle..."

"Whoa there," Athena interrupted. "Z, she clearly has some Power. In fact, she may be at least as strong as the rest of us, if she knew what to do with it."

"Interesting. Maybe you should concentrate on teaching her how to defend herself. Hephaestus is strolling around like nothing is wrong, so it would appear that he is feeling pretty confident. I think he might be getting ready to move on us."

Another rap on the door, and Hermes came in, followed by Angie. "There you are, Z. We've been looking for you."

Angie walked straight over to Dyo and studied her face carefully. "You are just as beautiful as Aphrodite. Hermes said that you were." She reached out and took Dyo's hands in hers.

"She knows about all this?" Zeus asked Hermes.

"I didn't know you could get more than four people into one of these rooms," said Athena to nobody in particular.

"If we're going to get our power back, Z, it might help if mortals believe in us."

"Possibly," said Zeus. "But you could be exposing her to danger."

Dyo smiled at Angie. "You are very pretty yourself. Your red hair is just beautiful, and your skin is absolutely lovely. In fact..."

"Down girl," said Athena. "That is way beyond inappropriate."

"I don't think there is much danger, Z. And I think there may be more to Angie and her mom than we might have assumed."

Angie looked deeply into Dyo's eyes. "You are not very old," she said. "You're not even as old as me. But I can see something else in there." Her eyes narrowed. "Can you make Lindsay Martin into a toad for me?"

"And her mother knows as well?" asked Zeus.

"Yes, and she is totally on our side. The more time I spend with her and Angie, the stronger I feel." He raised his hand and a full-grown goat fell through a portal and onto the bed next to Dyo. "A couple of days ago I couldn't have done that."

"Maybe we can tear out the wall to the room next door and make it a suite," said Athena. "The goat could do the demolition, since we now have a goat."

Another polite knock, and Artemis came into the room. "Athena, Ares is going bat-shit crazy down in the kitchen," she said. "He is convinced that the Argonauts broke in and stole his cheese grater. Oh, hi! You must be Dyo. I'm Artemis."

"Tell Ares that the Argonauts have all been dead for thousands of years," said Athena. "And remind him that he broke his cheese grater yesterday, throwing it at Apollo."

Dyo, still holding Angie's hands, looked up at Artemis. "So you're the other virgin! But then, I guess I am, too," She giggled. "In fact, if not in spirit. There just hasn't been enough time for me to do anything about..."

"Hello. Child in the room," said Angie.

"So you're thinking that the time you've been spending with these mortals is working to restore your Power," said Zeus to Hermes. "Have you noticed any new manifestations?"

"Well, there's this." Hermes spread his arms and grew larger, until his head was bent against the ceiling.

"Yeah, we definitely needed somebody to find a way to use up some more space in here," said Athena.

"Intentional up-sizing - great! But what do you mean there may be more to Angie and her mom?" asked Zeus.

"Like I said, I think Angie might have been sensing Aphrodite earlier." said Hermes. "And Sarah knew Phil before we woke up."

"Really. Angie, can you tell where Aphrodite is?"

"She is right here," she said, nodding at Dyo. "And she is also in a cage in the air, in a golden room. A messy one."

"How do you know this?" asked Athena.

"I just do."

"Do you know where the golden room is?" asked Hermes.

"Sure. It's under the mountain."

"What mountain?" asked Artemis. "Do you mean Olympus?"

"I guess." Angie again looked into Dyo's eyes. "The path is here. And the Power." As she squeezed Dyo's hands, Dyo began to grow, like Hermes had, until the back of her head was bent against the ceiling.

"OK, I'm not too sure about this," said Dyo. "Do guys like big girls?"

"Guys like any kind of girls," said Artemis.

"Did Angie do that?" asked Zeus.

"Or maybe Angie gave Dyo the Power to do it," said Hermes, returning to his normal size. "I don't know."

The door opened without any sort of preliminary knock and Apollo walked in. "Oh for pity sake," said Athena.

Apollo looked around the room. "Cool, a Giant Aphrodite. And a goat!" He crossed to the goat, who was still standing on the bed, munching on one of Athena's pillows, and scratched it behind the ear. "Where did you guys get a goat?"

"Angie, do you know how to get to Hephaestus' workshop?" asked Zeus.

"Hey, that's my pillow," shouted Athena.

"Mahahahahahahahah," said the goat, munching on the pillow.

"There is a portal," said Angie, still looking up into Dyo's eyes.

"Yeah, she told me about the one in Aphrodite's room," said Hermes. "I checked it out, and it's gone."

"There are a lot of portals," said Angie, "some open and some closed. Dyo can see them, and she can use them."

"OK, now this is like the old days," said Apollo, growing to match Dyo's size. "I can feel the Power." He smiled at Dyo. "Hey, 'sup?"

"Now we're getting somewhere," said Zeus.

"Now we're going to have to take turns breathing," said Athena.

"Dyo, can you see where there may be more portals?" asked Hermes.

"With my head stuck against the ceiling like this, all I can see is my chest," said Dyo. "Wow, this is pretty impressive..."

"Still a child in the room," said Angie.

"OK everybody," said Zeus, "grab your weapons and meet me in the hotel lobby."

"We can find the golden room, and release Aphrodite," said Angie. "But only three can go."

Zeus narrowed his eyes at the girl. "Excuse me?"

"Only three can go to save Aphrodite."

"How do you know this?" asked Athena.

"I just do."

"She's right," said Dyo. "I feel it too."

Zeus looked at them and nodded slowly. "All right," he said. "Apollo, Hermes, you're with me."

"No, sorry," said Angie. "It has to be Dyo. And Athena..."

"And me," said Artemis. "I'll get my bow..."

"No," said Angie. "It has to be me."

"Mahahahahahahahah," said the goat.

Preparations

"Do you seriously expect me to send my ten year old daughter into combat against an evil God?" Sarah, Hermes and Angie were in Sara's beige-on-beige office in the bank. The door was closed, and she was talking in an explosive whisper. "Damn it, I can't even believe that I actually just said that sentence out loud!"

"Combat is such a harsh word."

"What do you call it when Gods do battle in an underground lair?"

"Um, well OK, it's combat-ish. Believe me, Sarah, it's not my choice. Angie says that's the only way."

"Because the fifth grader is the senior tactician on the operation. Yeah, that gives me way more confidence in the whole concept."

"With us, it's like that a lot," said Hermes. "Remember how I was explaining senses to you that I couldn't really explain to you?"

"Red to a blind man, I get it. That is not going to keep her from having somebody change her into a ficus tree with a back story."

"Mom, I'll be fine. Mr. Hephaestus won't do anything to hurt me."

"You have to break into a magical place and rescue an actual Goddess from being tortured and possibly destroyed by a maniac God, and you're telling me that the maniac God can't hurt you?"

"Maybe he can, but he won't."

"OK, Angie, that's not really helping," said Hermes. "Look, Sarah, Angie is more than a ten year old girl..."

"I'll be eleven in September..."

"Right, see? She's almost eleven. Even better, for some reason she has some of our kind of Power in her, and it looks like she is able to channel it. A lot of it."

"Yeah, now that makes no sense at all to me. She's a kid!"

"I know. But Zeus did a quick test with her, and found that she has some serious Power of her own. The squirt whipped up a totally effective defensive shield, on the fly, with no training at all."

"That stapler would have hit me right in the head," said Angie.

"Zeus tried to bean my daughter with a stapler?" asked Sarah.

"... and she was able to up-size Dyo just by holding her hands."

Angie giggled. "She was gigantic! If you know what I mean."

"Tell me again why I let my daughter hang out with you?"

"Because you trust me, we're falling in love, and I'm cheaper than day care. Look Sarah, I promise that I will never, ever, let anything happen to her."

"You won't even be there."

"Ah, well, that's true. But Athena will, and she can outfight any of us... except Ares. She can even beat him, if she's fighting on her own terms. And she is smarter than all of us put together."

"I just don't see how I can..."

"... and Athena has been working with Dyo, so that she can handle Aphrodite's sword, she can up-size whenever she wants, and she can fire off some pretty impressive energy waves."

"Energy waves? Hermes, do you hear what you're saying?"

"Athena taught me how to deflect an energy

wave that she said would be enough to crush a rhinoceros," said Angie.

"Do what to a what?"

"Angie," said Hermes, "why don't you go find Artemis and see how she's doing with those goat burgers. Ask her to save me one."

"That is so transparent," said Angie. "And you're supposed to be the clever one. Why not just come out and tell me to beat it so you can talk to my mom alone."

"Angie, beat it, so I can talk to your mom alone. But do go ahead and check on those goat burgers. I'm starving."

Once Angie was out of the bank, Hermes took Sarah's hand and said, "Sarah, I swear to you, nothing will happen to her. Angie can't know it, but I'm going to make myself invisible and follow them."

"You can make yourself invisible?"

"What exactly did you do in that Greek mythology class you took? Of course I can, with my uncle Hades' hat. It does that. Look, I have quite a bit of my Power back, and between just Athena and me, we can easily take Hephaestus – especially if I surprise him. Add in Dyo, and Aphrodite after we release her, and there's no way we can lose. And I am completely serious when I say that Angie is tapping some serious Power on her own."

"She's my baby."

"She's not a baby, she's… well, we're not sure what she is. Sarah, do you think I would let this happen if there was the slightest chance of her getting hurt. I promise, I will not let any harm come to her."

Sarah looked down for a long moment, gazing at the "Loan Officers Collateral-Palooza 2005" commemorative paperweight on her desk. Then she looked up at Hermes and said, "Can you make me invisible too?"

"I suppose I could, by continuously touching you while I'm invisible… Oh no, wait. We're not doing that!"

"Oh yes we are."

"No way. You'll turn out to be my Reel Five Fight Foil!"

"Your what?"

"Don't you ever watch action movies? At some point toward the end of the fifth reel, after the big battle has been going on for a while, and just as the good guy is about to take down the bad guy, the good guy's love interest stumbles into the line of fire. Then the bad guy grabs her and puts a gun to her head, and the good guys all have to put their guns down, and eventually the fight flares up again so they can get another ten minutes out of the action footage."

"Wait, what's all this stuff about guns? You never mentioned guns."

"No, no, that's just the movie reference I was using to make my point..."

"So the messenger of the Gods is also a movie freak. I'm not sure why, but I find that disturbing. And you're leaning pretty hard on that whole 'love interest' thing."

Hermes looked down at Sarah's hand, still resting in his. "You know exactly what I'm talking about. You know how I feel about both of you."

"I have no idea what that means when you're dating a God."

"Honestly, neither do I. I've never been in exactly this position before."

"In seven thousand years, you were never interested in a woman?"

"Sure there were some. And really, it's been way more than seven thousand years if you add it all up. But remember, I was asleep for a pretty big chunk of that time, so you would have to subtract hundreds from the potential total, just based on the averages..."

"There is such a thing as way, *way* too much information."

"... but I have never really known anyone quite like you. I can't really explain the way I feel about you guys. But I do know that where we're going I can protect Angie. And I know that I could protect you. I'm just not completely sure that if it came down to it, I could protect both of you at the same time. Sarah, you really will have to trust me on this."

Sarah shook her head. "Why is this starting to make sense to me?"

"Because it does make sense. Look, if we can take care of this situation with Hephaestus right now, before he gets any more Power stored up, we can head off what could become a real war. I'm not sure how it happened or what it means, but it seems like Angie is an important part of getting that done."

"And there is no way you can do it without her?"

"Nope."

"And you won't let anything happen to her?"

"I swear it."

"Do you have any idea how miserable I will make your existence if anything does happen to her? You would find immortality to be a distinct disadvantage."

"Oh, yeah. I'm totally clear on that."

– λατερ –

As Artemis helped Athena strap on her armor, Athena laid out her plan to Angie and Dyo. "So once we find the portal, we'll need to move quickly. There will be a locked door just before we enter the workshop."

"Dyo can open it," said Angie.

"How how will I do that?" asked Dyo. With Angie's help she was putting on Aphrodite's armor, which had apparently been designed by the ancient Greek version of Victoria's Secret. It featured an Olympian Bronze bustier, a short white cape, a tiny white skirt, a stylish Gold helmet with a long, flowing white plume, sandals with Gold laces wound up to the knee and svelte Gold gloves.

"We'll know how to open it when the time comes," said Angie. She stepped back and looked thoughtfully at Dyo. "Doesn't the amount of coverage you're getting from that armor kind of miss the point?"

"Angie, I'd feel better if you had some kind of armor too," said Athena. "Unfortunately, the one person who could make some in your size is the guy whose butt we are going down there to kick."

"I won't need it," said Angie.

"I have a cute little shield of Aphrodite's that you could take," said Dyo. "No, wait, that's a compact. A really big one. Wow, who has a compact this big?"

"I don't want a shield," said Angie. "I have this." She reached into the pocket of her shorts and pulled out a bright blue chunk of sidewalk chalk.

"Well, that's a relief," said Artemis, tightening a leather strap on one of Athena's greaves. "I was worried that you wouldn't have any way to protect yourself."

"You can stop worrying," said Angie, stuffing the chalk back into her pocket. "I'll be fine."

"What you will be," said Athena, "is behind me or behind Dyo at all times. Got that?" It was more a statement of settled fact than a question.

"Got it," said Angie.

"But how will you guys actually deal with Hephaestus?" asked Artemis.

"I'm still kind of working that out," said Athena. "If his workshop is anything like it was in the old days, there will be a lot of stuff lying around. Dyo can supersize and throw a compression wave to blast one of his junk piles at him, which should at least distract him. Then I can attack and keep him off balance. While I have him busy, Angie and Dyo can find Aphrodite and set her free. Then we can all gang up on him and beat him to a pulp with his own stupid cane."

"Sounds like a pretty good plan," said Artemis. "Gods, I wish I could come along and pump a few arrows into his fat head. Talk about a distraction!"

"I wish you could," said Angie, "It would be

pretty cool to see you in action."

"Another time," said Artemis, settling a plumed golden helmet on Athena's head.

There was a heavy rap on the door and a frowning Zeus walked in, carrying a pulsing golden lightning bolt. "Here," he said handing it to Athena. "If my daughter is going to fight my battles, she should at least have my weapon to do it with. I've spent most of the afternoon getting as much charge as I could into it."

Athena turned the lightning bolt over in her hands. "You have trusted me with this in battle before. I'll use it well."

"Just don't rely on it too much," said Zeus.

"It's the thunderbolt of Zeus. That's just bound to come in handy." She tucked it into her belt, just behind her sword.

Zeus nodded, and his frown softened slightly. "Don't underestimate this. A battle is a battle, and there is a lot we don't know right now."

"I'll take care of her, Mr. Z," said Angie.

Zeus laughed. "You know, little one, I believe you will."

A Quest Begins

Dyo stood in front of Hephaestus' steel outhouse with her eyes closed. "He built a portal here, and I can sense that it's still open, but he has it well sealed. If I can only work out his code..." She walked slowly around the outhouse, still with her eyes closed.

Athena reached out with her spear and tapped on the side of the outhouse, eliciting the beautiful ringing tone. "That's odd," she said, and tapped it once more. Again, the beautiful tone, an octave higher. "Steel shouldn't have this sort of resonance." She tapped it a third time, this time answered by the dull thud, and the door swung open.

"Really?" said Dyo. "The code is three taps? He's not a master of evil, he's a complete imbecile."

"Let's go," said Angie, scampering through the door. Athena and Dyo followed after her.

At the bottom of the stairs, they stood in front of the glowing door and examined the shape indented in it. "That looks really familiar," said Dyo.

"I think it's the shape of his cane," said Athena. "He must be using it as a kind of key." She ran her hand thoughtfully over the embossing.

Angie squatted down next to the pool and began to dig out handfuls of wet clay. "Mud pies!" said Dyo, kneeling down by the pool. "That looks like fun!"

Athena leaned on her spear. "Look girls, we don't have time to play in the... Oh!" She moved to join them.

Within a few minutes they had a tube of wet clay formed, roughly the length of Hephaestus' cane. Working together they picked it up, carried it to the door, and carefully pressed it into the embossed area. As soon as all the intricate shapes of the embossing were filled, the impression began to rotate clockwise.

Athena shoved Angie behind her, raised her shield and lowered her spear. Dyo moved next to Athena and drew Aphrodite's sword, an elegant saber with a vibrant etched blade and a spare lipstick in the handle. The two women crouched slightly, ready to spring into action. The door swung open.

Athena and Dyo charged through the door. Dyo shot up to massive size, raised her left hand, and fired off a deafening explosive blast of compressed air. Athena drew her spear back and scanned for a target, ready to strike.

Angie stepped around from behind Athena and gazed around the vast and, as far as the eye could see through the golden haze, totally empty room. The concession from Dyo's blast echoed off into the distance. "He's not here," Angie said. "But I'm pretty sure he knows that we are."

Athena took off her helmet and looked around. "This looks like his workshop."

Dyo returned to her normal size and sheathed her sword. "It is the workshop. But where is all the junk?"

"The junk is where it always was," said Angie. "I think he moved the door."

Athena took a long look at Angie. "That's a... remarkable deduction. You were born a mortal, and you've lived your entire life with a mortal's 3-dimensional frame of reference. How could you conceive of the multi-dimensional manipulations it would take to reposition the outlet of a portal?"

"I just figured he used magic," said Angie. "Let's go." She started walking away from the door.

They had walked for nearly an hour before they saw a figure standing in the distance. They stood at the ready and watched for a few minutes, then decided that the utter lack of movement by the figure meant they were looking at a statue. As they drew nearer, still cautious, they saw that they were right.

It was an oversized image of Hephaestus himself, roughly modeled in clay. The head was mostly obscured in the mist above, but the body was unmistakable, right down to the misshapen leg. His right hand was raised above his head and disappeared into the mist.

"Why would he make such an unattractive statue of himself?" asked Dyo.

"He sees what is - no more, and no less," said Athena. "So most of his work mirrors reality."

"He told me that he made a woman before me, a mortal named Pandora." said Dyo. "I am an exact copy of Aphrodite. Was Pandora a copy of anyone in particular?"

Athena pursed her lips and kept her eyes fixed on the statue. "Yes, she was."

"I read about Pandora," said Angie. "She was maybe too smart for her own good. She got too curious and opened the box that released all the evil into the world. The only thing left in the box was hope."

"It happened something like that," said Athena. "Only it was a jar, not a box."

"Sounds like she really messed up," said Dyo. "So who was she patterned after?"

Athena, still staring at the statue said, "Me."

"Oops," said Dyo, "Awkward!"

"We should fight now," said Angie, diving to the side. The right hand of the statue came swinging down from the mist, holding a giant version of Hephaestus' cane, which smashed into the floor where Angie had been standing and splattered into a huge blob of wet clay.

Athena jumped into the air and drove her spear down through the statue's hand, pinning it to the floor. Dyo drew her sword, in one smooth motion striking at the left leg of the statue. The sword sliced neatly through the clay, separating the leg at the ankle, and the statue dropped to its knee. As it fell, the statue roared and swept its left hand around in an arc that caught Dyo, lifted her, drove her into Athena, and sent the two of them sailing nearly out of sight.

The statue grabbed Athena's spear with its left hand and tried to pull it out. Angie rolled to her feet and ran around behind the statue, scooping a handful of clay from the remnants of the cane on her way by.

By the time the statue freed its hand and turned around, Angie was standing facing him, feet apart, and holding in her hand a small gun-shaped hair dryer sculpted from clay. The statue raised its left arm to strike. Angie pointed her gun and said "Go ahead, make my clay."

A slight groan came from the air just to the right of Angie, and a searing stream of hot flame blasted the statue's left shoulder. The clay hardened almost instantly, freezing the arm in place. Angie dodged a blow from the right arm and pulled the trigger on the hair dryer, sending out a jet of hot air that immobilized that shoulder. The statue tried to kick at her, but another blast of flame from her right hardened the leg. "Thanks, Hermes," she said.

"Make my clay?" said a disembodied voice. "For that, I should have let it have you. So how did you know I was here?"

"You smell like soap. It's the kind you always use. Irish Spring?"

"Oh. Didn't think of that." The blast of flame widened to engulf the rest of the statue. "Let's not let the ladies know I'm with you just yet. Element of surprise and all that."

"OK."

By the time Athena and Dyo had limped back, the entire statue was cooked solid. "I'm impressed," said Athena. "How did you manage to pull this off?"

"I just made my little hair dryer with a super, super, super high setting."

"How would you even think to do that?" asked Dyo.

"Didn't you ever play with clay and a hair dryer? No, I guess you wouldn't have."

Athena took the gun from Angie and examined it. "How come this is not the least bit hot?" she asked.

"Well, duh!" said Angie. "It's just a make-believe hair dryer made of clay."

Athena sighed, tossed the clay hair dryer at the foot of the statue and said, "OK, so he knows we're coming. I doubt he seriously believed that this would stop us. Angie, what did I say about staying behind me?"

"If I'd been behind you, I would have flown farther than you guys did."

Dyo giggled and Athena sighed again. "OK, fair enough. But seriously, that thing could have killed you."

"I'll be more careful from now on."

They set off again. After another hour of walking they began to encounter piles of scrap metal, wire, tubing, and other Hephaestus-like material. "This room is really long," said Dyo. "But we must be getting close to the other end."

"Hephaestus always did like to leave himself plenty of room to expand," said Athena. She kicked at a pile of used hockey pucks. "Where do you suppose he gets all this stuff?"

"Why do you suppose he gets all this stuff?" said Dyo.

"Bad news," said Angie. "Here comes some more stuff."

With a furious clatter, hundreds of insect-like metal creatures, each one the size of a small dog, charged from the mist, running on legs made of water pipes and bits of conduit, and waving coat hanger arms.

"They don't look very dangerous," said Dyo.

"Don't assume anything, said Athena. "Angie, behind me!" She brought her shield and spear to the ready.

"I've got this," said Dyo, up-sizing again and thrusting her hand out in the direction of the attackers. The blast of air hit them and blew them into their component pieces. "There you go," she said as she returned to her normal size.

"I'm not so sure," said Angie, peering around Athena's skirt. "Look!"

The parts were not clattering to the floor. Instead, they were whirling into a vortex of nuts, bolts, pipes, coat hangers, and other metal bits. As they spun in the air, they began to stick together, in what at first seemed to be random clumps.

Then a pattern began to form. A gigantic handle emerged at the back of the cloud of parts, with an oversized trigger. A pair of blades, stacked one on the other, with deeply serrated teeth that looked a bit like the mouth of an alligator, grew from the front of the handle and toward where the women stood.

"Is that what I think it is?" asked Athena.

"A ginormous cordless hedge trimmer?" said Angie. "Uh huh, I'd say that's what it is." As the words left her mouth the hedge trimmer sprung to life, the blades sliding over each other ominously. It floated slowly toward them, it's teeth gnashing.

"Seriously?" said Dyo. "You would have to try to let that thing catch you. We could saunter away from it."

"Yeah, but you'd have to keep on sauntering forever," said Angie. "If you stopped for a long lunch it might catch up."

"Yep, we had better destroy it now," said Athena. "I'll take care of it." She sprinted off to the right of the hedge trimmer, flanking it, and moved in with her shield in front of her.

As she got near, the hedge trimmer lunged at her, moving with blinding speed. Startled, Athena didn't have time to jump clear, so she shoved her shield into the teeth, pulled her arm out of the straps, and rolled away.

The blades jammed against the shield and stopped for a few seconds, then with a shriek of tearing metal, sliced right through it. "Hey," shouted Athena, climbing to her feet. "That was my good shield."

The hedge trimmer made another lunge for her, and even though this time she was prepared, she was barely able to avoid the teeth. Dyo drew her sword.

"Your sword will just break," said Angie. "We need to find another way to..." She dove out of the way of a lightning-fast strike by the hedge trimmer, "...beat this thing."

"You know, I'm..." Dyo flipped backward out of reach of the blades, "... getting tired of my first impressions about this stuff being ironically wrong." She crouched down and sent a blast of air at the hedge trimmer, to no effect.

The blades swung toward where Angie was getting to her feet. She stumbled backward trying to avoid them, but this time she was off balance and could not jump clear. As the teeth were about to close on her, a metal street light pole shot up from the floor, jamming the blades for the few seconds it took for Angie to roll clear.

Athena dove in and smacked the side of the hedge trimmer with her spear shouting, "Come on, you piece of junk. Try to get me!" It wheeled around to take a swipe at her, and she skipped out of the way "Dyo, up-size and see if you can get to that switch on the handle. Maybe you can turn it off!" she shouted.

Dyo, now behind the handle, inflated again, soaring from the waist up out of sight into the mist. Then her enormous and perfectly manicured hand swooped down, picked up the hedge trimmer, and flipped the switch. As soon as the blades shuddered to a stop, she threw it to the ground and stomped on it with a very large spike-heeled pump, smashing the contraption into millions of random pieces.

Angie, Athena, and Dyo all stood around the wreckage, ready for the parts to re-form again, but they stayed put, inanimate, on the ground. After a few minutes Dyo shrank back to her normal size. "Shoot, I broke a nail," she said. "I'll bet I would hate doing lawn work."

"This is getting more dangerous," said Athena, looking at the halves of her shield. "That thing should not have been able to cut through Olympian Bronze. Angie, that light pole trick was quick thinking. I had no idea you could do that."

"Neither did I," said Angie. "But it seems like this beating thing was still too easy. I think Mr. Hephaestus might just be messing with us."

"Maybe it was not all that hard for you," said Dyo, waving her hand in the air. "My nail?"

"So why was Dyo's shoe tougher than your shield?" asked Angie.

"It wasn't," said Athena. "Hephaestus made my shield and our swords, and he would know that we would use them to try to stop the blades. He designed this thing for that. It was made from a heap of scrap metal reconstructed on a quantum level. After the inter-dimensional forces were disrupted by turning off the switch, it lost all cohesion, so then Dyo could smash it."

"Yeah," said Dyo. "Whatever she said."

"I just wonder why he's doing this," said Angie. "Couldn't he have just made an army of big cutting things and had them attack us?"

"Yes, he could," said Athena. "It took a lot of energy to set that up the way he did. I think he mainly wanted to disarm me. For some reason, he is testing us. And if he's watching, he now knows that Dyo is more than mortal."

"And he knows the same about Angie," said Dyo. "He should be pretty well prepared for us by the time we get to him."

"I'm afraid you're right," said Athena.

"Maybe we should go back and get some help," said Dyo.

"No," said Angie. "We have to do it with who is here. You know I'm right."

"I still don't really understand why," said Dyo.

"We don't need anyone else."

"I'm not so sure," said Athena. "I'm still not up to my full Power, and it looks like Hephaestus might just be getting pretty near his."

"Maybe the Power is not where you think it is," said Angie.

"How do you know all this stuff?" asked Dyo.

"I know that I have everything to learn," said Angie, "and that helps me out a lot. I don't know what won't work, so it does. Usually. Sometimes."

"And you don't fear the learning," said Athena. "Why don't you ever get scared like little girls are supposed to?"

Angie thought for a few seconds. "I do get scared, lots of times. But not about this stuff. I know I'll be all right."

"How do you?" asked Dyo.

Angie shook her head. "I don't know how. I just know."

Athena smiled. "Yeah, I really do get that. Look, it's clear that you have abilities, and some insights that I don't have. But I have to admit, I am getting pretty curious about where those abilities and insights are coming from."

"Isn't it obvious? We're girls." Angie raised her hands over her head and twirled in a little circle.

"Yeah!" said Dyo, "We're girls. Who needs Power? Hey, I'm getting the hang of irony!"

"That is Power," said Athena.

"Girl power!" said Angie.

Athena looked at Angie and shook her head. "Sometimes I'm not so sure who the wise one is in this gang."

"You are," said Angie. "You see, I'm the innocent one, and Dyo..."

"Right, right, I got all that. So I guess what we need to do now is get all that girl power cranked up. Let's walk and talk."

The Battle of the Workshop

They walked on, passing larger and more frequent piles of scrap, until they were constantly threading their way through them. Dyo and Athena both had their swords drawn, and Athena held her spear at the ready.

Olympian Bronze is not only incredibly strong, it is nearly weightless, so Angie was "wearing" Athena's shield, an arm stuck through the strap on each half. This made Athena feel better, and it made Dyo comment that Angie looked like a clam that had swallowed a little girl.

"We have no idea what he might hit us with next," said Athena, "So we'll have to be ready to respond to just about anything. I think we'll be best if I stay in the center of any attack, and you two move to the sides, until we know what we're dealing with."

"Are you sure?" asked Dyo.

"I'm sure. We want me to take the brunt of whatever happens," said Athena. "You both know the plan."

Dyo nodded. "Yes, we know the pla..."

A fireball exploded in front of Athena, blasting a crater in the ground and throwing them all violently backward. Dyo and Angie landed on their backs, while Athena rolled over and sprung back to her feet, her sword in one hand and spear in the other.

Hephaestus limped out from behind a pile of chrome hubcaps, chuckling. "My noble sister," he said. "I am more than happy to let you take the brunt of this..." He pointed his cane and another fireball shot out, striking Athena squarely in the chest, lifting her into the air, and driving her right into the center of a mound of old carburetors, which cascaded on top of her.

Dyo, still lying on the ground, raised her right hand and sent a blast of air at Hephaestus, pushing him several feet straight back.

"Ah, my traitorous little art-project bitch. You should not be able to do that," said Hephaestus, firing a fireball at Dyo.

She rolled to the side, dodging the fireball, and blasted him again, this time with both hands, and knocked him off his feet. "Nice talk," she said. "Asshole."

Hephaestus landed sitting up, still grinning, and tapped the cane on the ground between his knees. A towering pile of old pc housings arced into the air and buried Dyo.

"Why are you being so mean to us, Mr. Hephaestus?" asked Angie. She had climbed to her feet and was standing off to the side, holding her piece of sidewalk chalk in her hand.

Hephaestus fired a fireball at her. Angie dropped to one knee and snapped the halves of Athena's shield together in front of her. The fireball broke harmlessly around her.

"You puzzle me, child," said Hephaestus. He struggled to his feet, leaning on his cane. "What exactly are you?"

"I'm exactly what you think I am. I'll be going into the sixth grade next fall."

"I hate to harm a child."

"Then don't."

"You will forgive me, but it seems that you are no ordinary child." Hephaestus raised his arms and grinned at Angie. "Goodbye."

A 1997 Toyota Corolla materialized in the air above Hephaestus and fell directly on his head, driving him to the ground. Then a Hyundai, a

Ford Fiesta, and a Chevy SUV popped out of the air and formed a pile on him.

"Thanks, Hermes," said Angie. "And thanks for the light pole back there." She stuck the chalk back into her pocket. "He wouldn't have hurt me, you know."

Hermes appeared next to Angie, holding a black helmet. "Forgive me for not taking the chance," he said. He raised his hand and a bright blue Winnebago fell onto the pile of cars, followed by a red Dodge Ram pickup truck, a blue Volkswagen, a rusty El Torino with a rebel flag in the back window, and two Honda motorcycles. "That ought to hold him for a while."

"Where are you getting all those?"

"Walmart parking lot."

The pile of carburetors exploded and Athena sprung out, landing in a fighting crouch with her weapons at the ready. "Where is he?" She looked around, then stood up and looked at Hermes. "How did you get here?"

"Long story," he said, showing her his helmet. He pointed at the pile of vehicles. "I've got him parked in, but probably not for long."

Dyo dug herself out from under her computer housings and stood up, staring at Hermes. "How did he get here?" she asked.

"Long story," said Athena. She walked over to Hermes. "Hephaestus is a lot more powerful than we figured. He dusted me off like I was an insect."

"I saw it." He raised his hand; a Jeep Liberty, a Volvo station wagon, a Ford van, three bright red extended-cab pickup trucks, and an eighteen-wheel tanker truck full of milk crashed onto the pile. "Just in case."

"We need to find Aphrodite quickly," said Athena. "Hephaestus is a little tougher than I thought, and we could use her to fight. Then we need to try to get on neutral ground. Hermes, he hasn't seen you, so why don't you put that hat of yours back on. With a little luck you can surprise him again."

Hermes grinned, flipped the helmet back onto his head, and vanished.

"Aphrodite is not far ahead," said Angie. "Over this way."

They all ran, following Angie, weaving around Hephaestus' junk piles. Sprinting around a mountain of broken clocks, they nearly ran into Aphrodite's cage, still hanging in the air. Aphrodite was slumped inside, lifeless.

"Is she dead?" asked Dyo.

"No," said Angie, "but it looks like she's had a really crummy day."

"We have to get her out of there," said Dyo, drawing Aphrodite's sword and swinging, hard, at the near wall of the cage. The sword bounced off, flew out of Dyo's hand, and skittered across the floor.

Angie walked over to the sword, picked it up, took the lipstick out of the handle, and handed the sword back to Dyo.

"You're too young for makeup," came Hermes' voice from the air next to Dyo.

Angie smiled. "Just too young to use it on my face."

She walked over to the cage, then skipped all the way around it, drawing a red line in lipstick about an inch from the bottom. When she got back to where she started, she took a step back, closed her eyes and said, "Bzzzzzzzzzzzzzzzzzzzzzzz zzzzzzzzzzzzzzzzzzzzzzzzzzzzzzz," doing a pretty fair impression of a chain saw.

After a few seconds the bottom of the cage parted at Angie's red lines, and Aphrodite crashed to the floor.

"Well now, that was pretty neat," said Hermes.

Dyo and Athena ran to Aphrodite, kneeling on either side of her. Dyo lifted Aphrodite's shoulders and cradled her while Athena examined her. "She is not going to be much help in a fight," said Athena. "At least not right away."

Angie bent down next to Dyo and pushed the lipstick back into the handle of her sword. "You're right. We need to find a way out of here," she said.

"And soon," said Hermes' voice. "Here he comes, and he's brought some friends."

Athena and Dyo stood up, moved in front of Aphrodite, and drew their swords. Hephaestus was running toward them in a sort of loping trot, flanked by more animated collections of junk. This crew looked more formidable than the last, each one brandishing some kind of blade or bludgeon. Two of them, made in basically human shapes from copper tubing and old car mufflers, were riding the two motorcycles Hermes had dropped on Hephaestus.

Athena and Dyo, in perfect synchronization, thrust their fists toward the charging army, sending a massive burst of compressed air at them. Without slowing down, Hephaestus raised his cane, and a fireball shot out, meeting the blast from the women and neutralizing it.

Hephaestus laughed. "Is that all you ha..."

A large anvil materialized in the air just above and in front of him, perfectly timed to land on his head and drive him face-first to the ground.

"What is this, Hermes," asked Athena, swinging her spear and knocking aside the first wave of attacking machines, "a Road Runner cartoon?"

"What's a cartoon?" asked Dyo, demolishing one of the motorcycle riders with her sword and knocking the other off his bike with a blast of air.

"A source of inspiration," said Hermes' voice. A grand piano fell on top of Hephaestus, then a wave of fire melted a path through the second and third waves of machines.

Athena ran forward through the machine army, slashing with her sword and spear, so that ruined parts flew aside like the wake breaking around the bow of a boat. Using her spear to smash a soldier made of a microwave, a toaster, a chain saw, and four hockey sticks, she called back over her shoulder, "Angie, can you find us a way out of here?"

Angie was on her knees next to Aphrodite, protecting her from flying nuts, bolts, and bits of pipe with half of Athena's shield, and drawing on the floor with the sidewalk chalk in her other hand. "I'm already working on it," she said.

Hephaestus crawled to his feet, shrugging off the anvil and remnants of grand piano. "I don't think so," he said. He skipped to the side with surprising agility, dodging a large safe that crashed out of the air, and shot a fireball from his cane. It caught Hermes squarely in the chest, blowing his helmet straight up in the air, and carrying him, now visible, past Angie and Aphrodite. He landed on his back, skidded a few feet, and stayed down, not moving.

Dyo shot up to maximum size and brought her now-Giant sword down out of the mist toward Hephaestus. He casually swatted it aside with his cane, picked up a large steel flywheel and launched it like a Frisbee, so that it slammed into Dyo's shin. She screamed and fell to her knees, crushing dozens of Hephaestus' machine soldiers and barely missing Athena, who rolled to her feet and waded back in to destroy the few remaining machine soldiers.

"I don't care how big you are," said Hephaestus, "a whack on the shin hurts." Another blast from his cane lifted Dyo up out of sight into the mist, then she fell, limp and back to normal size, next to Hermes. He turned his attention to Athena. "So, sister, it's down to just you and me."

Athena sheathed her sword and pulled out Zeus' thunderbolt. "And this," she said.

Hephaestus took a half step back and his smile faltered. "Zeus gave you that? You don't have enough power to wield it."

"Well, I guess we'll just have to find out about that, won't we?" She raised the thunderbolt, throbbing with a dull electric glow, over her head, then lowered it, pointed directly at Hephaestus, who fell into a crouch and covered his head.

The thunderbolt brightened briefly, then a spark of static electricity snapped over to the remains of a nearby machine warrior that had been made mostly of coat hangers. With a little wheeze, the thunderbolt went dark.

Hephaestus opened one eye and peeked under his elbow. Then he laughed and stood up. "Well, that was terrifying," he said. "So I guess it is just you and me after all."

"You forgot about me," said Angie, standing next to Aphrodite with what appeared to be a thunderbolt drawn with blue chalk in her hand." She pointed it at Hephaestus, and a blinding blue fountain of pure energy flowed out. It twisted and turned deftly to track with Hephaestus as he tried to avoid it. When it hit him, a massive burst of blue light enveloped him, forming a sort of energy bubble that lifted him into the air.

The bubble contracted, but just as it seemed it would crush Hephaestus, it burst on one side and violently spat him out so that he flew, screaming, in a low arc up into the mist and completely out of sight back toward the far end of his workshop, his scream fading into the distance. After what seemed like an interminable wait, a muffled explosion echoed back to them.

Athena tucked Zeus' dormant thunderbolt back into her belt. "What," she asked, "was that?"

Angie tossed her thunderbolt aside. When it landed, it melted into the floor and became a simple chalk drawing. 'It's a drawing of Mr. Z's thunderbolt. I wasn't sure exactly how it should work, since I never saw Mr. Z's in action."

"I'd say yours worked just fine." She nodded at Aphrodite, Dyo, and Hermes, lying unconscious on the ground. "We need to get out of here before he gets back."

Angie looked off in the direction Hephaestus had flown. "I'm pretty sure we have quite a bit of time. But I've got an exit taken care of." She walked over to a drawing of a large rectangle on the floor next to where Aphrodite lay, and reached down to grab a chalk doorknob. A big blue chalk door swung up from the floor, and daylight flooded into the workshop.

"You made a portal, just like that?"

"It leads to your room at the hotel. The door is in the wall there, so coming out might be kind of goofy."

"How do we keep Hephaestus from following us?"

"Silly, we just erase it once we're through with it."

"Of course we do. What was I thinking? OK, help me get these three through."

Regrouping

Aphrodite, Dyo, and Hermes stretched out next to each other, still unconscious, on Athena's king-sized bed.

Artemis stood guard at the window, dressed in a short, softly glowing white tunic, belted at the waist with a golden strap. Her hair was tied back with a long white ribbon, and she wore golden sandals strapped up to the knee with golden laces. She had a short sword sheathed in her belt, a quiver of golden arrows over her shoulder, and a golden bow, one arrow nocked and ready, in her hand.

Athena, still wearing her armor and holding her spear, stood by the door next to Zeus, who was dressed in fresh dockers and an Aerosmith t-shirt, and turning his thunderbolt over in his hands. "I'm sorry this thing didn't work," he said.

"It did, in a way. It bought us just enough time for Angie to do her thing."

"What do you make of that girl?" Angie had left the halves of Athena's shield on the floor, and Apollo had taken her home to fetch Sarah. Before they left, Zeus and Athena had debated at some length over whether Angie would be in serious danger from a new attack having only Apollo with her. Angie had simply smiled and showed them her sidewalk chalk.

"I don't know what to make of her," said Athena. "Goddess, or child, or demigod, or something entirely different. I have never seen anything like what she did with her version of your thunderbolt. And she seems to perceive things that even we don't."

Hermes came around first, sitting up with a start. "Where's Uncle's helmet? He'll kill me if I lose that helmet."

"Yes, we're all fine, thanks," said Athena. "The helmet is over on the dresser."

Hermes rubbed the back of his head. "Ow! What happened?"

"Our attack plan didn't pan out," said Athena.

"There's a masterpiece of understatement," Hermes said, and he swung his feet over the edge of the bed. "How did you get us out of there?"

"I didn't. Angie did."

Hermes smiled and shook his head, winced, then looked down at Dyo and Aphrodite on the bed next to him. "How are they doing?"

Apollo took a damp washcloth off Aphrodite's forehead and replaced it with a cooler one. "Dyo is just stunned, like you were. No major damage. I'm not so sure about Aphrodite. I've never seen anyone in this condition. It's like all the life has been sucked out of her body."

"Oh no," said Artemis, "we're not going to get into some kind of vampire thing here, are we? I hate vampires."

"Dyo stirred and opened her eyes. "Does my hair look all right?" she asked.

An hour later Aphrodite began moaning and talking in her sleep.

Apollo sat next to her on the bed, put a hand on each of her shoulders, and gently touched her forehead with his. A glow surrounded the two of them for a few seconds, then Aphrodite opened her eyes. Apollo pulled his head back a few inches, smiled, gave her a brotherly kiss on the forehead, and said, "Welcome back."

She smiled up at him. "Thanks. I can't tell you how much the last couple of days have sucked."

Zeus decided to move their base of operations

down to the bar, where there would be more room to maneuver if Hephaestus should mount an attack. Hermes went ahead to chase out any customers. Zeus carried Aphrodite, who was still too weak to walk on her own, while Artemis, Athena, Dyo, and Apollo spread out and gathered up all the Olympian weapons they could find.

In the bar Zeus found Hermes squared off with Hera near the door. Hera was shouting, "This will ruin our business!"

"My dear," said Zeus, "Our business can wait. We are at war."

"War?" Hera's eyes narrowed. "What are you talking about?"

Zeus settled Aphrodite into a chair by the bar, while Hermes hung up a "Closed For Repairs" sign and locked the door. "Is Ares in the kitchen?" he asked.

"You know he is."

"Go get him, please, and ask him to come out here. I only want to tell the story once."

Without replying, Hera stalked into the kitchen. "Do you think we can trust them?" asked Hermes, sitting next to Aphrodite.

"Definitely not."

A few minutes later Hera reappeared, followed by Ares, who clutched a meat cleaver in one hand

and a string of sausages in the other. "What's all this bleedin' furphy about a war, then?" he asked. "Stone the crows, mate, nobody ever tells me nothin' 'round here."

"So you're what, Australian now?" said Hermes.

Hera gave Hermes a frosty stare, then turned to Zeus, "Well, My Lord?"

"Hephaestus captured and tortured Aphrodite," he said.

"Impossible! The tramp is lying!"

"We just went through a full-scale battle to rescue her from Hephaestus' workshop," said Hermes. "That would be one really elaborate lie."

"When do we fight, Mate?" asked Ares. "And who we bloody fightin'? And why? Nah, who cares about all that doovalacky. Bring 'em on!"

"Ares," said Zeus, "I want you to stay in the kitchen and defend the door to the alley. While you're there, maybe you can cook us up a pile of those sausages. We're all pretty hungry."

"I'll fetch me bleedin' weapons," said Ares.

"The one in your hand will be adequate for the time being," said Zeus. "Get to it." Ares nodded, smiled, gave his cleaver a twirl and headed back into the kitchen.

"Our son is the God of war..." said Hera.

"... And that is exactly why I am entrusting this important tactical post to him," said Zeus. "Hera, I need you to take the van, go to my brothers and bring them here. You will find Hades in his funeral parlor over in Sparta, and Poseidon should be in his office by the swimming pool at the high school."

"You could telephone them..."

"... I already have. Now I would like you to pick them up."

"Hermes is the messenger..."

Zeus turned, fire flashing in his eyes, and moved his nose to within inches of Hera's. He said in a barely perceptible voice, "I would like you to do this thing as I have asked you to do it."

Hera glared back at him for an instant, then lowered her eyes. "As you wish, My Lord."

After the door had closed behind Hera, Zeus chuckled. "If I'm wrong, and those two are not in league with Hephaestus, they will at least be out of our way for a while."

"We could use Ares' sword."

"If we could be sure in which direction he would swing it."

"Swing it," said Aphrodite. "Cute."

Five

That was not at all what I expected.

It was exactly what we knew it would be.

Was it?

You were the author.

True. Nevertheless, I was surprised.

I understand.

I'm still not sure that I do.

Two Gods Walk Into a Bar

"So, what exactly did Hephaestus do to you?" Zeus asked Aphrodite.

Apollo stood behind her, his hands resting on her shoulders and his forehead lightly touching the top of her head, while Zeus, Dyo, Hermes, Angie, and Sarah sat at a large round table nearby. Artemis stood guard between the front door and the door from the hotel lobby, while Athena leaned on her spear and kept an eye on the kitchen door.

Aphrodite shook her head. "He has built another generator thingie, and this time it didn't blow up. When he hooked me up to it and turned it on, I felt an incredible surge of energy, then pain, and then I must have blacked out. I can only assume that while I was out he somehow pumped all that power back out of me and into himself.

Every time I woke up, he'd do it again."

"How many times did you go through that?"

"Three. No, four. Then after the fourth time I woke up in Athena's room.

"What's happening with Apollo right now?" asked Dyo. "Would I be interested?"

Without moving Apollo said, "I'm giving her a sort of energy transfusion."

Dyo scratched her head. "Do you have enough Power to do that?"

Apollo smiled. "It doesn't use up any of my Power. This sort of energy is all around us. I'm just sort of channeling it."

"Speaking of Power," said Zeus, "can anybody explain what's going on? How is it that Hephaestus was able to defeat a God, two Goddesses, and... excuse me Dyo ... whatever Dyo is, and then is overcome by a ten year-old..."

"Almost eleven." said Angie.

"... almost eleven year-old girl?"

"I've been thinking a lot about that," said Athena. " It really does look like Hephaestus has found a mechanical way to remotely tap the Power of the Amulet. Obviously it's pretty potent, at least temporarily."

"And the rest of us are just getting our Power back..." said Hermes.

"Some of us are," said Zeus.

"... without really knowing how. I think Angie might be the key to understanding all this."

Zeus pounded the table hard enough for the salt shakers to leap into the air and topple over. "Never mind understanding it! How are we supposed to capitalize on it?" There was a hint of thunder in his voice.

"Easy there, Z," said Athena. "We're all working on that." She leaned over and gently stroked Sarah's wrist. "Hermes is right, you know. Angie might be the key. Is there anything you can you tell us about her father?"

Sarah looked uncomfortably at Angie, who smiled back."I know all about how the whole thing works," said Angie.

Sarah sighed. "You people don't really ever have to raise your children, do you. That's why you had time and energy to be rulers of heaven and earth. OK, so I met him right in this room. I was sitting over there by the window, having a glass of wine after work with my friend Cindy, and this really striking guy came in."

"Striking how?" asked Athena.

Sarah thought for a few seconds, and shifted in her seat. "Striking, like I could not take my eyes off him. And all I wanted to do..." She stopped and turned bright red.

"I know that feeling," said Aphrodite.

"Boy, so do I!" said Dyo. "Say, when do you suppose I can..."

"OK, so maybe this kind of thing isn't exactly what you want to be hearing from your mom after all," said Angie. She hopped up and grabbed Hermes by the hand. "Would you take me over to the bar and pour me a Coke?"

"Sarah, we don't need all the details, " said Athena. "but it might be important to know more about this person. Can you describe him at all?"

Sarah shook her head slowly. "That's the funny thing. I can't, not really. When I think about him, I feel like I know exactly what he looked like, but then when it gets down to it, I can't quite picture his face."

"How did your friend react to this amazing guy?" asked Athena.

"I'm not sure she even noticed him. And now that I think of it, I don't remember what even happened to her, when or how she left. The next thing I knew, I was sitting at the table alone with him, looking into his eyes..."

"Can you describe his eyes?" asked Aphrodite.

"Kind of. They were grey. No, dark, dark blue. No, wait, they were... I guess they kind of changed as he talked. And there was this flash in them, kind of like lightning..."

Aphrodite, Hermes, Artemis and Athena all turned to look at Zeus.

Zeus sat up straight. "What? Me? No way! I was asleep with the rest of you."

"I don't know, Z, it sure sounds like the way you used to work," said Aphrodite.

Athena nodded. "She's right. The veil of confusion, the irresistible aura, the seduction eyes? You went through half the women in Mesopotamia with that schtick."

"You crafty old fox," said Dyo, moving a little closer to Zeus.

"Let me get this straight," said Sarah, "you used your eyes to roofie half the women in the ancient Middle East?"

"No, no, nothing like that. They knew what they were doing, just not exactly who they were doing it with. And it was never more than two, maybe three percent of the women in the ancient Middle East. Tops."

"Ew," said Sarah.

"More like double Ew," said Hermes, sitting back down with Angie and her glass of Coke. "No offense, Z."

"Mmmm," said Dyo. "Maybe you could give me a demonstration."

"No demonstrations," said Zeus, "And no offense taken. It wasn't me. Things have changed a lot since the old days, but even so, if I had done this I would admit it."

"So who was around in the years before we woke up?" asked Hermes. "Not just everybody has that magical roofie-eyes thing in their repertoire."

"More to the point, who was around and had Power in the years before we woke up?" said Athena. "We were all pretty helpless when Phil got us up."

"Hmm, Phil. You don't suppose..." said Zeus.

"No," said Sarah, "it wasn't Phil Theos. That much I'm sure of. Look, I wasn't drugged or helpless. I was just... well, sort of overwhelmed."

"Don't be so sure it wasn't Phil. We are capable of modifying our forms," said Hermes. "Zeus used to do some pretty great animals."

"He did birds, mostly," said Artemis. "His swan was a work of art."

"The goat was usually pretty effective too," said Zeus. "Hermes, do you remember those twins in Ithaca?"

"That's another big 'ew,'" said Sarah, "Seriously, you were able to seduce women by turning into barnyard animals?"

"Times have changed a lot," said Hermes.

"Women have changed a lot," said Zeus. "Mind you, I haven't even considered giving that swan thing a try since Carthage was a cow town."

"Come to think of it, would a swan really be considered a barnyard animal?" asked Hermes.

"Will you two pigs please shut up," said Athena. "Look, it sounds like Angie's father might have had some Power, and he passed it on to her. We can worry about exactly who he was later."

The door to the street swung open and two men walked into the room, followed by Hera. "Here they are, My Lord," she said. "Now if you'll excuse me, I will check on the kitchen." She strode out of the room.

"Thanks, sweetie," muttered Zeus.

The taller of the two newcomers, dressed in a red sweat suit with "Olympus High" embroidered on the back of the jacket and the word "Coach" on the front, moved with the sure, easy stride of an athlete. His deep green eyes scanned the room from beneath a shaggy mane of curly blonde hair. His gaze lingered briefly on Aphrodite and Dyo, then he caught sight of Zeus and broke into a gentle smile. "Hello, everybody," said Poseidon, God of the sea. He looked back to Dyo. "You've got yourselves a spare Aphrodite - nice."

The second man was slight and pale, with startlingly black hair and eyes. He wore an immaculately tailored black suit, with a blood-red necktie and brilliantly polished black shoes. The face of the God of the underworld was completely expressionless, and he said nothing.

"Hades, Poseidon, nice of you guys to come over. As I said on the phone, we have a problem with Hephaestus."

"You have a problem with Hephaestus," said Hades. "I'm not certain that it has anything to do with us."

Poseidon chuckled, a sound like surf breaking on a coral reef. "What I believe our brother means is that he is not certain that there is any way for us to help you. In my case, we're 800 miles from the nearest ocean, so unless you want me to try whipping up a tempest in the lap pool, I've got nothing. Maybe Hades could crank you out a zombie or two."

"Oh ha, ha," said Hades, without the slightest hint of humor. "I never get tired of those zombie jokes. But Poseidon is correct; I can think of nothing I can do that would assist you with this situation."

"We were hoping that you could help us work out a plan to consolidate our power," said Athena. "Zeus explained what happened in Hephaestus' workshop?"

"He did," said Poseidon. He smiled at Angie. "This must be our new little Goddess."

"Where's your trident?" asked Angie.

"At home, in my closet."

Angie nodded. "You would probably be more comfortable if you had brought it."

Poseidon opened his mouth, closed it again, and looked at Zeus.

"As I said, she is not exactly what you might expect. Right now our main task is to figure out what she can do."

"I can do anything I need to do," said Angie.

"Can you search your instincts and tell us where Hephaestus is right now, and what he's doing?" asked Hades.

"Sure. He just came through the back door into the kitchen. He's talking to Hera and Ares."

The Prodigal

Athena drew her sword and crouched into a fighting stance, her spear at the ready. Artemis and Apollo, moving together as one, each nocked arrows and pointed them at the door to the kitchen. Hermes jumped to his feet and pushed Sarah and Angie behind him. Dyo grabbed Aphrodite's hand and drew her sword.

Zeus stood up, feet apart, knees slightly bent, and his left hand clenched in a fist. In his right hand he held his darkened thunderbolt. He tapped the thunderbolt on the table and gave it a little shake to see if he could fire it up. He couldn't.

Poseidon and Hades moved to either side of Zeus, so that the three brothers stood shoulder-to-shoulder.

Angie hopped out of her chair, skipped over to the kitchen door, and pushed it open. "It's OK,

Mr. Hephaestus, you can come out."

"Angie!" shouted Sarah. "Get back! Get away from that door..."

Hephaestus hobbled through the door and into the bar, leaning heavily on his cane. His left arm hung limp at his side. His nose was clearly broken, and both eyes were swollen nearly shut. As he passed through he shied slightly away from Angie, who was still holding the door. Hera followed him into the room.

Zeus lowered his thunderbolt and stood up straight. "I have to say, this is really not at all what I was expecting."

"The little tart did this to our son," said Hera.

"That being the case, I think I'd be extremely careful about who I was calling a 'little tart,' if I were you" said Athena.

Ares followed them through the door carrying a large platter heaped with steaming sausages, grilled onions, and asparagus spears. "Got us a plate of hot snags here," he said. "Who's hungry?"

– λατερ –

As luck would have it, everybody was pretty hungry, so they all settled around the dining room to have some food. Apollo attended to Hephaestus, gently probing his shoulder. "This arm is really messed up," he said.

"I was blasted right through the wall of my workshop and into a shoe store in Prague. I have never been hit so hard." He smiled weakly and nodded in Angie's direction. "This child packs a punch."

"Wait... Prague?" said Zeus. "I thought your workshop was under Mount Olympus."

"I thought so too. But then I never crashed through one of the walls before. Turns out the other side of that particular wall was a shoe store in Prague."

"So now there's a tunnel between your workshop and a shoe store in Prague?" asked Hermes.

"No, the seals I have on the workshop held up, so after I crawled back into my workshop the hole repaired itself."

"But how could going through a wall, no matter how hard the blow, injure you like this?" asked Apollo. "Your arm is broken and the shoulder is dislocated! That should not be possible."

"I imagine it happened the same way my leg was injured when I was cast from Olympus..."

"Look, I still feel bad about that," said Zeus.

Hephaestus waved a bite of sausage on the fork in his right hand, shook his head, and winced as Apollo popped his left shoulder back into the socket. "Forget it. As I was very recently reminded, when you attack, the ones you attack are likely to fight back. I was out of line."

"You sure were," said Aphrodite. "I'm not so sure I'm ready to forgive and forget..."

"Well, it's not like you have always been the ideal spouse..."

"Look you two, this is well-traveled territory," said Athena. "How about we talk about where we go from here?

"The first thing, Hephaestus, is to bind you with an oath," said Zeus. "This kidnapping and torture stuff has just got to stop."

Hephaestus sat up as straight in his chair as he could and touched the fingers of his right hand to the center of his forehead. "I hereby swear my unswerving loyalty to the Lord of Olympus," he said "I exist only to serve the throne until the last star burns from the sky." Then he spat generously into the palms of both hands, rubbed them together, and slammed them down on the table top. "To this solemn oath am I bound."

Zeus spat likewise into the palms of both hands, rubbed them together and slammed them down on the table across from Hephaestus, sending up a little spray of oath juice. "To this solemn oath are you hereby bound," he said. "Welcome back, Hephaestus."

"Thanks, Z. Honestly, it's good to be back."

"Yeah, well you better watch your back," said Aphrodite. "What makes you think you can swear your way out of this one?"

"If I was you, I'd make something really nice for her," said Dyo. "Maybe whip up a really good-looking guy this time. And while you're at it, you could whip one up for me…"

"We will accept his oath in good faith," said Zeus. "That is our law."

"That was a really interesting ceremony," said Sarah. "You people do wash these tables every day with chlorine, right?"

"One thing this little skirmish has accomplished," said Hermes, "is to get us all a little further toward getting our Power back."

"I don't know about that," said Hephaestus. "What I was trying to do didn't really work. Or I should say, it was only temporary. My generator was able to crank up enough juice to scrap with you guys, but most of it is gone now."

"Hmmm," said Hermes. He raised his right hand and a large recliner chair dropped through a portal and landed between the tables. "I still have a pretty good charge." Hermes plopped into the chair and leaned back, raising the footrest.

Athena closed her eyes, lowered her chin, and disappeared. She reappeared a few seconds later, carrying a loaf of French bread and a bottle of

Bordeaux wine, and wearing a little green beret. "Me too. So it seems that even though Hephaestus' generator thing might not have worked out, something is letting us tap into our old selves, at least partially."

Zeus spread his arms and closed his eyes, clenching his jaw in concentration. His hands began to quake. Everybody drew back and braced themselves. Zeus slowly raised his arms, palms up, threw his head back and clenched his fists.

The three light bulbs in the overhead fan popped, raining a fine dust of glass down on Zeus' head. "OK," said Dyo, "maybe some of us a little more than others."

Hephaestus pushed his chair back. "I'll get some new bulbs."

Hermes hopped up and said, "I'll take care of it. You sit tight and let Apollo do his job." A package of light bulbs dropped into his hand and he rose into the air, hovering there to change the bulbs in the fan.

"Damn it," said Zeus.

"It's OK Z," said Artemis, examining her now-glowing quiver of golden arrows. "It'll all come back to you, sooner or later."

"Yeah Z," said Aphrodite, together with Dyo bathed in a soft pool of amber light. "You'll catch up."

Poseidon held his hand over his glass of water and watched a small vortex swirl slowly. "I'm about where you are, Z. There's not a lot of fuel in the tank."

Hades wiped the corner of his mouth on a napkin and pushed his plate away. "Other than lending my helmet to Hermes, I'm afraid I don't have much to contribute either," he said.

"Lord love a duck," said Ares, "these here bangers is ace. Think I'll knock us up another batch. Bob's your uncle."

"Oh, come on Ares, " said Hermes, "Now you've got Liverpool mixed up with some kind of Irish-Cornish thing. Are you just getting this stuff off the internet?"

Hera pushed her chair back and stood up. "You may all make light of my husband, the Master of the Heavens, and our son, the God of war, but I'll have no part in it. If I may be excused, my Lord, I have work to do." She turned on her heel and stalked out of the room.

Poseidon watched her walk away. "Whenever that woman is polite to you, Brother, you can bet she's up to something."

Zeus nodded. "I thought she was plotting with Hephaestus."

"Funny, other than egging me on a bit, she didn't have all that much to do with it this time around," said Hephaestus. "You know that she has been trying to talk me into dumping you since the sun was a spark."

"That's a long time," said Dyo.

"Hera has different allies now," said Angie. "And these are dangerous."

Combat Training

Athena showed Angie a short brilliantly gleaming sword, its blade intricately inscribed with images of Gods and monsters. They were in the barn, standing next to Hephaestus' outhouse-portal. Dyo and Aphrodite were on the other side of the barn, teaching Dyo how to turn various objects into other things. She had just succeeded in changing an empty oil drum into a watermelon.

"This sword belonged to the demigod and great hero Perseus," said Athena, offering the hilt to Angie. "He used it to lop off Medusa's head and a lot of other things." She turned the weapon over in her hands. "That man could carve anything from a Minotaur to a roasted goose with this thing. Handy at feasts."

"I don't need a sword," said Angie. "I still have plenty of chalk."

"I'll admit the chalk is good. No, it's great. But it won't hurt you to learn to use a sword. And if we get into any other troubles, I'd like to have this one with us."

"Why don't you carry it?"

"It was meant for the human child of a God."

"So you've decided that's what I am." She took the sword and waved it experimentally in front of her. "It's not as heavy as it looks."

"It was made to adapt itself to the needs of the bearer. When it was in Perseus' hands, it would have weighed more."

Angie held the sword, point up, in front of her with both hands. The images on the blade began to pulse with a soft glow. "Yeah, there we go," she said. "It seems like sooner or later, everything you Gods have lights up."

Athena nodded. "I guess that's pretty much true. Just remember, in the old days we didn't have LEDs or glow sticks. We had to make do. It seems like the Sword of Perseus likes you."

"Does it have a name?"

"Perseus called it 'My Sword.'"

"I think I'll call it 'Larry.'"

"Fair enough." Athena picked up a heavily-figured Olympian Bronze shield and handed it to Angie. "Perseus also had a shield, but that disappeared a very long time ago. I had Hephaestus make a new one for you."

Arrayed around the surface of the shield in two concentric circles were dozens of My Little Pony characters in various poses, acting out a story involving butterflies, some vaguely Troll-like creatures, and a unicorn. "Seriously?" said Angie. "He thinks I'm still into My Little Pony?"

"He wanted to surprise you. He means well."

After a long, awkward silence, Athena pulled her sword. "OK. So, to defend yourself properly, you need to be balanced. Bend your knees a bit and shift your weight to the balls of your feet. When I carry a shield, I like to have the shoulder of my sword arm just slightly away from the opponent. Without a shield, you would want to turn so that your sword arm is toward the opponent. This way your weapon will always be ready to strike or parry any threats. Plus, when you turn to either side, you present a smaller target. In either case, you should keep the tip of the sword above your hand."

She demonstrated, dropping into a fighting stance and pointing her sword at Angie, elbow low and sword point slightly elevated. "As you can see, since I have no shield, my left shoulder is further back. With my sword in this position, I can block any blow. Go ahead, have a go at me."

Angie reached out and took a casual backhand swipe. With a slightly ringing sizzle, Larry sliced through Athena's blade, and the two of them watched the tip clatter to the floor. "Oops! Sorry."

Athena poked at the blade with her toe. "What? Oh, yeah, no. No problem."

"Does this mean I'm good to go on the sword fighting thing?"

"Well yes, I guess it does. Just remember what I said about keeping your weight on the balls of your feet."

"Got it. Here, hang onto Larry for me." She handed the sword and the My Little Pony shield back to Athena. "Can I go play now? Callie and Carlie Shay are putting on a play of the Lion King in their back yard, and they want me to be a monkey."

"I guess so. How about we get back together after lunch to work on creating energy barriers and transforming objects?"

"OK. See you later!" She skipped out of the barn, singing "Hakuna Matata."

Aphrodite and Dyo suspended their transformation training and joined Athena standing over the severed blade of the sword. "That should not have happened, should it," said Aphrodite. "Like your shield."

"Right." Athena examined the sword hilt in her hand. "Olympian Bronze, indestructible alloy, blah, blah, blah. I'll have to have a word with Hephaestus about this."

"Here," said Dyo. "Have an orchid. Five minutes ago it was a screwdriver."

A New Threat

For the next few days things remained quiet around the Delphi. Athena worked on training Angie and Dyo while Hephaestus' wounds healed and the rest of the Gods went back to running the restaurant and the hotel. All, that is, except Hera, who had vanished the night of the visit from Poseidon and Hades.

At about four o'clock on Tuesday afternoon, Wilfred Smith caught up with Hephaestus on the sidewalk along the north side of the Hotel. "Excuse me," said Smith. "We need to talk."

"We do? What about, Smith?"

"Call me Big Will. We need to talk about this sidewalk." He gestured toward the sling still holding Hephaestus' arm. "What happened to you?"

"I injured it shopping for shoes. What about the sidewalk, Smith?"

"It does not meet the guidelines written in the Municipal Building Code."

"How so?" Hephaestus examined the sidewalk. "It looks perfectly fine to me."

"Ah, but looks can be deceiving. The tensile strength does not fall within the ordinance specifications."

"It's too soft?"

"Too hard."

"Excuse me?"

"Too hard. The code specifies that concrete sidewalks should test between 3,000 and 4,000 psi. Our inspector was unable to break this one at more than 8,000 psi."

"He tried to break my sidewalk?"

"It's his job."

"And if he had succeeded in breaking it, I would have had to repair the damage he caused?"

"Why yes, I suppose so."

"And since he didn't break it..."

"You'll have to replace it."

"Because..."

"If the concrete is too hard, you would have difficulty replacing it, should that ever become necessary."

"So you want me to replace it now, so that

it will be easier to replace, just in case we should ever need to replace it."

"It's the law."

Hephaestus tapped with his cane on a corner of the square of pavement he was standing on, and the corner broke off. He picked it up. "It is a tiny bit hard," he said. "I think, however, that I am going to tell you and your inspector to go stuff yourselves."

Smith flushed. "I'm afraid you don't understand. These ordinances were written to ensure the safety of the community, and..."

"I understand completely, you little shit weasel. You can stuff all your ordinances. And lame or not, I'm about ready to take this whole sidewalk and shove it up your..."

"You will live to regret those words! I am the Mayor of this town..."

"And I am a God." He dropped the chip of pavement, where it fused seamlessly back in place. "The way I look at it, that pretty much trumps being the Mayor."

Smith thrust his chin out. "Is that supposed to frighten me?"

Hephaestus raised his eyebrows. "Well, I'd think it would have at least surprised you. Maybe a little bit?"

"You would be surprised at what I am not surprised... what doesn't surprise... what I don't find surprising." He took a step back and pulled a small two-way radio from his pocket. "Send in Carl," he said into the radio, then he smiled at Hephaestus. "It might surprise you to know that I have a couple of surprises of my own to surprise you with. So, Surprise!"

The earth shook as slow, thundering footsteps approached from around the corner. Hephaestus watched with his head cocked to one side as a man the size of a beer truck approached, dressed in an enormous policeman's uniform. Tiny flashes of lightning danced around his head. Hephaestus gave a low whistle. "You have a Giant? Of your very own? Good for you!"

"Constable Carl is not a Giant," said Smith. "He is your equal, or possibly your better - Hephaestus, God of the Forge."

"So you already know about that. And somehow you've found a supernatural creature. Named Carl. OK, fair enough." Hephaestus smiled at Carl. "So where do you hail from, big guy?"

Carl stopped in the middle of the street, squared off to Hephaestus with his fists clenched. "I was forged in the fires of Tartarus, from the tears of Rhea and perspiration of Cronus."

"So... that would make you what, my uncle by

excretion? How is my grandfather these days?"

"You should know. He and the other Titans still sleep their eternal sleep, betrayed by my brothers and their offspring." The lightning increased in intensity.

"That's what I thought, but we've been getting a lot of new information lately. So Carl, how is it none of us have met you before?"

"I am newly born. Like I said, forged in the fires of Tartarus..."

"Yeah, so the whole sweat and tears thing was fairly recent. Got it. So that makes you a new guy. First one in quite a while. What exactly are you the God of?"

Carl looked puzzled. "What do you mean?"

"We're all Gods of something. Like the little nutwad here just said, I'm the God of the Forge. So what's your thing?"

"Perhaps time will tell."

A blue pickup truck came around the corner, honked its horn, swerved, and gunned around Carl. A young boy on a bicycle coming from the other direction skidded to a stop, then turned around and quietly rode back the way he had come.

Karen and Bill Wilson came around the corner, arm-in-arm, headed home from lunch and cocktails at the Delphi. "Hi Hephaestus. Hi Smith," said Bill Wilson.

"Call me Big Will,'" said Smith.

"Who's your tall, good-looking friend?" asked Karen Wilson, smiling at Carl. "Good afternoon, Officer."

Hephaestus shook his head. "Man, what does it take to get a rise out of folks around here?"

Smith shouted into his radio; "Damn it, I told you guys to shut down the streets!" He dropped the radio into his pocket and turned his attention back to Hephaestus. "So, impotent God, do you still want me to 'stuff' the ordinances?"

"Impotent?" said Hephaestus. "OK, Smith, there has to be a line you crossed in there somewhere. Where exactly does an idiot like you fit into all this anyway?"

"Your mother came to me last week and told me all about your little tribe. She was able to convince me by turning a stray cat into a bar of gold."

"My mother can be pretty persuasive, and she's always been kind of hard on domesticated animals."

"Once I understood the facts, and the limits of your power, she said that she would help me regain ownership of my family's property if I would finance a secret trip to Greece for her..."

"... So she could get to the gates of Tartarus, where she could whip up Carl." Hephaestus nodded. "She really is a crafty old bat."

Smith grinned. "And now that I have someone who can make you obey the laws of this community, I will take my family legacy back."

"Seriously? That's what you think this is all about?" Hephaestus turned to Carl. "Take my word for it, Carl, not all mortals are as stupid as this little twit."

"I wouldn't know about that," said Carl. "This mortal is of no consequence."

"Hey," said Smith. "Don't forget, Constable, you report to me. Well, you actually report to the chief of police, but still, I'm the Mayor, and he reports to me, which means…"

"Like I said, big guy, they're not all this stupid. So what comes next?"

Carl opened his hands and raised his arms toward Hephaestus, palms down. A blinding halo of lightning flashed, surrounding the Giant.

"Oh crap," said Hephaestus. "That's what I thought. Smith, you better run. Now!"

Smith took two stumbling steps back, looked from Carl to Hephaestus and back, then took off sprinting up the street.

Hephaestus raised his cane. "Look Carl, do

you think we could work something out here? Up to now, this has been a really rough summer for me."

"My sister-creator told me you were weak. She said that she has tried for millennia to hand you the Throne of Heaven and you were too timid to take it."

"Sounds like something she would say. That is not exactly how this whole thing works, though. Strictly speaking, there is no longer a Throne..."

"She said that you were defeated by a human. Even worse, by a human child."

"OK, well technically that's true. But she's more of a pre-teen than an actual child..."

"So now Carl will sit on the Throne of Heaven, and be Lord of all the Gods."

"Like I said, there isn't really..."

The blast was partially deflected by the shield Hephaestus had formed with his cane, but it still picked him up and threw him, hard, against the wall of the hotel. Chunks of sidewalk flew in all directions, leaving a cloud of dust and a deep crater where Hephaestus had been standing.

"Ow," said Hephaestus. "Geeze! I have to say, Carl, that was totally uncalled for. And thanks to you, I'm going to be up all night fixing this stupid sidewalk again."

The second blast hit Hephaestus directly, driving him part way into the stone wall of the building. Chips of paint and soot rained down around his head.

"Oof," he said. He slid out of the indentation in the wall and to his knees. He was bleeding from his nose and both ears, and his left arm was obviously re-broken. He coughed and spat out a little blood." I have to admit, it looks like this building could use a good power washing."

Hephaestus flinched as the third blast broke around him, deflected by an invisible barrier. Carl stepped back, surprised, then fired another blast, which also deflected around Hephaestus. He examined his hands, then aimed another shot.

This one stopped a few feet from Carl, then cascaded back and around him, revealing a huge bubble engulfing him. The shimmering sphere expanded and contracted silently, the sound and power of the explosion trapped inside. Carl stood still for a few seconds, his constable uniform singed and smoldering, then slumped to the ground, unconscious, as the bubble disappeared.

Angie, holding a pink bubble wand and a small pink jar of bubble juice, walked over to Hephaestus. "Are you all right?"

"I've been better." He smiled weakly. "Really? Blowing bubbles?"

"It was all I could think of."

"Nice. Do you think you can help me find a way to contain our friend there before he wakes up? He is a pretty rough customer."

"Sure." Angie walked over to where Carl lay, pulled out her sidewalk chalk, and drew a rectangular line around him on the pavement. The area inside the rectangle turned to glowing Olympian Bronze, then walls of Olympian Bronze grew up around him. Finally, a lid of bronze closed off the top of Carl's prison, which sank down until the pavement closed over it.

"Good work," said Hephaestus, struggling to his feet. Where did you send him?"

"To your workshop. Do you think I should have poked some air holes in the box?"

"Definitely not. Holes would weaken the containment, and if he's really one of us he won't need any. How about we find Apollo to reset this arm?"

Six

Was the new one your idea?

No, I believe it was yours.

Oh, yes. So it was.

And the creativity of the little one?

That was hers.

This becomes more interesting.

Someone will prevail.

Or not.

Precisely, or not.

A New Plan

The next day the Delphi had a pretty good lunch crowd, including Karen Wilson at her regular table with her husband. All the men in the bar were in high spirits, since both Dyo and Aphrodite were waiting tables. The Wilsons had their attention firmly focused on a pair of king-sized margaritas.

Hermes drew himself a large glass of ice water, then leaned on the bar across from where Zeus and Sarah sat. "Not that I'm complaining, Z, but why do we still have this place open? We have another war starting up, and I'm still spending time every morning printing up the lunch specials."

"Because Phil told me that the hotel was very important, and to keep it at all costs. It's becoming pretty obvious that he had some sort of a plan for all this."

"If you say so." Hermes scanned the room. "I can't figure out why these people aren't at least a little bit afraid of us. Smith has been running around town telling everyone that we're demons from hell. Watch this." Hermes grew to more than ten feet tall and in a thundering voice announced, "Hey everybody. All draught pitchers are half price until two o'clock."

The patrons cheered and a few applauded as Hermes shrank back down. The man seated on the other side of Zeus, a tractor repair man named Kevin, said, "Dude, you should totally try out for the Pacers. When you get all big like that, you wouldn't even have to jump to stuff with both hands."

Hermes gave Kevin a smile and a friendly nod, then shrugged at Zeus. "See what I mean? Where's the awe, the reverence?"

"Hermes, these people's parents watched on television as regular mortals walked on the moon. For generations they have gone to movies to see zombies, and goblins, and Death Stars blowing up planets. They sit in aluminum tubes with wings, and rocket across the continent without thinking twice about it. My guess is that running across a few regular old Gods is just not all that exciting for them."

"How do you even do that getting big thing?" asked Sarah. Since the battle on the workshop she

and Hermes had spent every possible minute together, and Angie had already confided to Tammy
Clinenbacher that she might be getting a dad of
her own. She was working hard on understanding
as much as she could about the Gods.

Hermes refilled Sarah's Diet Coke. "You know
how when somebody is far away they look small,
and they look bigger the closer they are?"

Sarah nodded.

"Well, it's just like that. Kind of. When we appear bigger, we are just closer to your reality."

Sarah looked at Zeus. "Does that make any
sense to you?"

"Not really," said Zeus.

Hermes chuckled. "Smith was in this morning, with an exorcist."

"Really?"

"Yep. It turns out that spraying Holy Water
around and shouting about the Power of Christ
doesn't particularly compel us."

"No, I wouldn't think so."

"Any sign of Hera?"

Zeus shook his head. "Artemis is still searching
for her, but she hasn't found anything yet. I sent
Apollo to hang out at the entrance to Tartarus in
case Hera tries to go back there."

"Hephaestus tried to have a little chat with

Carl this morning, shouting through the box. He didn't get any response, so the big dude's either sleeping, dead, or really pissed off. My bet is on the latter. Whoops, hang on a second." Hermes went to the other end of the bar to draw two pitchers of beer. When he got back, Zeus was staring at his cell phone. "What's up now, Z?"

"It's a text from Artemis. She has encountered some Wood Nymphs."

"Where?"

"Somewhere in Michigan. A place called 'Escanaba.' I didn't know there were any Wood Nymphs around any more."

"How many are there?"

"I don't know." Zeus tapped laboriously on his phone with his thumbs, then waited for the little "bloop" of Artemis' reply. "She says it's a small tribe, half a dozen. And get this, they have as much Power as they ever had."

"That's not saying much," said Hermes. "It means they can teleport, chat with trees, and sing enchanting songs."

"Yeah, well that's still more than I can do."

"Nonsense Z, As far as I'm concerned, everything about you is enchanting."

"Ha ha." Zeus tapped another message into his phone. "I'm having Artemis bring those Wood

Nymphs back here to the Delphi. If we get any more surprises, they might come in handy."

"Besides, Apollo and I could use a few good-looking backup singers."

– λατερ –

Wood Nymphs are very beautiful female creatures who generally wear little more than occasional wisps of gossamer. A few minutes later, when Artemis and six of them teleported into the bar, it caused a considerable stir among those male patrons. "Didn't I tell you this place was great," said Kevin, nudging the soy bean farmer on the stool next to him with his elbow.

Zeus' asked Aphrodite to hustle the Nymphs upstairs to get them into jeans and t-shirts, while Dyo did her best to get the customers refocused on their burgers and beers. Artemis joined Zeus at the bar.

"Hera is moving like a Goddess who has a lot of Power," said Artemis, sipping on an iced tea. "By the time I could sense her in a place and then get there, she would be gone. I chased her across three continents without ever really getting close."

Zeus nodded. "You and the others are getting stronger every day."

"True, but none of us are completely back up to speed yet. I think Hera might have found more in Tartarus than just our new colleague."

"You may be right. Why don't you resume the hunt, and take along a couple of those Wood Nymphs to help out. I think I'll see if Angie can help me communicate with Carl, God of Getting Himself Trapped In A Metal Box."

– λατερ –

Angie drew a small rectangle on top of the box containing Carl, then drew a small circle near one edge of the rectangle. She hooked a finger in the middle of the circle and pulled open a small door. A pair of well-polished but slightly singed policeman's shoes wiggled beneath the opening. Angie closed the door, wiped off the chalk, and walked to the other end of the box.

This time the door opened right over Carl's face. Angry flashes of electricity danced in his eyes as he snarled, "Release me. Immediately!"

"Not going to happen," said Zeus. "not just yet, anyway"

"What happened to me? Who did this?"

"You got trapped in a bubble by Angie."

Angie looked down through the door and smiled. "Hi," she said. "I'm Angie."

"This puny child did this to me?"

"You're lucky she only captured you."

211

Carl narrowed his eyes. "You are Zeus. You are like me, a son of Titans."

"Yeah, real pleased to meet you. What I want to know is exactly what you and Hera are trying to do."

"Our sister brought me into being, forged in the fires of Tartarus, from the tears of Rhea and the perspiration…"

"…of Cronus. Yeah, I heard. So, did you just wake up with Hera staning over you and wiping Titan drippings off her hands?"

"I came to my first awareness looking at her. I do not recall what she was doing with her hands."

"Right. What did she say to you?"

"She told me that you Olympian Gods had thrown away your dominion over the world. She told me that you had grown weak. She told me that I was born to return our kind to the greatness we deserve."

"And she told you that your name was Carl?"

"I picked that name. She had a book…"

"Yeah, trust Hera to bring a baby name book to a creation in Tartarus. Is there anyone else like you?"

"I am unique in the universe."

"Sure you are. What I mean is, would there happen to be any more Giant sweat puppets like you running around?"

"No, aside from Todd, our brother, there is only me."

"Wait, what? Our brother? So there is another one of you?"

"Yes. Our mother-sister named him Todd. He was also born in the fires of Tartarus, forged from the tears…"

"Whatever. Where is Todd now?"

"He is with our sister, searching for allies."

"Allies?"

"She knows that there may be lesser Gods and creatures scattered around who can aid our cause. She and Todd will find them."

"Your cause. I suppose that would be to take over as top God?"

"I am the most powerful of all, therefore I should rule."

"So why did Hera and Todd not tag along to help when you came to visit? Or wait until she had those reinforcements."

He thought about that for a moment. "She was confident that I would be more powerful than you. As I am."

"Right up to the point where you got yourself sardine-canned by a little girl."

Carl frowned. "Yes, aside from that."

"If I know Hera - and Gods, how I do - I'd say she was hedging her bet. She was tossing you at us as a test to find out if we could stop you. Since you failed, she'll just try to recruit more muscle, then come back and try to put Todd on the top of the bill."

Carl tried to struggle, but the box held him tightly, so that the only effect was an increase in the lightning around his eyes. "This is not so," he roared. "I will be king of the Gods!"

"I'm thinking that's not going to happen any time soon." Zeus reached for the little door over Carl's face. "Why don't you take another little nap while I sort all this out."

"Wait!" said Carl.

"What?"

"Scratch my forehead. Just above the left eye. Please."

Zeus did it. "Better?"

"Yes. Thank you."

"You're welcome. I'll be back." He flipped the door shut.

Angie, who had been standing quietly off to the side and listening, wiped the chalk door off the surface of the box with the palm of her hand and said, "We need to go to Tartarus."

"I was thinking the same thing," said Zeus. "And don't try to tell me I can't go."

"It's OK, Mr. Z, you can go. This time you have to go."

A New Quest Begins

"I'd like Hermes and Athena to come along with us," said Zeus." Apollo is already at the entrance, so he can cover our backs and help out if we run into any trouble."

They were gathered in the bar. All the lunch customers were gone, except for the Wilsons, who were snoring softly at their table surrounded by empty king-sized margarita glasses.

"So now you intend to literally take my daughter on a field trip to hell?" asked Sarah.

"Do we really have to go through this again?" said Hermes. "Besides, it's not really hell. Not the way you would be likely to think about hell, anyway. None of that pitchforks and brimstone stuff."

"She will be safe," said Athena, "I promise you she will."

"How's come I ain't goin' along wit' youse guys?" asked Ares.

"OK, that's it," said Hermes, whacking Ares on the back of the head with the Visa machine. "Brooklyn is the last stop. Just don't talk any more. Ever. Seriously. Don't. Not a word."

Zeus took Sarah's hand reassuringly. "I understand your concern, but Angie really is something very special. And very powerful."

"I'll say," said Dyo. "She's getting really great at turning things into orchids. There was this green Toyota..."

"That was an accident," said Angie. "I was trying to change just the 'Make War Not Love' bumper sticker."

"Wait," said Ares, "a green Toyota? My car is a green Toyota. And I have bumper sticker that says that. Think it's just a coincidence?"

"Nope," said Aphrodite. "You now drive a four-door orchid."

"Aw, man. I really liked that car."

"No accent! Thank you," said Hermes, "Tell you what, Ares, if it will get you to give up trying to sound like Dr. Who meets Jersey Shore, I will personally buy you another crappy green Toyota."

"It's a deal," said Ares, "But I don't remember where I got that bumper sticker."

Athena took Sarah's other hand. "Angie's skills are formidable. I gave her the Sword of Perseus..."

"Larry," said Angie.

"... I gave her Larry, the Sword of Perseus, and she has mastered the power of it."

"Him," said Angie.

"The power of him," said Athena. "With it – him – she is virtually invincible."

"She also turned a toilet brush into a unicorn," said Dyo. "That was very cool. And beautiful."

"A marble statue of a unicorn," said Aphrodite. "Be fair, making a real unicorn would be almost impossible."

"But it was still beautiful," said Dyo.

"Oh yes, gorgeous," said Aphrodite.

"In any case," said Zeus, "I don't think we will have any real problems in Tartarus. Artemis is keeping track of Hera and her new protégé, and Carl is safely tucked away downstairs in Hephaestus' workshop."

"Strictly speaking, it's not downstairs," said Hephaestus. The portal we've been using makes it seem that way, but in reality..."

"Z, I'm kind of worried about what happens if they hit us at the hotel," said Athena. "We would only have Aphrodite, Dyo and Hephaestus back here to fight them."

"And Ares," said Aphrodite. "He's good in a scrap, and I should be able to keep him pointed in the right direction."

"I think I got that bumper sticker online," said Ares. "AllKillerStickers.com, or something like that."

"I saw a sign on Facebook just yesterday that said, 'Make Dinner Not War,'" said Dyo. "That would be hilarious on your car."

Zeus stood up and paced over to the bar, his hands behind his back. "If Hera attacked the hotel, Artemis would follow her here. I think that even with Hephaestus still hurting, the two of them should be able to hold their own until we get back."

"What about your brothers?" asked Sarah. "Couldn't they help you?"

"You met them," said Zeus. "They haven't regained any more power than I have. And up to now they don't appear to be all that interested in any of this."

"That Poseidon is a cutie," said Dyo. "I love that surfer blonde hair of his. I'd like to..."

"Don't waste your time," said Aphrodite. "He's way too cute, if you know what I mean. Not all that interested in women."

"Correction. He's just not all that interested in you," said Hermes.

"Make Dinner Not War," said Ares. "Say, that's funny!"

"The Wood Nymphs could also help you out here," said Zeus. "They aren't much in a fight, but they can be pretty distracting."

"I had forgotten how cute Wood Nymphs are," said Aphrodite. "They have such adorable little shapes..."

"I wonder if we could dig up some satyrs," said Hephaestus. "Those little guys were always pretty handy with a bellows and hammer..."

"Good thinking," said Zeus. "I'll tell Artemis to keep an eye out."

"Sarah, you really don't need to worry about Angie," said Athena. "As far as we can tell, it would be almost impossible to harm her. And between Larry and her hunk of chalk, she is probably more dangerous than any of us."

"Oh yeah, my daughter has a sword called Larry," said Sarah.

"Well then, just think of it as the Sword of Perseus. Called Larry."

"Oh, right, way better. Look, this is all getting pretty weird."

"It's been weird for a while, Mom," said Angie.

– λατερ –

Angie, dressed for combat in blue shorts and a little red Indiana University t-shirt, drew a chalk door on the wall of Athena's room. Larry and the My Little Pony shield were strapped across her back. "This portal should take us directly to the entrance to Tartarus," she said.

Athena, wearing her armor over a short white dress and carrying her freshly-repaired sword and shield, leaned on her spear. "With Apollo there, we should have nothing to worry about. But even so, be on your guard."

Hermes was dressed in army surplus combat fatigues and holding Hades' Helmet of Invisibility under his arm. "I'll go through with the hat on, just in case." He put the helmet on and vanished.

Zeus wore jeans, a Rolling Stones t-shirt, and sneakers. His faintly glowing lightning bolt was stuck through a weathered brown leather belt with a large Lone Star buckle. "Good plan," he said. "We need to be prepared for anything. Angie, you stay behind me and..."

Before he could finish his thought, the portal door swung open and Angie walked through.

Apollo was in the center of a small gray room, seated at a card table with a silver longbow and a quiver of silver arrows on the floor next to him. Around the table with him sat three more-or-less female creatures with pterodactyl wings, wearing scales instead of clothing. The one to his left was dealing a hand of five-card stud poker. Piles of gold coins sat in the center of the table and in front of each of them. Apollo's pile was considerably smaller than the others.

Hermes materialized next to the table. "Cool," he said. "Where did you find the Harpies? Hi there, ladies."

The Harpies all gave Hermes a friendly wave with sharply taloned hands and turned their attention back to their cards. "They were hanging out in Tartarus," said Apollo. "Did you bring us that little gift I asked for?"

Hermes held out a hand and a large pizza box dropped into it. "Feta cheese, Gyro meat and olives. Ares just pulled it out of the oven."

Athena came through the portal with her sword drawn. When she saw Apollo and the Harpies she relaxed. "Hi girls. I see you conned Apollo into a card game."

Zeus followed Athena through the door and the Harpies jumped to their feet, bowing their heads. "Lord Zeus," they said in voices like the air being let out of a truck tire. "We are here to serve you."

"No, no, don't get up," said Zeus. "It sure is good to see you three again."

Angie picked up one of Apollo's gold coins. "Is this real gold?"

"Sure," said Apollo. "We couldn't find any matchsticks."

She turned to the nearest Harpy and smiled. "Hi. I'm Angie."

"My sisters call me 'Sister,'" hissed the Harpy.

"What do you call your sisters?"

"'Sister.'"

"That must be confusing."

"Not really. We know who we are."

Zeus walked over to an ordinary-looking wooden door on the far side of the card table and tapped on it. "Where are the guys?"

Apollo smiled. "They've been stuck here playing three-handed card games for eighteen centuries while we were snoozing, so I gave them a little time off. I think they wanted to hit the beach at Naxos. I told them to have fun and be back here on duty tomorrow morning."

"My book said that there were three Giants who guarded the Gates of Tartarus," said Angie. "Is that who you're talking about?"

"Yes, the Hecatoncheires, " said Zeus. "But I wouldn't exactly call them Giants. More like linebackers. Very, very large ones, who command hurricane winds. I left them here to watch this door, so that they could let me know if any of the Titans woke up and tried to get out."

"They are pretty nice guys," said Athena. "And handy in a fight."

"It's going to be a real interesting day on the beach at Naxos," said Hermes.

He turned to the Harpies. "Were you in Tartarus when Hera came?"

"She summoned us to this place," said Sister.

"In your name," said Sister.

"So of course we came," added Sister.

"What did she want from you?"

"She demanded that we and the Hecatoncheires work together to create a vortex of wind in the center of Tartarus, near the resting place of the Titans," said Sister.

"For what reason?"

"She needed to harness the Power in our wind," said Sister.

"She was creating two new Gods," said Sister.

"She told us she was merely doing your bidding," said Sister.

"And you believed her?" asked Athena.

"Sadly, yes," said Sister.

"Apollo told us of her treachery," said Sister.

"We are sorry, Lord Zeus," said Sister.

"Not your fault," said Zeus.

"You're going to call with that hand?" asked Hermes, looking at Apollo's cards. "No wonder the Sisters are kicking your butt."

Tartarus

"This is not exactly what I was expecting," said Angie. Athena, Hermes, Zeus and Angie were walking down a long gently-sloping walkway in a brightly lit hallway, with the Harpies following and hovering over them like big scaly humming-birds. Apollo had stayed behind to play solitaire and guard the entrance.

The walls and ceiling of the walkway were made of smooth featureless gray stone, and the floor was slightly darker. "My book said Tartarus was an enormous evil pit reaching to the center of the Earth. This is more like the walkway at the Colts game."

"Really?" said Hermes. "Your mom took you to a Colts game?"

"With Uncle Rick."

"Uncle Rick? I didn't know your mom had a brother," said Hermes.

"He's not my real uncle."

"But..." said Hermes.

"I'd leave it at that," said Athena.

"Stay alert," said Zeus. "Angie, this is just taking us to the entrance. Tartarus is a prison for the Titans, my parents and their brothers and sisters, who are trapped in an eternal sleep. I don't see any reason the entrance to the place has to look like some kind of dungeon."

"How did you beat the Titans, anyway? My book isn't too detailed on that."

"I gathered all the forces of the world together, except the Titans themselves, and their allies the Giants, and I attacked. I freed the Hecatoncheires, and the Cyclopes, and the Harpies, and some other allies from right here in Tartarus, where my father, Cronus, had imprisoned them. The Cyclopes made my thunderbolts and other weapons for me. The Hecantonchieres and the Harpies threw pretty nasty storm winds at the Titans."

"After that, he got them all drunk," said Hermes. "They're still sleeping it off."

"OK, that too," said Zeus."

"I get mad at my mom sometimes, but I've

never been mad enough to clobber her with a bunch of hurricanes."

"The whole parent thing is a little different for us. Plus, it was never really about getting angry," said Zeus. "It was about getting control. That's always been kind of a thing in our extended family."

"Yeah, you might say that," said Hermes.

"And has it always been the most powerful who got control?" asked Angie.

Zeus thought a moment. "Of course it has," he said. "How else would it work?"

"We're almost there," said Athena, lowering her spear. The ramp had leveled out, and they were approaching a huge bronze double door. "Hermes, why don't you make yourself invisible and open the doors?"

"Good plan," said Hermes, vanishing.

The Harpies, still hovering, moved together nearly wing-to-wing above and ahead of Zeus. Athena assumed the fighting stance that she had been teaching Angie, who pulled out Larry and her shield, and copied her pose.

Zeus drew his lightning bolt from his belt, shook it, smacked it against the palm of his hand a couple of times, sighed, and said, "OK, let's go."

The bronze doors swung open away from them.

A blast of hot air, tinged with the odor of sulphur, swept over them. A red light glowed on a light mist hanging in the air beyond the doors. The rough stone floor stretched off and disappeared into the distance, with no walls or ceiling visible.

"What's with the red light?" asked Athena. "It used to be pretty gloomy in here."

"We did that," said Sister.

"We thought it would be pretty," said Sister.

"We were bored," said Sister.

"It's really hot in there, too," said Zeus. "Was that Hera's doing?"

"She was cold, Lord Zeus," said Sister.

"She's always cold," said Athena.

"We did both the heat and the light with lava pools," said Sister.

"We're sorry if this displeases you," said Sister.

"No no, it's fine," said Zeus. "In fact, it's pretty clever. Hermes, why don't you scout ahead to make sure there are no unpleasant surprises waiting for us."

"You got it," said Hermes' disembodied voice.

Zeus, Athena and Angie moved into Tartarus with the Harpies flying low cover for them. "What do you expect to happen? Will someone attack us?" asked Angie as they veered around a perfectly round pool of bubbling lava. She had replaced Larry and the shield on her back and had her chalk in her hand.

"There is really no way to tell," said Athena. "In a sense, this place is death for Gods. As we fell asleep all those centuries ago I assumed we would somehow end up here, where we would spend the rest of time."

They passed a pile of lava rocks and a broken-off stalagmite. "There's really not much to it, is there?" said Angie.

Zeus chuckled. "When we fought the Titans this was the scene of some of the most violent battles in the history of this world. It was on this very spot that I defeated the hundred-headed serpent Typhoeus to free our winged friends here."

Angie scanned the utterly featureless landscape. "Really? Right here?"

Athena laughed. "You are so full of it, Z."

"Well, it may have been over that way a bit," he said, gesturing with his thunderbolt. "Anyway, the point is there have sometimes been some pretty nasty creatures wandering around in here, so it pays to keep your guard up."

Hermes materialized in front of them. "It's all clear," he said. "They're sleeping like baby Titans."

"Where exactly did Hera brew up Carl and Todd?" Athena asked the Harpies.

"Among the Biers," said Sister.

"She had us make her an incubator there," said Sister.

"We'll show you," said Sister.

They walked on.

– λατερ –

The Biers were twelve long, low marble slabs, arranged in a circle. On each one lay a sleeping Titan. There were six enormous men and six enormous women, all dressed in pure white robes. They all had their hands folded across their laps, and their chests rose and fell in the gentle rhythmic breathing of deep sleep. "These are the children of Gaea," Athena told Angie. "Once Cronus was too tired to fight any more, they all had a few drinks with Zeus and then came here to rest."

"That's not exactly how the stories go," said Angie.

"Yeah, well you know how writers are," said Hermes. "What they don't make up, they fabricate. It's a miracle those clowns ever get anything right."

In the center of the circle bubbled a small pool of lava. An empty platform of marble, supported by blocks of marble at each end, stretched across the pool, so that volcanic vapors curled up and around it. "This is the Incubator we built," said Sister.

"Fueled by the wind," said Sister.

"Hera commanded it," said Sister.

"... all in my name," said Zeus. "Athena, what do you think?"

Athena examined the marble platform. "There is a really strong Power residue here," she said.

"The afterbirth of a God," said Hermes.

"Ew, gross," said Angie.

"Carl told Hephaestus that he was created from the perspiration of Cronus and the tears of Rhea," said Zeus. "What do you think that's all about?"

"It's been a really long time since any new Gods came into being," said Athena. "And you know as well as I do that we don't just get born. Even so, creating a couple of Gods by wringing out a sweaty toga would be pretty unique."

"Yet we met Carl," said Zeus, "and we have no reason to assume he was lying about Todd."

"Hephaestus made Dyo out of, basically, Play-Doh," said Hermes.

"Good point," said Athena. "Only he had no idea he was creating a Goddess."

"More like modeling clay," said Angie. "Play-Doh is way different. It cracks when it dries."

A long thundering yawn came from the Bier at the top of the circle. Cronus, Supreme

Lord of the Universe (Ret.), sat up and stretched.

Athena and Hermes drew their weapons, while the Harpies took up attack positions hovering overhead. Zeus shook his thunderbolt and cursed softly.

Angie walked to where Cronus sat, his head more than ten feet above her, and said, "Hello, Mr. Cronus."

Cronus scratched his chest and smiled down at her. "Well, hi there," he said, his voice rumbling like an earthquake. "Who would you be?"

"I'm Angie."

"Pleased to meet you, Angie." he looked around. "Hi Son," he said to Zeus. "Nobody's destroyed you, or overthrown you, or put you out to pasture yet?"

Zeus tucked the thunderbolt back into his belt. "Not yet, although Hera's still working on it. Have a good snooze?"

"Not bad. What time is it?"

Athena closed her eyes and did some silent calculations. "It's the year 119,358, in God time. I'd say that you've had a little over seven thousand years of sleep."

Cronus yawned again. "Yeah, well I could use six or seven thousand more. So, what are you kids up to?"

"Hera came down here and cooked up two new Gods. We're trying to figure out exactly what she's doing."

"Angie here defeated one of them," said Hermes. "Kicked his butt."

"Hermes, you little rascal" said Cronus. "You're looking good." He looked back to Angie. "You snagged yourself a God, did you?"

"Yes, with this," said Angie, holding up her chalk. "Oh, and my bubble wand."

Cronus raised his eyebrows and nodded. "I see. So you're the one."

"Angie is THE ONE?" asked Athena.

"No, just the one. The Oracle once told me that there would eventually be a Goddess of Chalk Art. And here we are."

"Don't forget the bubbles," giggled Angie.

"Right," said Cronus, chuckling. "Goddess of Chalk Art and Bubbles."

"So father," said Zeus, "did you wake up to fight with us or against us?"

Cronus looked at Zeus, tilted his head to the side, and raised his right hand. A black cloud formed in the air above his hand, then grew, billowing, larger. Finally, with an enormous crack of thunder, a flash of lightning lashed out and struck Zeus in a blinding explosion of pure energy.

When the smoke cleared Zeus sat in a shallow crater, his hair singed and smoking, wearing the shredded remains of his Rolling Stones t-shirt and a smoldering pair of Alvin and the Chipmunks boxer shorts. His thunderbolt, pulsing with energy, lay on the ground next to him, right beside the molten remains of the Lone Star belt buckle. "What was that for?" he asked.

Cronus closed his hand and the cloud dissipated. "Just wanted to see if I could still do that," said Cronus. "Apparently I can. And I wanted to get those things off your legs."

"Pants," said Angie.

"Yes, those stupid pants. A God should wear Godly robes."

Zeus stood up and grabbed his thunderbolt, trying to act like he was dressed in something other than Alvin and the Chipmunks boxer shorts. "So, I take it this means that you'll be fighting against us," he said.

Cronus yawned a third time, stroked his beard, and said, "Nah, I don't think so. I've had enough fighting. I was enjoying my rest, and I think I'd prefer to return to it." He stretched back out on his Bier, folded his hands on his lap, and turned his head to look at Angie. "It was a pleasure meeting you, Little Sister." He nodded to the chalk still in her hand. "Be careful where you point that thing." Then he turned his face upward, closed his eyes, and resumed the deep rhythmic breathing of peaceful sleep.

"OK, that was different," said Hermes.

"Unexpected," said Sister.

"Astonishing," said Sister.

"My wings are getting tired," said Sister, fluttering down for a landing.

"Cronus was never that mellow in the old days," said Athena. "Who knew, the old guy just needed a nap."

"He's way different from what they say in my books," said Angie.

"I don't suppose anyone has a spare Godly robe. Or a pair of pants," said Zeus.

Seven

That was rude.

Absolutely.

Cronus deserves his rest.

It was necessary.

True. They have to learn.

But they don't seem to be learning much.

How can they?

True enough. None of it makes any sense.

But do they really know that?

I would be amazed if they didn't at least suspect.

Back From Tartarus

When they returned to the little room at the Entrance to Tartarus, they found Apollo lying on the floor in the corner, wrapped from head to foot in a wild tangle of golden wire. Artemis was kneeling over him.

"Lord Apollo!" said Sister.

"Oh my!" said Sister

Are you hurt?" asked Sister.

"Mmmmmmmf," said Apollo through a mouthful of golden wire.

"I just found him like this," said Artemis. "I think he's all right, but help me get this stuff off him."

Angie pulled Larry from his sheath and used him to carefully cut Apollo free.

"So, what happened to you?" asked Zeus.

Apollo sat up and stretched. "I had a run-in with a strange God, who I presume is our new friend Todd, along with a Giant and a couple of automatons. Wait, are those Alvin and the Chipmunks boxers?"

"Never mind," said Zeus. "A Giant? Really? And what kind of automatons?"

"What's left of one of them is over there," said Apollo, gesturing to a pile of bronze in the far corner of the room. "They were like big mechanical spiders, and they shot out all of this Olympian Bronze wire. I was able to blast that one, and I gave the Giant a pretty good headache with an arrow too. But then I got tangled up in all the wire."

Athena poked at the pile of bronze with her spear. "Who besides Hephaestus could have made something like this?"

"Who indeed? The real question might be not if he made this thing, but when," said Zeus. "Is it possible that he has broken his oath and is messing with us again?"

"Carl worked him over pretty thoroughly," said Hermes. "That seems like a long way to go to try to mislead us. Plus, that oath should be unbreakable."

"Unless he found a loophole," said Zeus.

"I don't think Mr. Hephaestus made this," said Angie, examining a leg of the spider. "The things he makes are always pretty and polished."

"She's right," said Athena. "There are burrs and scratches on all these parts. Hephaestus would never be this sloppy. Maybe a Cyclops or a Satyr?"

"Crazier things have happened," said Hermes.

"Artemis, how did you happen to come here?" asked Athena.

"We were tracking Hera, and we could tell she had others with her. I couldn't believe I was sensing at least one Giant, along with that Todd guy. When they split up, I sent the Nymphs to keep track of her, and I followed Todd and his oversized sidekick here."

"And they just legged it when you showed up? Hermes, why don't you send this stuff back to the hotel so Hephaestus can look at it," said Zeus. Hermes raised a hand and the pile of spider parts dropped through a temporary hole in the floor. Zeus helped Apollo to his feet. "So, after they tied you up, did they even try to enter Tartarus?"

"No, that's the weird thing," said Apollo. "They attacked me, grabbed my bow and the arrows, and when Artemis got here they just left."

"They jumped you just to get your bow." said Hermes. "That doesn't make any sense. Nobody but you can even use that thing."

"Todd may not know that," said Athena, "but of course, Hera would. So if she sent him here, we can assume it wasn't specifically to get the bow."

"Maybe she was just testing him," said Angie.

"There's an interesting thought," said Zeus. "It's a good idea to get a sense of what your troops can do before the real battle. The bitch is conducting war games."

"Or," said Hermes, "maybe she just wanted to disarm Apollo."

– λατερ –

Hephaestus squinted through a magnifying glass at a piece of the spider automaton's carapace, scraped at it with his fingernail, and then handed it and the glass to Zeus. The two of them were in Hephaestus' workshop, with the wreckage stacked in front of them on a well-worn workbench.

"See that?" said Hephaestus. "It was made by a coarse file. Two seconds with a bit of emery cloth would have taken care of it. Disgraceful. No pride of workmanship."

Zeus nodded. "I see what you mean. But what I really want to know is who could have put this together? Crude or not, two of these things were able to spit out enough Olympian Bronze thread to overcome Apollo."

Hephaestus scratched his head. "I've worked with the Cyclopes and trained the Satyrs, and I can tell you that the Cyclopes are better craftsmen than this. I would not have thought that any Satyr would be able to make a functional automaton like this on their own, but I guess it is possible."

Zeus paced over to Carl's box and sat down on it, drumming absentmindedly on the top. A muffled tapping came back from inside the box, and Zeus jumped back to his feet. "So Hera has Satyrs, and they might have had help with these things. The question is where would they get the help?"

Hephaestus whacked the side of Carl's box with an automaton spider leg and listened with satisfaction to the responding thud. "Well, what do we know about Todd's capabilities? Those automatons were powered by Olympian Power, so it's logical to assume that they were made by a God. Maybe the new dude has some of my kind of talent." He tossed the leg back onto the workbench. "Just no standards."

Zeus looked down at Carl's box. "Maybe we should have another chat with our friend here. Can you open a window in this thing?"

Hephaestus shook his head. "Nope. This box is Angie's doing, and I can't put a scratch on it."

"You've tried?"

"Sure I have. I can't think of anything I'd rather do than open a port, tickle this moron with a stick, then seal him back up."

"Wow. That's really unkind of you."

"Well, he did try to blow me to bits."

"Haven't we all tried to blow you to bits at one time or another? Even Angie was rougher on you than Carl was."

"True. But she was just doing what she had to do." He nudged the box with his toe. "It was like this guy was really enjoying it."

"Still, I'd like to find an alternative to keeping him locked up like this."

Hephaestus shook his head. "I don't know, Z. It's not like you to get all soft and squishy."

"I'm not getting all soft and squishy. I just know that I would hate it if I was locked up in there."

"Whatever. So, what did you do with the Harpies? I haven't seen them since they got here."

"They're on the roof of the hotel, doing surveillance. They are prepared to fly close air support if something happens. The Hecatoncheires are back at their post, securing the gate to Tartarus."

"OK, General Patton, that all makes sense. When I get a chance I'll have to go up and say hi to the girls. In the meantime, let me have a look at that thunderbolt."

Zeus handed it to him. "Ever since Cronus zapped me, it's been supercharged."

Hephaestus turned it over in his hands. "Have you tested it?"

"Just once. Oh yeah, I meant to tell you, there's a good-sized hole in the floor of my office."

Hephaestus sighed. "I'll take care of it. As far as I can see, it looks like this baby is pretty much back up to its old strength. How about you?"

"To be honest, I've been too busy to try anything." He stepped back and raised his hands, palms up. A dark cloud formed in the air over his head. A rumble of thunder shook the workshop. The cloud grew larger, and larger. Then, with a little wheeze it blew apart and drifted away.

"OK, well, yeah, Z. There you go, that was good. Real good. Yeah," said Hephaestus.

They were interrupted by Dyo bursting into the workshop, sobbing. "They've taken Angie and her mother!"

Zeus caught her by the arms. "Who took them? When?"

"Hermes said that Hera has them. He went over to see Sarah and found this in what was left of their house." She handed Zeus a square bronze plate with a peacock inscribed on it.

"That's Hera's calling card." Zeus handed the plate to Hephaestus. "I wonder what that woman is playing at."

"I just wonder how they could grab Angie without the kid turning them all into cat food," said Hephaestus.

– λατερ –

Hermes sat at the bar with his head in his hands. Dyo gently rubbed his shoulder and said, "Try not to be upset, Hermes. I'm sure we'll get them back somehow."

Hermes looked up. What was in his eyes was rage, not any sort of sadness. "I'm trying to locate them," he said. "If I can just find the right wavelength, I can feel Sarah. Then we can take those pigs apart and bring the girls home. If that pathetic hag hurts either one of them..."

"Take it easy," said Athena.

"She could easily kill Sarah," said Hermes. "And we don't really know just exactly how immortal Angie really is."

"True," said Athena, "but I don't think she will. As we have discovered, that little half-pint can be a pretty tough customer. Hera would only have any kind of leverage over her as long as her mother is unharmed. I think Hera's overall plan might be to pick us off and disable or neutralize us one at a time. She may not believe that she's strong enough to destroy us in an all-out fight."

"Then why didn't Todd take Apollo when he had the chance?" asked Aphrodite.

"We're not exactly dealing with Socrates here," said Apollo. "I'd say he was doing exactly what he was told to do."

Hera's Hideaway

A gigantic Todd sat on the concrete floor of an abandoned factory, the back of his head jammed against the beams overhead. He glared down through the gloom at Angie and Sarah. They were side by side on the floor, bound with Olympian Bronze chains strung through Olympian Bronze eyelets sunk into a cinder block wall. Hera stood over them and held Angie's sidewalk chalk in her hand. "Skank and mini-skank," she said.

"My daughter is ten," said Sarah. "She doesn't even know what that word means."

"Yes I do," said Angie. "And no, I'm not. And neither is my mom."

Hera grunted, then tossed the hunk of chalk up in the air and let it fall back into her hand. "So this is the mighty weapon you used to defeat and confine my son."

"Technically, I think he would be more like your brother," said Sarah.

"Silence!" shouted Hera. She flipped her fingers toward Sarah and a burst of air pinned her against the wall. "I created him and this one as well. They are my children. Together we three will rule Olympus!"

"You sound just like the nasty queen in one of those movies on TV where everything's all black and white," said Angie. "And the girls wear long gowns, and the guys wear tights and do a lot of sword fighting. I like those movies a lot."

"Will you SHUT UP!" shouted Hera. She pushed both palms toward Sarah and Angie. This time the blast broke around them and carved a circular groove in the cinder blocks.

Hera took a step back. "How are you able to do that?"

"I didn't want you to bump my mom's head. You might have hurt her."

Hera narrowed her eyes and shook the chalk in Angie's face. "You will show me how to use this weapon of yours."

Angie shrugged, setting off a melodious rattle of Golden chains. "It's not a weapon. It's just a piece of chalk. You draw things with it."

"How did you use it to defeat a God?"

"I just drew a box. By then he was already pretty much defeated, though. You see, I had my bubble wand..."

"Enough!" Hera drew a large rectangle on the floor with the chalk. "Now what?"

"What does it look like to you?" asked Angie.

"A chalk rectangle."

"Then that's what it is."

Hera stared at the rectangle then snarled at Angie, "You will show me how this works."

"I just did."

"Whelp," shouted Hera, and she threw the chalk against the wall over Angie's head. It shattered and rained blue shards down over the girl.

Sarah strained against her chains. "You will not talk to my daughter like that!"

Hera drew herself up until she towered over them with her head pressed against the ceiling. "Harlot," she said. "I am Hera, Goddess, Queen of the Heavens. I will speak as I please to whomever I please, and you will worship me."

"Worship you?" Sarah gritted her teeth. "When the time comes, I am going to kick your enormous ancient ass."

"Enormous? Ancient?" Hera fired another blast with her hands, which again broke harmlessly around Sarah and Angie and scored the wall.

"That's not really working, Mistress," said Todd. "Can I kill them now, just a little bit?"

Hera returned to her normal size. "Not just yet," she said. She turned to look at Todd. "Haven't you worked out how to re-size yourself yet? That looks really uncomfortable."

Todd closed his eyes and grunted for a few seconds. "Nope, no luck."

"You just think about... Never mind. Go, wait outside for the Giant to get back with his brothers." She watched him crawl out through the factory's loading dock door.

"So what are you going to do with us?" asked Sarah.

"Nothing for now," said Hera. "You may have some value as hostages. With any kind of luck, once I am mistress of the universe I'll have a little spare time to squash you like the insignificant insects you are."

"That's not very nice," said Angie.

Hera laughed. "No, I suppose it's not. I need to run a few errands, but I'm going to leave a couple of Giants behind, just to make sure you stay put. Since you're new to this, I feel that I should warn you that a single Giant is nearly a match for a true God. You two will not fare well if you try anything." She turned and swept out after Todd.

Sarah watched her leave, then sagged back against the wall. "Why did I let Hermes drag us into this," she said.

"This is not Hermes' fault," said Angie. "I need to be part of these events."

Sarah studied her. "How do you really know that you're so important to all this?"

"I'm not sure. But I can see things, and feel things, and do things and it all feels like this is exactly how it's supposed to be."

"You're just a little girl."

"I know, Mom. But I'm more than that, too." Angie stood up and her chains clattered to the floor behind her. She held a tiny bit of chalk in her hand. "Lean forward, and let me get those things off you." She drew a chalk line across Sarah's chains, and they parted.

Sarah stood up, rubbing her wrists. "OK, I give. Now what?"

"I think we should get out of here." She walked over to the chalk rectangle Hera had drawn on the floor. "To me, this looks like a door to Hephaestus' workshop." She pulled it open. "Careful. When you jump down here, you're going to pop up out of the floor on the other side. You go first."

Sarah hopped through the door and immediately shot back up into the factory, landing on the floor next to the door. Angie helped her back to her feet. "Sorry Mom, I should have told you that you have to jump at an angle, so you'll clear the hole. Try it again."

Sarah rubbed the elbow she'd landed on and shook her head. "I work in a bank. In Indiana. Now my fifth-grader is teaching me the proper way to leap through trans-dimensional portals."

"You'll get the hang of it," said Angie.

Sarah took a deep breath and jumped again, this time at a slight angle. When she didn't re-appear after a few seconds, Angie followed her, jumping and pulling the door shut behind her.

She landed on her feet next to Sarah, who was lying on the floor next to Carl's box and rubbing her other elbow. "No, I don't think I'll ever get the hang of that," said Sarah.

"It is pretty weird," said Angie. She looked around the workshop. "Help me find something I can use to wipe this chalk door away and seal off..."

The door swung back open and Hera popped into the room. She landed nimbly on her feet, grabbed Sarah by the arm, and pressed the thin golden blade of an elegant dagger against her neck.

She was followed by Todd and three Giants, who piled up in a very large, noisily grumbling heap.

"Seriously?" said Hera. "Get up, you idiots." She drew Sarah closer and circled away from the tangled mass of enormous bodies. "Despite the breathtaking ineptitude of my invasion force, I am now in a position to kill your mother. Unless, of course, you choose to save her by setting my other son free."

"I wondered why you drew such a big rectangle," said Angie. "That was a clever plan."

"I'm honored," said Hera. "Now, release him." She pressed the knife and a trickle of blood ran down Sarah's neck.

"You cut my mom!" said Angie.

"I'll do far worse if you don't..."

Angie clenched her fists and pursed her lips. Hera's knife turned into a piece of red licorice. She gestured with her hand and swept the pile of Todd and Giants, who had barely managed to stand up, back into the hole in the floor. She raised her hand and the door slammed shut. Sarah kicked Hera hard in the shin and twisted herself free.

"I don't need a weapon to destroy the likes of you," said Hera.

Angie raised the palm of her right hand toward Hera. "Neither do I," she said.

The blast caught Hera in the chest and drove her, screaming, out of sight down the length of

Hephaestus' workshop. Angie walked over to the portal door on the floor, slipped off her shoe, and began to wipe away the door with her sock.

"Where will she land?" asked Sarah.

A muffled explosion and a faint scream reached them from the other end of the workshop. "My guess would be Prague. Come on, Mom. We need to talk to Hermes and Mr. Z."

A New Ally

"You didn't have much trouble dealing with Hera," said Zeus. He, Hermes, Athena, Hephaestus, Sarah and Angie were gathered around Carl's box in Hephaestus' workshop.

"I took her by surprise," said Angie. "And it was lucky that I had an easy way to get rid of Todd and the Giants. Next time it might not be that simple."

"She's right, Z," said Athena. "Hera's not dumb. And I'm not sure any of us are really ready to take on a bunch of Giants."

"There were only three," said Zeus.

"She talked like they were still finding more," said Angie.

"Where do Giants even hang out so nobody notices them?" asked Sarah.

"Walmart?" said Hermes.

"Not all that big a fan of Walmart, are you?" said Sarah.

"No, not really."

"So what now, Z?" asked Hephaestus.

"I'm not real sure," said Zeus. "I've got Artemis, Apollo and the Harpies positioned around town watching for an attack, while Aphrodite, Dyo, the Nymphs, and Ares run the restaurant."

"I get why we have to stay here, but why are we even messing around with keeping the restaurant open?" asked Hephaestus.

"Well, for one thing, between Ares' obsession with cooking and having our two versions of Aphrodite and a gang of Wood Nymphs hanging out there, we can keep our God of War pretty much occupied and out of trouble. When the fighting starts, I want him where I can see him."

"Plus, until we get more of our Power back, we can use the cash flow," said Athena. "We can't just manifest all our needs anymore."

"I can," said Hephaestus.

"You're pretty handy with pipes and sheet metal," said Hermes, "but nobody really wants to eat your swords and spice racks. You have to admit it, that lunkhead Ares makes a great feta cheese burger."

"So, for the time being, we stay with the hotel," said Zeus.

Athena shook her head. "As much as we need the money and the diversion, I don't know if staying around town is such a good idea, Z. We should think about what would happen to all the humans in Olympus if it came to an all-out battle there."

"Speaking for all the humans, I can totally relate to that," said Sarah. "My house is a pile of rubble in a shallow crater, and I'm not sure my homeowner's insurance covers warring deities."

"You don't need insurance when you're dating a God," said Hermes.

"Yeah, Hermes, and you're so good at repairing things," said Hephaestus. He smiled at Sarah. "I'll take care of it."

"We'll take care of it," said Hermes.

"Athena, what do you suggest?" asked Zeus.

"I'm not sure," said Athena. "It would be nice if we could find a way to move any kind of battle to open ground, away from people. Let me work on a plan."

"You do that," said Zeus. "In the meantime, I've made a decision. We're going to let Carl out of this box."

"What?" shouted Hephaestus.

"Wow, I don't know Z," said Athena.

"Back in the day, you'd have had a chicken hawk plucking out his spleen, every ten minutes until the end of time," said Hermes.

"Yeah," said Hephaestus. "What he said."

"I'm pretty sure it was an eagle," said Athena.

"I think letting him out is a good idea Mr. Z," said Angie.

"That's sweet of you," said Sarah. "Why do you say that, Honey?"

"She sees compassion as a noble end in itself," said Zeus.

"Not really," said Angie. "Of course it would be pretty cool if just because we're nice to him, he would be on our side against Hera. But if that doesn't work out, we can bind him with an oath, then force him between us and Hera's forces in a fight, to soak up some of the punishment from the Giants."

"OK, now that's cold," said Hermes.

"But downright tactical," said Athena.

"I like the concept," said Hephaestus.

"I'm not sure if I should be proud right now, or really worried," said Sarah.

"Probably both," said Zeus. "So Angie, can you open a window so we can talk to our friend?"

A minute later the door opened over Carl's face. "I DEMAND THAT YOU RELEASE ME AT ONCE," he roared.

"We're going to," said Zeus.

"IF YOU DO NOT COMPLY I WILL SMITE YOU AND... wait, what? Oh. All right then," said Carl.

"First, we have to clear up a few things between us," said Zeus.

"Yes?"

"To begin with, this whole thing about you sitting on the Throne of Olympus? Not going to happen," said Zeus.

"I was bred to rule!" said Carl.

"You're made of pit-sweat" said Hephaestus.

"That's beside the point," said Zeus. "Look, Carl, Hera is kind of crazy, but she has also been my wife for a really long time, and I know her pretty well. She pulls this whole Seizing the Throne of Olympus routine every few hundred years, and it's never worked yet. For one thing, this time there isn't really any kind of Throne. We run a hotel."

"As Gods we can be masters of this world!"

"Not so much," said Athena "The world is a lot bigger now than it was back in the day. If it came down to it, these people have bombs that could turn Mount Olympus itself into a smoking hole in the ground."

"Impossible!" said Carl. "We are immortals!"

"But even we can be destroyed," said Zeus. "And we can destroy each other. Look, Carl, what I'm trying to say here is that we don't really need mankind to worship us and do our bidding. In fact, over the past year since our re-awakening, we've discovered that it's really kind of fun to hang out with them."

"Yeah, it's a lot less stressful to sell people stuffed grape leaves than to guide the course of human history," said Hermes.

"You only say these things because you have no Power."

"I have the Power to shut this little window and leave you alone with your thoughts for the next ten thousand years," said Zeus.

"Hera will free me."

"Hera will do no such thing" said Zeus. "Didn't you hear all the commotion when Angie defeated her, right here on this spot?"

"It was over that way a little bit," said Angie, pointing to the spot on the floor where the portal had been.

"The child defeated Hera?"

"Hera, three Giants, and your brother Todd,"

said Hephaestus. "And she did it just as easily as she kicked your butt."

"It was a little bit harder than that," said Angie. "My chalk was all busted up, so I had to improvise."

"So here's the deal," said Zeus. "You renounce Hera and swear a binding oath of eternal loyalty to me, and I let you out of this box."

"And if I refuse?"

"I could always turn this thing into a kind of smoker," said Hephaestus. "Suspend it over an eternal flame and sprinkle some mesquite chips down around your feet."

"Could you rig the box up to turn like a rotisserie?" asked Athena.

"Great idea," said Hephaestus. "You'll get some really juicy Briskit of Carl that way."

"Or," said Hermes, "we could attach some speakers and a subwoofer right against the side of the box and treat you to a continuous loop of Taylor Swift music."

"What is Taylor Swift?" asked Carl.

"Trust me, you really do not want to find out," said Sarah.

"What's wrong with Taylor Swift?" asked Angie.

"The bottom line is, Carl, if you come over to our side, it will work out better for all of us."

"Speak for yourself," said Hephaestus. "I'm kind of leaning toward the rotisserie idea."

"*All* of us," said Zeus.

"You're asking me to do battle against the one who created me," said Carl.

"Yeah, well that's a really old story in this crowd," said Hermes.

"I'm hoping it won't come to that," said Zeus. "If Hera sees that you are on our side she may be willing to back off, and with luck we could avoid a major battle."

Carl rolled his head back and closed his eyes for a few seconds. Then he looked at Zeus. "Alright, Lord Zeus. I will completely and forever renounce Hera and swear my eternal loyalty to you. How do I go about doing this?"

"How about saying, 'I hereby completely and forever renounce the rule of Hera, and swear my eternal loyalty to Zeus,'" said Hermes. "You guys can do all the hand-spitting stuff later."

"Works for me," said Zeus.

"And these words will be binding?" asked Carl.

"Words are powerful," said Angie.

"Yes, they will be binding," said Athena.

"Violate the oath and you'll find yourself back in the box. And we'll make you the most tender slow-roasted Taylor Swift fan in Southwest Indiana," said Hermes.

"Very well," said Carl. He closed his eyes. "I hereby completely and forever renounce the rule of Hera, and swear my eternal loyalty to Zeus." A green glow enveloped Carl for a few seconds, then faded away.

"What was that?" asked Sarah.

"That was an unbreakable vow binding itself," said Athena. "Like Angie said, words really are powerful."

"All righty then," said Zeus. "Angie, would you please do the honors and get our new brother out of this thing?"

Angie rubbed her right hand across the top of the box and it disappeared, leaving Carl lying on the floor in a police uniform considerably more scorched than when Angie captured him. "Have you been trying to blast your way out of there?" she asked.

Carl sat up and stretched his arms. A thin sheet of lightning rippled from his fingertips down to his shoes. "I tried once. Or twice. OK, quite a few times."

Angie shook her head then spread her hands apart, and as she moved them back together Carl shrank down to human size.

"Kid, you have got yourself some serious moves," said Hephaestus.

"Who is this child?" said Carl.

"That is a real good question," said Zeus.

Eight

Who is that child?

What an unoriginal question.

Is she one of us?

You should know.

Oh yes, I guess I should. So is she?

Is she what?

One of us.

That would be my guess.

Mine too. She's clever.

Maybe too much so. What should we do about it?

Good question.

Thank you. I try to come up with good ones.

Peace at the Delphi

A quiet month went by.

Hermes actually did pitch in and help Hephaestus rebuild and restore Sara's house, with the addition of a portal straight to Hermes' room at the Hotel (according to Hermes, strictly as a safety precaution) and a jacuzzi made of Olympian Bronze in the back yard.

Zeus put Carl to work in the restaurant as a bus boy, clearing tables and fetching water for the customers. Once they got him out of his scorched police uniform and cleaned up, he became an instant favorite with the female customers – especially Karen Wilson. He was diligent about his work and stayed true to his pledge, obeying every order Zeus gave him.

He and Ares hit it off right away, so Ares was teaching Carl how to make souvlaki and, trying to exploit an apparent loophole in his agreement with Hermes, working to convince him to speak with a really annoying Danish accent.

Artemis rounded up twenty-four more Wood Nymphs, along with a dozen or so Cyclopes, and deployed most of them around the world to keep tabs on Hera. They were able to sense an occasional glimpse of her, along with Todd, some Giants, and a handful of other immortal creatures, but they were never able to get any good information as to exactly what she was up to. Zeus dispatched a small group of the Wood Nymphs to continue to comb the Indiana countryside for any sign of the Amulet.

Athena and Hermes worked with Angie, honing her fighting skills and trying to figure out exactly how much Power she really had. Angie was pretty patient for an almost-eleven year old, and she went along with every training exercise they came up with. She got to the point where she could create a trans-dimensional vortex nearly as well as Hermes. She could transform objects, plants, and even small animals as well as Athena. She splintered a dead elm tree with a blast from her chalk thunderbolt, after which Zeus locked himself in the barn for six hours practicing with his own weapon. He finally succeeded in setting fire to one of the wooden workbenches and blasting a hole in an old Richard Petty poster on the back of the door.

One thing Angie was not interested in learning was how to supersize herself, mostly because she didn't see any point in being any bigger than she was.

They also had trouble getting her to wear the Olympian Bronze armor Hephaestus made for her. She didn't care for the little white skirt made of indestructible Olympian Silk that Athena wanted her to wear with it, and she didn't like the way the greaves looked with her favorite lime green Sketcher shoes.

Apollo located a colony of Centaurs, half men and half horses, hanging out in a state forest near Terre Haute. Centaurs on the whole have never been too crazy about Zeus, but they were offspring of Apollo (twice removed). Carreth, the colony's leader, allowed Apollo to position them around the outskirts of Olympus, where they could work along with the Harpies as sentries.

Most of the people of Olympus were getting pretty accustomed to the idea of a restaurant full of Gods in their town, and the Delphi was becoming a popular tourist destination for folks from as far away as Evansville. Hermes and Apollo were doing concerts in the bar to sellout crowds every weekend. When none of the other Gods were around, they sat together and spoke in low, excited tones about going up to Indianapolis to record a CD.

The only disturbance came during one happy hour, a couple of weeks after they released Carl, when Wilfred Smith burst into the bar with an AR-15 assault rifle in his hands. "Alright, you miserable demons. I've checked every statute in this state, and there is no law against an honest American shooting lousy subhuman scum like you people."

Hermes came around from behind the bar. "You know Smith," he said, "I'm not sure you're quite getting this whole 'we're Gods' thing."

Smith slid his sunglasses onto the top of his head. "And I don't think you get the whole 'Second Amendment with armor-piercing bullets' thing." He caught sight of Carl standing by the Wilsons' table with a bus tray. "Former Constable Carl, I'm starting with you!" He aimed the gun and flipped the safety off.

Most of the customers in the bar hit the floor in a panic. Carl stood with a bus tray in his hands, cocked his head to one side, and watched with a slightly detached interest.

When Smith opened fire, Hermes raised a hand, and a disc of pure darkness appeared in the air between Smith and Carl. The bullets disappeared into the vortex and traveled through a portal to Smith's Escalade parked outside, where the slugs shredded the deluxe leather interior and set the fuel tank on fire.

The customers thought that was easily the best trick they'd seen at the Delphi yet, so they gave Hermes an enthusiastic round of applause. The clapping became a standing ovation when Carl walked over, took Smith's gun away from him, bit it in half, and handed it back.

"Looks like you'll be walking back to your office, Smith," said Hermes, nodding in the direction of the Escalade. "And maybe, just as a favor, you could send someone from Public Works to haul that flaming piece of junk away from our front door."

Hephaestus spent most of the month in his workshop trying to design a device that could help the Wood Nymphs find the Amulet. He finally came up with an Olympian Bronze automaton in the shape of an Giant Schnauzer, and programmed it to sniff out Olympian Power.

When Hephaestus flipped the switch to activate his golden dog, it began cavorting around the workshop, barking joyfully and wagging its woolly tail. Hephaestus was surprised by all the noise, so he decided to name his creation "Demosthenes," after the prolific Ancient Greek orator.

The Wood Nymphs immediately fell in love with the dog. They have their own language, in which the name Demosthenes becomes "Dü-mass," pronounced pretty much the way you might think. Unfortunately, the Wood Nymphs' version of the name stuck.

Dümass went to work in the forest and fields with the Wood Nymphs. While he wasn't successful in the search for the Amulet, he did have a real talent for sniffing out Morel mushrooms, which made Ares and the dinner customers at the Delphi very happy.

Predictably, the first time Dümass saw Angie he fell madly in love with her, and insisted on spending each night at the foot of her bed. Angie was a little bit nervous at first about a three hundred pound metal dog jumping in bed with her, but it didn't take long to get used to the way he clanked when she patted his back and licked her with his golden tongue.

Sarah was less enthusiastic about a solid gold tail smashing her furniture to splinters, but Hephaestus was willing to repair or replace everything the dog broke, so she eventually relaxed to the inevitable.

Aphrodite spent the month working with Dyo, mostly on fine-tuning her makeup and hair styling skills.

Hera's Homecoming

The first hint of trouble became apparent when one of the Harpies smashed through the Delphi's front window and into the bar, screaming "Trouble! Trouble!"

"The door, Sister," said Zeus. "You have to learn to use the door."

"Apologies, Lord Zeus." The Harpy darted into the air, rocketed over the heads of the Wilsons at their normal table and out through the second window pane, then smashed back in through the door.

Zeus sighed. "So what's the trouble?"

"Hera and an army of Giants approach from the south. Sister and Sister are harrying them, along with the Centaurs. They are slowing their advance, but barely."

Zeus led Sister to the map he had spread out on the bar. He pointed to a spot on the map. "Based on their route, would this be the place to meet them?" he asked.

Sister studied the map carefully. "Yes, they should pass that place exactly," she said.

"OK, so there it will be. Any sign of Todd?"

"No, we did not see the God Todd."

Zeus turned to Hermes. "She is going to try to have Todd flank us. So I guess it's going to be Plan B."

"Plan B it is," said Hermes, and he walked over to the Wilsons, the bar's only customers. "Sorry folks," he said,"family emergency. We have to close down. Your tab is on the house."

"How nice," said Karen Wilson. "Bill, leave a nice tip."

"No need," said Hermes. "Have a nice evening." He smiled as they slugged down the last of their drinks, stood up, and headed out the door. He turned back to Zeus. "The Nymphs should have all our senior citizen guests out of the hotel and over to the high school by now. Your brother Poseidon is showing them 'The Little Mermaid,' then Hades will keep them occupied with a presentation of funeral pre-planning."

Zeus chuckled. "And the guys thought they

couldn't help us. OK then, go ahead and round up the troops, and have Angie get started. When you see Hephaestus, ask him to bring along my thunderbolt," said Zeus.

"No problem." A large black hole appeared in the air. Hermes hopped into it and vanished.

Carl came out of the kitchen, followed by Ares. "My mother is coming," said Carl. "She summoned me with a waking dream."

"I'm sure she did," said Zeus. "And what was your reply?"

"I did not reply. I will honor my pledge to you, Lord Zeus."

"That is refreshing. And much appreciated." Zeus turned to the Harpy, who had been sitting on the bar, pecking peanuts out of the basket. "Go back and tell Carreth to have his Centaurs go ahead and engage, then fall back as planned. You sisters are to support them. Carl, Apollo and Artemis, along with the Cyclopes, will be waiting for you at the first defensive line."

"It will be done." Sister crashed out through the remaining unbroken pane of glass, then looped back into the room. "Apologies, my Lord, I forgot about the door," she said, then sailed away, taking the last fragments of the door frame with her.

Zeus shook his head and turned to Carl. "Did Hephaestus get you hooked up with a weapon?"

Carl reached into his pocket and pulled out a small red Swiss Army knife. "Lord Hephaestus has armed me, and I have been training hard with it. At long last we will test its steel in combat."

"Let me see that." Zeus took the knife and turned it over between his fingers. The little white cross throbbed with a faint glow, but other than that it looked like any other pocket knife. "When this is all over, remind me to have a little chat with Hephaestus. Well, at least it's convenient to carry."

"And versatile," said Carl. "With your permission, I should gird my armor and get to my assigned post."

Zeus dropped the pocket knife back into Carl's hand. "Yes, go and fight well. And remember our battle plan."

"I shall, Lord Zeus."

Zeus turned to Ares, who was flipping his meat cleaver in the air and catching it by the handle. "And you, Ares. Do you remain loyal to me?"

"Huh? Oh sure. Haven't I always?"

"Not really."

"Oh, right. Well, this time for sure. I promise." Ares touched his fingers to his forehead and glowed green for a second..

Zeus raised his eyebrows and nodded. "All right, then. As we have discussed, your task will be to engage the new God, Todd. I expect him to try and flank us, so he will appear from the side or the rear. You stay here at the hotel until he shows himself, then you and Hephaestus will take him on."

"Right. I can go ahead and chop him up?"

"That would be the idea. Son, you will need to be careful. You're not up to full charge and he should be powerful."

Ares stopped flipping the cleaver and tilted his head to one side. "Zeus, you called me 'son.'"

"You are, after all, my son."

Ares drew himself up as tall as he could manage. "And I am also Ares, God of war. I'll fight well for you. Father."

Zeus smiled and patted Ares on the shoulder. "I know you will. Go gather your weapons and hurry back here."

As Ares disappeared back into the kitchen, Angie stepped through the remains of the front door, clutching a large yellow piece of chalk and followed by Dümass. "All set, Mr. Z."

"Good. Stay right here until we have everyone else in position. Is your mother out at the high school, helping my brothers with our old folks?"

"Yes, and I drew a protective shield around the grounds like you said. My mom was not happy drawing Depends duty."

"I can appreciate her feelings, but she'll get over it. She's way too mortal for what's coming. Where's your sword and armor?"

Angie's shoulders slumped. "Do I have to?"

"It would mean a lot to Athena. And you'll look like the Goddess that you are."

Angie sighed and drew a circle in the air with her chalk. A vortex opened and a small set of golden armor dropped onto the floor, complete with Larry the Sword and the hated little white dress. "Can't I just wear the stupid thing over my jeans?"

"I don't see why not," said Zeus. "You'll be celebrated in song as the Olympian Fifth Grader. Angie, Goddess of Fractions."

"I'll have you know we had a whole month of pre-Algebra last year," said Angie, pulling the little white dress over her Olympus Junior Soccer t-shirt, fastening the belt, strapping on the bronze breastplate, and fastening Larry across her back.

"What happened to your shield?" asked Zeus.

She looked around. "I'm not sure. It was right here a minute ago."

A growl, a crash, and a clatter from the end of the bar answered the question. Dümass sat among the splinters of a table, tossing the My Little Pony shield up in the air, catching and shaking it, then throwing it to the ground. When he noticed Angie and Zeus looking at him, he looked up hopefully and wagged his tail, launching a bar stool through the broken front window and into the street.

"Bad dog," said Angie. "Bring that here."

Dümass picked up the shield, trotted over to Angie, and dropped it at her feet. Zeus bent down and picked up the shield. "That's funny," he said. "There are tooth marks in it. And a dent on the edge."

"Yeah, he's pretty hard on stuff," said Angie. "So where's your armor, Mr. Z?"

Zeus looked down at his Kinks t-shirt. "Until I can fight like the rest of you, this is all I get," he said.

"The Kinks Shirt will throw 'em off for sure, Z," said Hermes, stepping out of a large vertical vortex in full battle armor, followed by Dyo and Aphrodite. "We're all set to go. Artemis, Apollo, Athena, and Carl are at the first line, along with the Cyclops brigade, and things should be getting under way out there any time now. The Nymphs are waiting for us at the second line."

"Hephaestus?"

"He said that he had to put the finishing touches on his little project to help Ares hold the hotel. He said he'd send your thunderbolt along once it's charged up."

Ares came out of the kitchen, wearing a helmet, breastplate and greaves made of a metal so black that it seemed to absorb all light. A blood red plume sprouted from the top of the helmet and cascaded to where the black belt at his waist cinched in his scarlet tunic. In his right hand he held a massive sword made from the same black metal as the armor. In his left hand he held his meat cleaver. He flipped the cleaver in the air, caught it, and said, "All right, Pop. It's show time."

The First Line

The first defensive line was farm land five miles outside of Olympus. Athena had calculated it to be a place where a battle would cause a minimum of collateral damage to humans. The only buildings around the perimeter, a handful of farmhouses and barns, were protected by invisible shields Angie had drawn weeks ago.

Carl, Athena, Artemis, and Apollo stood in the middle of a field of soy beans, the exact spot Sister had shown Zeus on the map. On either side of them stood a row of Cyclopes, half the size of Giants and twice the size of normal men, armed with clubs and tridents.

Athena, Artemis, and Apollo wore pure white tunics and gleaming armor made from polished Olympian Bronze.

Carl stood off to the left of them. His Swiss Army knife was clutched between his thumb and index finger. He wore the armor Hephaestus had made for him: a breastplate made from an old steel Standard Oil sign, greaves made to look exactly like soccer shin guards, and what appeared to be an ice hockey helmet. His shield was shaped like a garbage can lid.

Apollo looked Carl over and shook his head. "Hephaestus can be a real asshole," he said.

Artemis nodded. "That he can."

Athena looked at the Standard Oil logo and said, "Carl, are you sure you're all right with wearing that gear?"

Carl looked at her and his lips compressed into the hint of a smile. "I will be fine. After all, although I am merely a sweat stain, I have come to the realization that I am the God of Sweat Stains. This means that I am not without Power."

Athena smiled back at him and saluted with her sword. "I am proud to fight at your side, Brother. Cousin. Uncle. Um, Carl."

A thundering cadence began in the distance, faint at first, then growing stronger. "BOOM tromp tromp tromp, BOOM tromp tromp tromp, BOOM tromp tromp tromp, BOOM tromp tromp tromp…"

A small herd of Centaurs burst out of the woods and into the field, followed by the three Harpies overhead. "Oh, no," said Apollo. "There are only eleven left. I sent out thirty."

Artemis pulled an arrow from her quiver and bit her lip. "Maybe the rest are just… maybe…" Her voice trailed off and she nocked the arrow.

The leader of the Centaurs reached them. He was bleeding from a deep head wound. "We tried, Lord Apollo. We did our best. So many Giants…"

Apollo stroked the side of the Centaur's face with the back of his hand. "Oh, Carreth, look what they've done to you. You did well, my friend. More than I could have asked."

The remaining Centaurs gathered in front of Apollo, panting and nursing many wounds. Carreth blinked and shook blood from his eyes. "Where shall we deploy?" he asked.

"I want you to fall back to the second line and present yourselves to Lord Zeus. You need to take a few minutes to catch your breath. We can handle this stage." He looked up at the Harpies, hovering over the Centaurs. "You go with them."

"Please, My Lord," said the Centaur, "We wish to stand here with you. We owe that to those of our brothers we left behind."

Apollo shook his head. "This is only a delaying move, and one Hera will recognize. We will be joining you at the second line for the real fight, after leading them to you, as you have led them to us." He stroked Carreth's back. "I only wish I had time to treat these wounds properly."

The Centaur bent his front legs and dipped into a deep bow, echoed by the rest of the Centaurs. "We can deal with such matters after the battle is won, My Lord."

Apollo dipped his head to return their salute. "We can indeed."

As the Centaurs made their way to the rear, the "BOOM tromp tromp tromp…" of the approaching army grew louder. The ground shook with the cadence. "BOOM tromp tromp tromp..."

"It sounds like Hera has her Giants marching in unison," said Athena.

"I'm impressed," said Apollo. "It's tough to get Giants to agree on anything."

"It sounds to me like there are a lot of smaller creatures marching too," said Artemis. "Satyrs maybe? Trolls?"

"Maybe," said Athena. "Although from the sound of it, I would guess that they are a little bigger than that."

Carl clenched his jaw and stared at the forest at the end of the field. "Are Giants difficult to defeat?" he asked.

Apollo nodded. "They can be killed, but it takes a lot. We had a pretty big war with them once, and I was able to kill their leader with my bow - the one Hera stole from me, which now explains a lot. Other than that, we have mostly had to just subdue and contain them."

"So mostly," said Artemis, "Our job right now is to follow Zeus' orders - try to beat them up a little bit, then retreat and draw them to the second line."

"And what about the smaller creatures?" asked Carl. "How must we deal with them?"

"No idea," said Apollo, drawing his sword as the first Giant's head appeared over the tree tops, "but we're about to find out."

The entire row of trees at the end of the field seemed to burst into the air as eight Giants came striding out of the forest, kicking the trees ahead of them. Each Giant was more than thirty feet tall and each clutched an enormous club.

Apollo, Artemis, Athena, and Carl all super-sized themselves.

"Alright," said Athena, "Number them one through eight, left to right. Carl, you take One and Two. I have Three and Four, and Artemis, you take Five and Six. Apollo, Seven and Eight are yours. Cyclopes, move outside and prepare to take on the second wave."

"Got it," said Apollo as he circled to the right, his sword at the ready.

"One and Two," said Carl as he circled to the left, sparks of lightning dancing around his head and around the Swiss Army Knife clutched in his right hand.

The Cyclopes split up and trotted out to either side of the field.

Artemis and Athena unleashed two enormous arrows, catching Giants Three and Five directly between the eyes. The two Giants dropped to their knees, clutching at the arrows in their foreheads, then crashed to the earth face down. The women fired two more arrows, and Four and Six went down.

Apollo launched himself into the air and landed next to number Seven, stabbing the Giant through the heart with his sword. Then with a backhand stroke, he skewered Giant Eight.

Carl charged across the field, roaring an incomprehensible battle cry, and plunged his Swiss Army Knife into the neck of the Giant One, who straightened up and looked at Carl with a low growl and a sneer.

Carl smiled, jerked the knife up toward One's chin, sending a waterfall of purple blood cascading into the air as the Giant crumpled to the ground. He aimed his garbage can lid in the direction of Two and blasted him over backward with a massive bolt of pure energy.

Carl looked over the prone bodies of the eight Giants and shouted at Apollo, "That wasn't such a hard thing..."

"Run!" said Apollo, sprinting back toward Athena and Artemis.

Giant Number One, with the blood now just barely trickling from his neck, swung his club, striking Carl on the right shin and bringing him to his knees. The four Giants felled by Athena and Artemis sat up and plucked the arrows from their foreheads. Seven and Eight wiped at the purple blood on their chests and picked up their clubs. Number Two, the one Carl had blasted with lightning, stood up and coughed out a puff of smoke.

Number One swung his club again, catching Carl under the chin and knocking him onto his back.

Then all eight Giants mounted a rumbling charge at the other three Gods. Athena and Artemis pumped arrows into them, while Apollo parried clubs and slashed at them with his sword. As they fought, all three retreated slowly.

Carl rolled over and struggled to his hands and knees, then crawled around looking for his knife among the soy beans. As he picked it up, he heard a rapid "tromp tromp tromp" coming from the forest behind him.

He stood up and turned to see hundreds of golden ostriches, each the size of a farm tractor, charging toward him. Sitting on the back of each metal bird was a mud-colored lump of some sort of creature. Their black eyes glowed above noses that looked like rocks, and their grins revealed brown, gnarled teeth. Each rider was holding a small black box and manipulating a joystick poking out from it.

Carl aimed his garbage can lid at the leading ostrich and used it to send out a column of lightning. The fire struck the creature in the chest and simply broke around, with the rider protected by the bird's neck. Carl lowered the lid and fumbled with the Swiss Army Knife.

The first ostrich charged at him, but he rolled to his right and grabbed the bird by the leg, tripping it. The rider flew off, and Carl blasted him out of the air with an energy bolt from his left hand. Then he grabbed the ostrich by the neck and used the can opener from his Swiss Army Knife to cut the golden bird in half.

The rest of the birds rushed forward, and the Cyclopes closed in from both sides, knocking riders off their ostriches with their spears and crushing the birds with their clubs. They were only twelve against thousands, though, so the best they could do is strike and retreat, each harrying attack picking off a few on the outside edge of the golden horde.

Carl managed to use the can opener to destroy another bird, then another, and then five more, blasting each rider with lightning, before he too was driven back by sheer numbers.

Golden ostriches surrounded Carl and pecked at him while he shrank back to human size and struggled to remain conscious. He looked up and caught a pair of black eyes and grinning brown teeth, leaning out over the side of the bird to look down at him and rhythmically twitching his joy stick so that the bird pecked at Carl's chest with its golden beak. Carl smiled back, winked, then flicked his finger and burned the rider's head off with a lightning bolt. Then he relaxed content to discover what death is like for a God.

A few seconds later Carl realized that he was not dead, and that in fact the pecking had stopped. He opened his eyes and looked up at Angie, standing over him and holding a bubble wand. Dümass pranced in a circle behind her, wagging his tail, tossing the front half of one of the ostriches up in the air, and catching it.

"Mr. Z thought you might need a little help," she said.

Carl looked around to see the horde of golden ostriches circled around them, fifty feet away, pecking furiously at the shimmering bubble that had pushed them out and was keeping them at bay. "I am indebted to you," he said. "I can't tell you how incredibly unpleasant that last part of the fight was."

"I'm glad my bubbles are on your side this time," said Angie. "Now come on. I'm supposed to get you back to the second line." She helped Carl climb to his feet and handed him his Swiss Army Knife and his garbage can lid. Then she led him over to a door in the ground. Dümass dropped his ostrich toy and followed them through.

The Second Line

Zeus had set up a command post at the top of a hill on the edge of town directly in the Giant army's line of attack. The hill was, in fact, the highest part of the county's sanitary landfill, overlooking a nearly mile-long flat field – an ideal spot for battle.

Zeus stood next to one of the Harpies with his hands behind his back, watching Apollo, Artemis, Hermes, and the other two Harpies fighting the Giants and retreating slowly toward the hill.

The Centaurs stood off to the side stamping nervously to get back into the fight, but respecting the order from Apollo to stay back and recuperate. Aphrodite, Dyo, and a bevy of Wood Nymphs surrounded them and treated their wounds. The women were all dressed in matching silver armor with pink accents and pink skirts. Instead of helmets they each had their hair plaited in a sort of complicated French-braided up-do that probably served no military function, but looked really nice.

The battle was a virtual stand-off. As one Giant would go down, another would stand back up and resume the fight. The Giants were showing some wear and tear, some having eyes plucked out by Harpies, some taking extra time to re-attach severed hands or arms, and all sprouting Artemis' arrows like porcupine quills. But still, they were advancing slowly across the field.

Angie and Carl popped out of the door in the ground next to Zeus at the top of the hill. Angie closed the door and scrubbed it away with the toe of her sneaker.

Carl sat down to rest, and Zeus went down on one knee in front of him. "Are you all right, son?"

Carl drew a deep breath. "Yes, my Lord. Thank you for sending the child to save me. I fear I would not have lasted much longer."

"You'd be amazed at how long you can last and how much you can take. Just so you know, Apollo wanted to fight his way back to try and get you, but they were pretty busy with the Giants. Athena made the right decision to fall back as we planned and let me send help for you."

"What sort of creatures was I fighting? They were some kind of large metal birds."

"They were ostriches," said Angie. "Hundreds of really big ones made of gold."

"Gold?" said Zeus. "Are you sure they weren't made of Bronze?"

"The metal birds were impervious to my fireballs," said Carl.

"Yep, that would be Gold," said Zeus. "No Satyr or Cyclops I've ever known could work like that in Olympian Gold."

"... and they were ridden by small, nasty, grey creatures, who were surprisingly easy to kill. To be fair, I only killed a few..."

"Ridden?" said Zeus.

"Trolls!" said Sister.

"Were they ugly, stubby little guys?" asked Zeus. "Look like they're made from dirt mixed with mucus?"

"I suppose so. Definitely ugly."

"Sounds like Trolls." Zeus scratched his head. "Why would Trolls ride automatons?"

"They all had video game joysticks," said Angie. "I think the Trolls might have been controlling them."

"Interesting," said Zeus. "And that gives me an idea. Sister, would you fly a reconnaissance lap for me, then come back and tell me how close those ostrich-riding Trolls are?"

"As you wish, Lord Zeus." Sister flapped up into the air, turned, and shot off in the direction of the battle.

"Carl, do you feel well enough to go help Apollo and Artemis with the Giants? I could use Hermes back here."

Carl stood up and flexed his arms and legs experimentally. "I believe I do. And I would enjoy killing those Giants a few more times." He squared the hockey helmet on his head, switched his weapon from can opener to blade, picked up his garbage can lid, super-sizing himself as he trotted down the hill toward the battle.

Sister swooped back to the ground. "Lord Zeus, there are nearly a thousand of the Gold ostriches just over a half mile away from this battle," she said. "They appear to have spent some time attacking a large bubble a mile or so back and there are still a few there, but most of them are now advancing on us. And they are indeed being controlled by Troll riders."

"Definitely not the brightest cavalry you could recruit. Thank you, Sister. Aphrodite, are you about ready to go?" he shouted.

"We're all set, Z," said Aphrodite.

An explosion rocked the hill, and a Giant's ear sailed over their heads. Zeus watched the ear disappear into the distance. "You have to admit, young Carl is a real artist with a fireball and a pocket knife. Aphrodite, I need your team to stop their second wave. It seems that there are a whole lot of big Olympian-Gold ostriches, controlled by Trolls, coming in just behind the Giants. I need you to circle around past the Giants and engage them. Sister will lead you to them."

"You want us to take down all the Giant Golden birds?"

"No, I want you to take down the riders. As I said, Trolls."

Aphrodite nodded slowly and smiled. "Got it. Yes, I think we can deal with a few dozen of those little snotballs."

"I told you we needed this armor to show more cleavage," said Dyo.

Aphrodite surveyed her troops and smiled again. "We'll manage. Let's go, girls." The Harpy launched herself into the air, and the Goddesses and Nymphs trotted after her down the hill, passing Hermes coming up.

Zeus turned to Angie. "Angie, are you able to tell where Hephaestus is?" he asked. "I can sense Ares at the hotel, and Hephaestus is supposed to be with him, but I'm coming up blank."

She shook her head. "No, and I have no idea where he is," she said. "Mr. Ares is alone."

Hermes joined them, his armor covered with mud and bits of Giant. He had a big grin on his face. "I have to admit it, Z. This is kind of fun. Just like old times."

Zeus aimed his right hand at a Giant down the hill and fired off a spark that disappeared into the air a couple of yards out. "It would be more like old times if I could make a difference in the fight," he said. "Hermes, can you sense Hephaestus?"

Hermes closed his eyes for a few seconds, then shook his head. "No, I can't. He never showed up with your thunderbolt?"

"Nobody has seen him since this whole thing began. How about Hera - can either of you get a bead on her?"

Angie and Hermes both closed their eyes in concentration, then shook their heads. "It's weird, Z," said Hermes, "it's like they don't even exist. I can usually get at least a hint of Hephaestus even when he's shielded in his workshop."

"I have a bad feeling about this," said Zeus.

Angie stood up straight and turned to look back toward town. "Mr. Ares is in trouble," she said. "A lot of trouble."

Zeus looked at Hermes. "Better check it out. I'm going to pull the trigger here."

"I'm on it, Z," said Hermes. He whipped up a Hermes-sized vortex and hopped through it.

A Harpy arced overhead and crashed to the ground on her back just behind Angie, holding a fair portion of a Giant's nose in her talons. She stood up, shook her wings, and tossed the nose aside. "I am reminded that I strongly dislike Giants," she said.

"Ah, Sister," said Zeus with a little shudder, "perfect timing. I need you to go back down to the battle and tell everyone that it's Go Time."

"Yes, my Lord," said the Harpy flapping a little unsteadily into the air, then zooming back into the fray.

"Angie, you and Dümass get to your position and wait for my signal." He turned to the Centaurs. "Carreth, could you please give her a ride down and wait for me there?"

"As you command, Lord Zeus," said Carreth.

"Right," said Angie, and she hopped onto the Centaur's back. They all galloped down the side of the hill away from the battle.

Given the word by the Harpy, Apollo, Artemis, and Athena began a more rapid fighting retreat, letting the Giants push the battle up the side of the hill and toward Zeus.

A vortex opened next to him and Hermes

staggered out of it, carrying Ares. He fell to his knees and the vortex disappeared.

Ares' helmet was gone, and he had a large bleeding wound across his forehead. A golden arrow protruded from his shoulder. One eye was swollen shut, and a trickle of blood ran from his nose. He looked up at Zeus with his uninjured eye, grinned weakly, and said, "You should see the other guy."

Zeus knelt by him and brushed some broken glass from the side of Ares' face. "So, you took care of Todd, did you? I hope you totally messed him up."

Ares cocked his head to one side. "Are you kidding? No, you should see him. He looks great. I never laid a hand on him."

"Is that one of Apollo's arrows?" asked Zeus. "Todd was able to draw Apollo's bow?"

"It is an arrow of Apollo," said Ares, "But the bow didn't work for him, so he just whacked me in the face with the bow and stabbed me with the arrow. It went right through this armor."

"Any sign of Hephaestus? He was supposed to whip up some help for us and be there at the hotel to stand with you."

"He never showed up," said Hermes. "Ares took that goon on by himself."

"I'm sorry, Son. I miscalculated and left you on your own to get hurt like this." Zeus patted Ares on the shoulder, which caused the arrow to shift, and Ares to grunt with pain. "OK, I'm sorry about that, too."

Ares grinned, showing several missing teeth. "No problem. I just want another crack at him when I get back on my feet."

The battle with the Giants had nearly reached the top of the hill. "Hermes, get him to the bottom of the hill, then go check on Aphrodite and Dyo. I'll take care of this."

"Got it, Z." Hermes helped Ares to his feet, made another vortex, and helped the injured God through it. Zeus walked to the back of the hilltop, where a two-foot fuse stuck out of the ground, and turned back to watch the battle.

As the fighting reached the very top of the hill, two of the Harpies disengaged and picked up the ends of a length of telephone wire that had been stretched around the perimeter.

Zeus shouted, "Now!" and the Harpies shot into the air and rocketed in opposite directions past each other, carrying the wire around in a loop. Athena, Artemis, and Apollo jumped up as the wire passed under their feet and wrapped around the legs of the Giants.

Zeus pointed at the end of the fuse and

snapped his fingers. A spark shot out to the side and struck his belt buckle. "Damn it," he muttered, as he fished a disposable lighter from his pocket and lit the fuse. Then he shouted, "OK EVERYBODY, TIME TO GO!"

The Harpies, who had flown in dizzyingly rapid circles and wound the cable many times up and around all eight Giants, flew a quick intricate pattern to tie it off. The third Harpy swooped down, picked Zeus up by the armpits, and soared back into the air carrying him. While the Giants struggled to disentangle themselves from the telephone wire, Athena, Artemis, and Apollo sprinted down the hill, with the three Harpies and Zeus flying close behind.

At this point in the battle it might be a good idea to take a short time out to catch our breath and consider an interesting fact about sanitary landfills. It seems that when a lot of garbage is buried for a number of years under tons of dirt, the garbage decomposes. This digestion of organic waste by bacteria produces several by-products, the most notable of which is methane gas. In the normal course of landfill events, the methane gas gets vented off into the air, with the vents often set on fire, to produce festive blue eternal flames scattered around the site.

On the other hand, when methane gas is not vented, it gets compressed, and compressed methane gas is explosive. Really, REALLY explosive.

When Zeus decided that this would be his second line of battle, he had Hermes shut off all the methane vents on the hill. Just to be on the safe side, he also had Hermes vortex a dozen large liquid propane tanks into the center of the landfill, with a fuse attached to the one in the center.

The retreating Gods and Harpies reached the bottom of the hill just as the burning fuse reached the propane tank. The hilltop erupted with a massive explosion, sending a blue fireball and eight still partly entangled and very surprised Giants a hundred feet into the air.

The Giants, knocked temporarily senseless by the blast, reached the top of their arc and Angie, standing next to an open toy box at the bottom of the hill, waved her hand at them. All eight Giants turned into Cabbage Patch dolls, tangled up in some black twine. All eight dolls tumbled through the air and fell into the box.

Angie slammed the lid shut, flipped the latch, and snapped an Olympian Bronze padlock through it.

The Last Battle

Tons of turf and sanitary landfill rained down around them in a driving storm of flying garbage.

Carl, his hockey helmet cracked in half and his oil company armor hanging in shreds, limped over and stared at the toy box. "This is all it took to defeat the Giants?" he said. "Not to second-guess the wisdom of your strategy, My Lord, but could we not have saved some effort by having the child do this a little bit sooner?"

Zeus picked a mostly-intact sandwich bag, containing moldy bread crusts with hints of peanut butter and jelly, off his shoulder. "I wish we could have done it sooner. Unfortunately, nobody can alter the form of a living being unless that being is unconscious or disabled. We had to come up with a way to knock them all out at once."

"I see." Carl nodded thoughtfully then

reached out with his foot, shook a Twinkie wrapper and a bit of orange peel off his sandal, and gave the toy box a little tap with his toe. "Are they as secure in this box as I was in mine?"

"Probably more so. The kid has had some training since then."

"And will they remain in the form of dolls indefinitely?"

"Let's hope so. If not, it's going to get pretty crowded in that box."

A portal opened and Hermes stepped out, followed by Aphrodite, Dyo, and the Wood Nymphs. All of the women were wearing new golden necklaces, hoops, bracelets, tiaras, and earrings.

"No problem with the cavalry?" asked Zeus, picking a banana peel out of his hair and tossing it aside.

"None," said Aphrodite. "The Nymphs did a little dance to get the Trolls hooting and hollering, I knocked the little scums cold with a blast, and Dyo turned them all into ceramic garden gnomes."

"Cute. What did you do with the ostriches?"

Dyo shook an arm weighed down with Gold bracelets. "We did a little re-purposing. We have a few stacks of Olympian Gold ingots left over."

Zeus nodded. "You ladies made your own armor, right?"

Dyo turned to the side and struck a pose. "Yes. Yes, we did!"

"So, would you consider a little more re-purposing to turn some of those leftover ingots into some decent armor for Carl here?"

Aphrodite studied Carl for a few seconds, and then smiled. "Give us five minutes," she said.

"But please, no pink trim." Zeus looked around at the rest of the Gods, recuperating from the fight with the Giants and brushing random trash from their armor. "OK, here's the situation," he said. "It looks like Hera outsmarted me. While we were tied up here, Todd managed to take the Hotel."

Athena took off her helmet and shook it. A red Solo cup, with the name, "Shane" scribbled in Sharpie on the side, fell out of the plume. "I thought Ares and Hephaestus might have trouble with him."

"Hephaestus never showed up," said Ares.

Apollo put the final wrap on a bandage around Ares head. "It looks like he sabotaged this armor, too," he said. "This junk wouldn't stop a spitball." He yanked the arrow from Ares' shoulder.

"Ow," said Ares.

"Hmmm," said Zeus. "Did anybody else have Hephaestus work on your stuff?"

"He made this stupid shield," said Angie, handing My Little Pony to Zeus. Apollo tossed the arrow at the shield, and it went through without slowing down.

"Well, at least now we know where we stand," said Zeus. "Anybody else?"

They all shook their heads. "Good. Ladies, we will need you to give Ares a make-over also. Assuming, Son, that you feel up to getting back into the fight?"

"I lost my meat cleaver – but sure, why not? Dad."

"I don't know about the rest of you, but all that 'father and son' crap is really starting to creep me out," said Hermes.

– λατερ –

Gods and other immortals recover fairly quickly from injuries and exhaustion, so in less than half an hour Zeus had his little army ready to go back into action.

Carl and Ares were resplendent head-to-foot in glittering Olympian Gold armor. They each held a glittering Olympian Gold sword and a glittering Olympian Gold shield. Neither of them complained about the images of Aphrodite's and

Dyo's heads, winking at each other, embossed on the face of the shields.

There had been plenty of Olympian Gold left over, so the Centaurs had new Gold breastplates and Gold-tipped arrows, while the Harpies were sporting new Olympian Gold talon extensions.

"All right, here's the plan," said Zeus. "Angie and Hermes can work together to whip up a large portal, but it won't be big enough for all of us to get through at once. I want Apollo, Athena, and Artemis to go through first to form a battle line, with Carl and Ares right behind them and spreading out to either side. You will have to try to respond to whatever you find there while Hermes, Aphrodite, Dyo, Angie, and I come along. After that the Nymphs, riding the Centaurs, will go through and spread out to the sides, with the Harpies overhead."

"Where will we come out?" asked Athena.

"It seems like Hephaestus has built up some kind of shielding around the hotel, and Angie and I have not been able to break through it," said Hermes, "so we'll be hitting the street just outside the main entrance to the bar."

"OK," said Zeus, "is everyone set?"

They all readied their weapons. Hermes took Angie's hand, and they both closed their eyes. A large portal appeared in the air. Zeus shouted,

"GO!" and they rushed through, according to Zeus' orders, and deployed in front of the Delphi.

Hephaestus sat in a patio lounge chair on the sidewalk just outside the entrance to the bar, with his feet crossed and a Piña Colada in his hand. He wore bright blue-and-green flowered shorts, a black aloha shirt with colorful pictures of beer bottles and palm trees on it, a straw hat perched on his dreadlocks, and flip-flops. He had repaired the window and door, and the Wilsons sat inside at their normal window table, toasting each other with Piña Coladas.

"Hey, good to see you guys," said Hephaestus. "We're doing a two-for-one piña colada special for happy hour. Turns out young Todd really knows his way around a rum bottle."

"You absolute sack of scum," said Aphrodite. "We should have known better than to trust you."

"Yes, I suppose you should have known better," said Hephaestus.

"You made those spiders that attacked me?" asked Apollo.

"No, they were the work of Satyrs, under my supervision. I wanted to use Satyrs to throw you off the scent. We located a couple dozen of the little rascals, wandering around in Kentucky and Tennessee. I have most of them down in my workshop right now, forging the unbreakable chains in which all of you will spend the next several thousand years."

"Speaking of unbreakable, how did you manage to find a way to wiggle out of your oath?" asked Zeus.

Hephaestus sat forward and chuckled. "This one was a real beauty, Z. I swore loyalty to the Lord of Olympus, not specifically to you. In fact, I'm sort of surprised you didn't catch that."

"Yeah, that makes two of us," said Athena.

Hephaestus laughed. "So after Carl got himself boxed up, my mother got in touch and pointed out that as long as you had less power than the rest of us, there is no way we could consider the Lord of Olympus to be you. Then she brought me in on this whole plan she had cooked up, making the Lord of Olympus," Hephaestus raised his glass in a toast, "...me. You have to admit, Z, it turned out to be a pretty good plan."

Hera came out of the bar, followed by a Satyr with a pitcher in his hand. The Satyr trotted over to freshen Hephaestus' drink. Hera put her hands on her hips and examined Zeus' army. "There you all are," she said. "You know, Zeus, I was just thinking that it would be a good idea to do sidewalk seating in the summer. In fact, you can wait on the tables out here yourself. That will be especially appropriate, since you will be chained to the sidewalk, and you will not be entering the hotel, ever again."

Zeus stepped out in front of the other Gods, who stood with weapons drawn.

"You know, that is just typical. I mentioned that whole sidewalk seating idea last spring," said Zeus. "You thought it was totally stupid back then."

Hera smiled. "That was before I was the boss," she said. "Being in charge gives one a very different perspective."

"Yes, I suppose it does," said Zeus. "So now you rule us all, do you?"

"Yes. I do," said Hera.

"Yes, we do," said Hephaestus. "You and I rule together now."

"Of course, Dear. That's what I meant to say," said Hera.

"And Todd," said Zeus. "Don't forget Todd. Doesn't he also share the throne of heaven with the two of you?"

"Yes, I suppose Todd does as well," said Hera.

"That is going to be one crowded throne," said Aphrodite. "Especially if you keep pounding down all those drinks. Think of the calories."

Hera set her pitcher on the table next to Hephaestus and smiled at Aphrodite. "Oh my, a fat joke at my expense. How very original of you. You can all have a good laugh about it as you bow down before me."

Athena stepped up next to Zeus. "And what, exactly, keeps us from kicking your fat butt and chucking all three of you into Tartarus?" she said. "Look around. Are you really that bad at math?"

"What protects and preserves me is very simple; you will all bow down before me, because I now have the most Power. And I have the most Power because I possess the Amulet."

Zeus raised his eyebrows in surprise. "The Amulet! You found it? Where is it?"

Hephaestus laughed. "You're not going to believe it, Z. It was here all the time."

"Here? What, buried under the hotel?"

Hephaestus laughed harder. "No, not under the hotel. It is the hotel. We've been living in the Amulet ever since we woke up!"

"The hotel! That's why Phil said this place was important." Zeus took a step forward.

Hephaestus picked up his cane. "Careful, Z. Don't come too close. We've got a pretty powerful rejection shield around this place, and I don't want it to mess up all your cool little outfits."

"But if we were living in the Amulet, why didn't it give me my Power back?"

"Because that's not the way it works. It seems like what you have to do is ask it for the Power in a certain kind of way. The way I figure it, back in the day, you were just naturally asking for power because you expected to have it. I think my generators worked because I accidentally came up with coils that 'asked.' They just concentrated the power so much that I kept blowing up my wife."

"Yeah, that's why you kept blowing me up," said Aphrodite.

"So why have the rest of us been getting our power back?" asked Hermes.

"Just because we wanted it. We were not sure that we would have to wait until Zeus found the Amulet."

"But I did believe that," said Zeus. "So I waited."

"Exactly," said Hephaestus.

"And now we have the Amulet, and we control the Power," said Hera. "More Power than all of you combined!"

She spread her arms apart, palm down. Zeus began to shake, then sank to his knees, face turned to the pavement, forced down by an invisible energy. One by one, the other Gods and immortals were also forced down to their knees, involuntarily genuflecting to Hera.

All except Angie and Dümass. Angie looked around at the kneeling army then walked up next to Zeus, the golden dog at her side. "Ms. Hera, why do you want power so much?"

"Insect!" said Hera. "You and your kind will serve me and worship me for the rest of time. Now, kneel!" She threw the palm of her right hand toward Angie.

Angie put her hands on her hips and cocked her head to one side. "Seriously? You think humans are going to worship you?"

"They will worship me, or they will all perish," shouted Hera, hurling a fireball.

Angie pulled Larry the Sword and held it up in front of her. The fireball split on Larry's blade and broke around her, the right half going on to set fire to a silver Prius parked behind her across the street, and the rest blasting the street lamp on the corner into a shower of sparks and glass.

Hera's eyes narrowed. "Is that the Sword of Perseus you hold in your sticky little hands?"

"Athena gave it to me."

"Perseus was a great hero. How dare you defile his weapon!"

"I call it 'Larry.'"

Hephaestus grunted up out of his lounge chair, reached behind it, and pulled out Zeus' thunderbolt. "I like you, Angie. I really do. Well, I admit, you did kind of smash me to pieces. But I don't hold that against you…"

"I like you too, Mr. Hephaestus."

"…So I'm not going to enjoy killing you. Not even a little bit. And you, you stupid metal mutt…" Dümass gave a happy bark and wagged his tail. "You were supposed to take care of killing her for me." Hephaestus fired the thunderbolt and blasted Dümass into thousands of golden parts. His tail, still wagging clattered to the street.

The Gods, Centaurs, Harpies and Nymphs all struggled to move, but they were still frozen, kneeling with their heads bowed. Zeus snarled, "Hephaestus, I swear, if you harm this child in any way, I will take your good leg and stuff it up…"

Hephaestus aimed the thunderbolt at Zeus and fired a blast that lifted him ten feet into the air. He seemed to hang suspended overhead for a few seconds, his clothing blasted into the shredded remains of his Kinks shirt and a pair of Curious George Christmas boxers. Then he crumpled to the ground. "That's the first payback for the leg, Z." He tossed the thunderbolt in the air and caught it. "I'm not sure if I can destroy you completely, old man, but I will thoroughly enjoy trying."

Angie, choking back tears and clutching one of Dümass' legs to her chest, said, "I take it back - I don't like you at all anymore." She squatted down and drew a chalk circle on the pavement in front of her.

"It really does break my heart," said Hephaestus. He aimed the thunderbolt at Angie. "But, business is business."

As Hephaestus fired, Angie lifted her chalk circle out of the street, so that it became a highly-polished golden shield. The blast reflected off the surface of the shield and caught Hephaestus full in the chest, smashing him back against the building and embedding him halfway into the limestone.

"TODD, YOU GET OUT HERE, RIGHT NOW!" shouted Hera. She fired a fireball at Angie, and then dove to the side as it reflected back, incinerating Hephaestus' lawn chair and the hapless Satyr.

Todd came through the door to the bar, holding pitchers of piña coladas in each hand. He scanned the scene around him, dropped both pitchers, and raised his hands toward Angie.

"No, wait," said Hera.

Todd's blast reflected off the shield, blasting him back and embedding him in the front of the building, so that he and Hephaestus flanked the door like gargoyles.

Hera jumped to her feet and up-sized, but she was standing directly under the green awning at the hotel entrance. Her head tore through the vinyl, while the aluminum frame wrapped her arms against her body. She staggered into the street and toward Angie, struggling to free herself.

Angie pointed Larry toward where Hera struggled to untangle herself. She flipped the tip of the sword upward, and Hera rose into the sky above the hotel. Then Angie swung Larry like she was making an overhand shot with a badminton racket, and Hera soared out of sight.

Olympus Rises

Released from their bondage, all the members of Zeus' army stood and stretched. Hermes gathered Angie into his arms and hugged her. "That was amazing, Squirt," he said. "I'm so sorry. I couldn't help. I was afraid she was going to..."

"I was fine, Hermes," said Angie, giving him a brief hug in return, then wiggling out of his embrace. "I'm not a baby."

Athena took the shield from Angie and looked it over. "So you made the Shield of Perseus for yourself," she said, and handed it back.

Angie grinned. "Yeah, well, good thing I read the book," she said.

Zeus sat on the street and wiped soot from his eyes. "Aphrodite, why don't you and Dyo go round up Hera, before she has a chance to regroup. Angie, where do you suppose she landed?"

Angie sheathed Larry and looked down for a moment at the golden dog's leg in her hand. Then she looked up at Zeus. "I'd try Prague," she said. She drew a rectangle on the pavement, pulled it up into a transparent box with a dark wood bottom, and handed it to Aphrodite. "You can put her in this for safekeeping. It's just like the display boxes I have for my American Girl dolls, only the glass is unbreakable. While she is in there, she will be Kit Kittredge." She drew another, larger rectangle. "Here's a doorway to Prague for you."

Dyo ruffled Angie's hair. "I have got to get me some of that chalk," she said, then she and Aphrodite hopped through the doorway.

Todd and Hephaestus began to stir, struggling to dis-embed themselves from the wall of the hotel. Hermes drew his sword. "What do you think, Z? Do you suppose that rejection shield is still up and operating?"

Apollo picked up a stone from the street and tossed it toward the hotel. Fifteen feet from the door it exploded into a cloud of dust. "Still there." He drew his sword and Artemis readied her bow.

Zeus climbed to his feet. "I was hoping we wouldn't have to tussle with these guys here in the middle of town. Angie, do you have any ideas?"

"I don't know how to get through that shield," she said. "We can fight off whatever they toss out at us, but if they stay behind the shield, that's about it."

Todd freed one arm, then the other, and then he burst out of the wall and dropped to the pavement, landing in a fighting crouch. Hephaestus wiggled free, then toppled straight down and onto his face, arms and legs splayed out to the sides. Fire danced around Todd's head and shoulders as he clenched his fists, while Hephaestus struggled to his hands and knees and crawled over to retrieve Zeus' thunderbolt from the ruins of his lawn chair.

Carl drew his sword and stepped in front of Zeus. "I will deal with these pretenders, My Lord," he said. "No harm shall come to you, not while I draw breath nor have any strength in this, my good right arm that I did pledge unto your eternal service."

Ares stepped up next to Carl, drew his sword and snarled, "Yeah, what he said."

Apollo, Artemis, and Hermes closed ranks with them and readied their weapons.

"Look guys, can't we talk about this?" said Zeus, over Carl's shoulder. "If we start throwing a lot of fireballs, and lightning, and other stuff around, who knows what will happen. We could take out the whole town, and all the innocent people in it."

"Mortals are of no consequence," said Todd, "and the time for conversation has passed. We still hold this place, and with its power, we hold the Throne of the Heavens. You will return our Queen to us, or you will suffer the consequences."

"Besides, the odds are we won't kill all of the people, Z," said Hephaestus, powering up the thunderbolt. "With any luck there will be enough of them left over to cower at our feet and serve us. You do remember that whole worship thing, don't you?"

The door to the bar opened and the Wilsons walked out, slightly unsteadily. "Oh my, Carl, don't you look nice," said Karen Wilson, winking and smiling at Carl in his golden armor.

"So here's where the staff has got to," said Bill Wilson. "Say, any chance of getting someone to come in and whip up another pitcher of drinks?"

Todd turned to face the Wilsons. "These two vermin will be the first of your precious humans to perish," he said, and he began to up-size.

"How rude," said Karen Wilson.

"Not the least bit friendly," said Bill Wilson, "and really, not half the bartender that young Hermes is."

"Although to be fair, those piña coladas were really quite passable," said Karen Wilson.

"Yes, I will give him that," said Bill Wilson.

"But that is no excuse for rudeness," said Karen Wilson. She looked up at Todd, now nearly as tall as the building. "And for your information, young man, my husband and I are not vermin. Or, for that matter, human." She snapped her fingers and Todd vaporized in a puff of smoke.

Hephaestus dropped the thunderbolt. It went off, firing off a shaft of lightning that went into one of the third-floor hotel room windows and exited through the roof. He backed away from the Wilsons. "Who are you?" he asked.

"I'm Karen Wilson," said Karen Wilson, "and this is my husband Bill. You really should know that by now."

"Did you destroy the idiot?" asked Athena.

"Not entirely," said Bill Wilson. "The idiot's molecules are still floating around here somewhere. At least I assume they are."

"Yes, they are," said Karen Wilson. "Assuming that you are correct."

Zeus stepped out in front of his battle line of Gods. "So you have the power to vaporize a God. What sort of Gods are you, then?"

Karen Wilson looked him over and wrinkled her nose. "You really should pay more attention to your appearance, like these young people do," she said. She smiled at Carl again, and winked.

"We are not Gods," said Bill Wilson. "And my wife is right – you look terrible. Good grief, is that Curious George?"

"Look, I've had a rough day..." said Zeus.

Angie moved next to Zeus, holding her shield and Larry in fighting position. "You people are dangerous," she said.

"You know, sweetheart, you might be right," said Karen Wilson. A hint of green lightning flickered across her eyes. "Cute dress. Looks nice with the whole sword-and-armor thing."

Zeus put his arm around Angie, forcing her out of her battle stance. "What exactly do you want?" he said.

"Aside from a refill on the piña coladas? Well, for one thing, we are here to test you," said Bill Wilson.

"Think of us as a couple of professors," said Karen Wilson.

"More like proctors," said Bill Wilson.

"Or profoctors," they said together, laughing.

"Either way, we pretty much hold your eternal fate in our hands," said Karen Wilson. "Wouldn't you say so, Bill?"

"Think of this as a galactic pass-fail class," said Bill Wilson.

"Yes, that's a good way to think of it," said Karen Wilson.

"Unless you want to think of it some other way, of course," said Bill Wilson

"No, I believe that's the best way to think of it," said Karen Wilson.

"So..." said Zeus, "did we pass?"

"Oh, heavens no," said Karen Wilson. She raised her right hand and prepared to snap her fingers.

"Well maybe," said Bill Wilson.

"Wait, what?" said Karen Wilson.

"They might have passed," said Bill Wilson. "For one thing, they worked to protect the humans."

"Who cares about humans?" said Karen Wilson.

"We do," said Bill Wilson.

"We do?" said Karen Wilson.

"We do," said Bill Wilson.

"Oh. Right," said Karen Wilson.

"Plus, they are not trying to attack us," said Bill Wilson.

"The child was," said Karen Wilson, nodding at Angie.

"Not really," said Bill Wilson. "She simply recognized us."

Karen Wilson nodded slowly. "You make a good point," she said.

"Excuse me," said Zeus, "Is it alright if I say a few words?"

"Last words?" said Karen Wilson.

"I hope not," said Zeus. "Mr. Wilson is right; we are not attacking you, because we do not know you to be our enemies. If you do intend to destroy us, then we would have to at least try to fight. But why would you want to destroy us?"

"It's sort of our job," said Bill Wilson. "Remember the whole galactic pass-fail thing I was telling you about?"

"But why destroy us," said Zeus. "Why not teach us?"

"Seriously?" said Karen Wilson. "You've had millennia to learn."

"Maybe so," said Zeus, "but I have no idea what we were supposed to be learning."

"He has a point," said Bill Wilson. "Maybe we should have provided some sort of study guide, or a workbook..."

"There is no workbook," said Karen Wilson. "Look, the Titans failed, and before them there were those horrible Prokans..."

"The who?" asked Zeus.

"Never mind," said Bill Wilson. "Way before

your time. That whole Prokan go-around really did not go well."

"That's an understatement," Karen Wilson said, and she shuddered.

"See, there you go. We're way better than those rotten Prokans," said Zeus. "Give us another chance. Please."

"We could just let them sleep, like we did the Titans," said Bill Wilson.

"I thought you vaporized the Titans," said Karen Wilson.

"Oh! Um, no. I never got around to it," said Bill Wilson.

Karen Wilson sighed and shook her head.

"Look," said Zeus, "if you have to destroy anybody, just destroy me. Let the rest of them keep learning whatever it is you want them to learn."

"Geez, like that was not totally predictable," said Karen Wilson. "Go ahead, try to melt our hearts with your selfless act of sacrifice."

"OK, I'll admit I was kind of hoping for a little heart melting," said Zeus. "But the offer stands. I can't seem to get any power back anyway. Go ahead." He closed his eyes and spread his arms to the sides.

"That does it," said Karen Wilson. "I'm going to do you first, just to put an end to this soap opera." She raised her hand again.

"Hold it, Karen," said Bill Wilson. "Remember, he's half human."

"What?" said Karen Wilson.

"What?" said Zeus.

"What?" said everybody else on the street.

Bill Wilson shook his head and pinched at his eyes. "Seriously Karen? You really don't remember Rhea and the island?"

"Oh, yeah," said Karen Wilson. "Rhea. The island. That king. Yada, yada..."

"What?" said Zeus.

"Well, go Rhea," said Athena. "Who knew the old girl was messing around?"

"Wow, Z. Half human. What's it like?" said Hermes.

"You're just like me! That's so cool, Mr. Z," said Angie.

"What?" said Zeus.

"OK, so maybe we could extend the Test a bit," said Karen Wilson.

"That's what I've been trying to tell you," said Bill Wilson.

"So... there will be no molecules of us floating around?" said Ares.

"Aside from Todd's," said Hermes.

"Aside from Todd's molecules, no," said Karen Wilson. "For now."

"I'm half WHAT!?" said Zeus.

After

Zeus leaned his head on his hand, supported by his elbow on the top of the bar, and watched the cockroach as it explored the beer-spotted territory behind his coffee cup. It probed at an English muffin crumb for a few seconds, then scuttled from the shade of the cup into the patch of morning sunlight on the counter top.

Zeus pointed a finger and got the drop on the bug just as it cleared the cover of the cream pitcher. A tiny flash of lightning, and a cockroach-sized pile of ashes settled softly down onto the bar.

"Nice shot, Z," said Dyo, coming off the street in a very short coral pink dress, and carrying matching very high heels.

"Looks like the voltage is getting better, too," said Aphrodite, close behind Dyo. She was dressed in a sort of sarong made of a tablecloth from the banquet room at the Holiday Inn. "You've been charging the old batteries."

"Meditating. I'm getting there, but I'm still not sure how it's working."

"Affirmations to kill bugs," said Hermes from the table where he'd been having breakfast with Sarah and Angie. "But what about the Test? Aren't you the least bit concerned with the sanctity of all life, and crap like that?"

"You have me confused with that Buddha guy," said Zeus.

"I'd better get the orange juice made before the Wilsons get here for their mimosas." Hermes hopped up and headed to the bar.

Athena came in from the kitchen carrying Zeus' Greek omelet and the coffee pot. "Hey Dyo. 'Morning Aphrodite. Wow, Girl! That's what I call a world-class Walk of Shame. Any idea where your clothes are?"

Aphrodite smiled a dreamy smile. "Nope. Not a clue."

"Coffee?"

"Absolutely."

Dyo gave Aphrodite an affectionate hug, nearly dislodging the tablecloth. "I am truly humbled to be learning from the best," she said.

Zeus dumped a generous layer of hot sauce

onto his omelet. "Have the Wilsons said anything to any of you about this whole Test thing?"

They all shook their heads. "Not so much as a word," said Hermes.

"So we're no closer than we were before to figuring out exactly what they're looking for."

Hermes grabbed a menu on his way to the juice maker behind the bar. "I think that might be the point, Z," he said. As he walked past where Zeus sat, he slapped the menu down on the counter top, blowing the little pile of cockroach ashes onto the omelet, and kept walking.

Athena wrinkled her nose. "Was that a roach?" she asked.

Zeus sighed and pushed the plate away. "And not the good kind."

She took the plate and dropped it into a bus tray. "I'll have Ares make you another one." She disappeared back into the kitchen.

"So what did you do with Hera?" asked Sarah.

"She is still frozen in the doll display box Angie made for her," said Zeus. "She occupies a place of honor on the knick-knack shelf in the lobby."

"She looks really nice up there," said Angie.

"I figure I'll leave her there for a few years, then bind her with an oath and assign her to housekeeping. You know, running the laundry, cleaning the guest rooms in the Hotel."

"Will an oath really do any better than it did with Hephaestus to keep her from causing more trouble?" asked Dyo.

"It should, at least until she finds her own loophole," said Zeus. "I intend to make the next one a little harder to break.

"What about Hephaestus?" asked Sarah.

Zeus chuckled. "We have him, along with the Satyrs, oath-bound and wrapped up with the chains he was going to use on us. They are all down in the workshop, repairing Dümass. After they're finished with that, I've assigned them to make a couple thousand of those little wind-up plastic toys that you send scurrying around on tables to entertain an infant. I want to put a treasure chest in the restaurant for all the kids who eat their spinach."

"OK, that should keep them busy for a while," said Dyo. "But if oaths work, why the chains?"

"Just to piss him off," said Hermes.

"That, plus that guy is really good at finding loopholes," said Zeus. "But yeah, mostly to piss him off."

"What I don't understand," said Sarah "is why you guys keep doing this. Why do you keep working in the hotel? You should not have to tend bar and wait tables. I mean, you're Gods. I get it that you have to stay in contact with the hotel, since it's the source of your power. But you could turn this place into some kind of palace and do anything you want."

"For one thing," said Hermes, pulling the juicer out from under the counter, "the Wilsons seem to enjoy the Delphi. And based on what we have recently learned, anything the Wilsons enjoy needs to be pretty high on our list of priorities."

"That's right," said Aphrodite. "We never did find a trace of Todd. Those people are scary!"

"But Mr. Wilson is kind of cute," said Dyo. "In a creepy old teacher way."

"I'm getting tired of saying it," said Sarah, " but ew. Ew, ew, ew. Look, I've been wondering why the Amulet never showed up as the source of your power in all the stories. It seems like that would be some important information."

"Because we never told anyone outside of the immediate family about it," said Zeus, shooting a withering look at Hermes. "Word tends to spread about things like that, and eventually your enemies learn your weak spot." He snapped his fingers and the orange in Hermes' hand exploded.

"Sarah and Angie are family now, Z," said Hermes, shaking bits of orange off his hands and wiping his face with a bar towel. "Angie even carries the Sword of Perseus."

"Larry," said Angie.

"Besides," said Athena setting a fresh plate of eggs in front of Zeus, "most of our most serious enemies have always been family."

"That's true enough," said Zeus. He took the lid off the bottle, and a searing jet of hot sauce blasted the eggs right off his plate.

"Seriously Hermes?" said Athena, picking bits of egg and hot sauce out of her hair. "What are you guys, ten years old?"

"Going on eleven," said Hermes.

"Never mind," said Zeus, pushing the plate away. "I wasn't that hungry anyway."

"So Sarah, are you going to send Angie back to school?" asked Dyo. "Should a young Goddess carry a lunch box and take spelling tests?"

"I want to go back to school," said Angie. "I'm going to wait until we're doing science, then I'm going to turn Lindsay Martin into a toad. Then this big ugly bird can eat her..."

"No," said Hermes, "There will be no turning mortals into toads."

"Besides, you would have to knock her unconscious first," said Dyo. "Even without the toad thing, that will probably upset your teacher and get you at least a time-out."

"Yes, you'd better just stick with doing the regular school stuff," said Aphrodite. "Besides, I understand there are boys there. And if there are boys, some of them are bound to be cute. I'll be happy to give you a few tips…"

"No, please," said Sarah. "No tips. At least not until she's, I don't know, say, thirty."

"Oh, I wouldn't dream of teaching her anything inappropriate," said Aphrodite, adjusting the drape of her tablecloth to show more leg. She gave Angie a wink and a knowing smile. "You can trust me."

"Another reason for staying here and running the hotel," said Athena, "is that by doing it we learn and understand more about the human world every day. And for all we know, that might be part of the Test."

"Maybe the real Test is for us to discover… what the real Test is," said Hermes.

"Whoa there, Plato, you're blowing my mind," said Zeus. He raised his hand and fired a bolt of lightning at the bottle of Amaretto on the shelf over Hermes' head. The bottle exploded, showering Hermes with sticky, almond-scented liqueur. "But you may be right, we just don't know. Our very existence may depend on it."

"OK, now that was a real nice shot," said Hermes, wiping Amaretto from his eyes. "You're getting some major zip back in your zap."

"Yes, and getting zip back in your whatever really moves us toward discovering our higher purpose and passing the Test," said Athena. "Z, I believe this thing about you being half human might be a key to the puzzle."

"I'm not really sure what to think about that," said Zeus.

"I've been thinking a lot about it," said Athena, "We always assumed that demigods were more than human and less than Gods. But look at Angie. We know that she's at least half human, and she's demonstrated more Power than any of us. We don't know how much more she may have tucked away in there."

"... While I'm still stuck with being a glorified bug zapper," said Zeus.

"Don't be so hard on yourself, Z," said Hermes. "You're an awesome bug zapper."

"Enough," said Athena, stepping between Zeus' raised hand and Hermes. "OK, so your Power is coming back more slowly. But you were the one God who defeated the Titans and wore the Amulet. You ruled Olympus for thousands of years. What if your human half is what made you the most powerful God of all?"

"It may be one of the reasons Cronus was never too crazy about me."

The door opened and the Wilsons came in from the street. Bill Wilson mopped his forehead with a handkerchief and stuffed it back into his pocket. "Man it's a scorcher out there," he said. He caught sight of Aphrodite and Dyo, and his face lit up. "Good morning, ladies."

Karen Wilson rolled her eyes, then scanned the room. "Isn't Carl working this morning?" she asked.

"He's in the kitchen helping Ares prep for lunch," said Hermes. "Have a seat, folks. The mimosas will be ready in just about two minutes."

Athena smiled at them. "Do you need a couple of menus?"

"No dear, we'll just have the usual," said Karen Wilson, smiling sweetly.

"Oatmeal, English Muffins and mimosas, coming up," said Athena, heading to the kitchen.

Sarah got up and crossed over to the Wilsons' table by the window. "Mrs. Wilson, I'm Sarah Cashen. I had you for Latin," she said. "And Mr. Wilson, I was in your Social Studies class."

"Of course we remember you, dear," said Karen Wilson.

"Oh yes, we certainly do," said Mr. Wilson. "You're Smoking Hot Sarah."

Hermes brought two mimosas to the table. "Really, even in high school?"

Sarah elbowed him hard in the ribs. "Anyway, I just wanted to thank you for the other day, for sparing everyone. Angie is my daughter, and these people are our friends. I never had any idea who you really were."

"You said it yourself," said Bill Wilson. "We were your high school teachers."

Angie came over, glared at the Wilsons, and took Sarah's hand. "Mom, we should go," she said.

"Your little girl is just adorable," said Karen Wilson. She gave Angie a sweet grin. "She looks just like you."

"Thank you," said Sarah. "Anyway, I just wanted to say that I really appreciate you not... harming her. For not harming any of them."

Karen Wilson's smile faded slightly, and a hint of green flashed in her eye. "Oh, you're more than welcome Dear," she said, and reached out to pat Angie's head. "I certainly hope that we will not find it necessary to do so in the future."

"I promise you," said Angie her own eyes flashing green, "if you do, it won't be as easy as you think."

335

Nine

That was interesting.

Definitely.

We should have done it.

Probably.

But they may not have deserved it.

Possibly.

They may get better.

Conceivably.

Or worse.

Undoubtedly.

But we will accomplish our task.

Theoretically.

Another mimosa?

Absolutely.

Appendix

If you are not a nerd, a geek, or pretty much any high school kid, you may be not totally familiar with the traditional Greek Gods. Here are a few facts about the major ones who are mentioned in this book. As I said in the preface, since I'm writing most of this from memory, or just plain making stuff up, you should probably not use this to resolve any beer-stoked bets.

Aphrodite is the Goddess of love, beauty, and desire. According to the myths, she was born from some "foam" floating around in the sea that may have been the result of a little bit of heavenly hanky-panky. At least that's the story she liked to tell, and for obvious reasons, nobody else has ever really wanted to talk about it.

Aphrodite's appetite for beautiful things and physical pleasure of almost any kind is unrivaled among the Olympian Gods. Her focus is mostly on men, but she does not like to discriminate or limit her options in any way. She is the wife of Hephaestus, the God of the forge, a fact that never really slowed down her adventurous nature very much.

The Romans called her Venus, which caused a lot of trouble when it came to keeping her credit cards straight.

Apollo is the son of Zeus and a fairly low-key Goddess named Leto, which has always been kind of a sore spot with Hera – who, as you'll see, has a lot of sore spots. Apollo is the God of healing, truth, light, and music.

Like his twin sister Artemis, he's good with a bow and arrow. He has a special bow that only he can draw, and his silver arrows can penetrate almost anything. The ancients believed that the sun was Apollo driving a flaming chariot across the sky, until they found out that the whole thing was done with mirrors.

As the God of music, Apollo is a fine musician, which means that he is always broke and hoping that somebody will buy him a beer.

Ares is the God of war. He is not necessarily the sharpest tool in the shed, but he's pretty good with any weapon. He once had a fling with Aphrodite, which sets him apart from hardly anybody.

He's the son of Zeus and Hera, who have never been real fond of him. In fact, since he is basically a bloodthirsty savage, nobody has ever been especially crazy about having him around.

When Ares and the other Gods woke up in twenty-first century Indiana, Ares immediately found out about television, and with it reality shows – especially one featuring a celebrity chef with a borderline-psychopathic personality.

After a little experimentation, Ares discovered that, in addition to creating absolute mayhem in the kitchen, he could whip up a very serviceable souvlaki, and a new culinary master was born.

Artemis is the Goddess of the moon, the natural environment, chastity, virginity, and, in an odd assignment for the Goddess of virginity, childbirth. Given all that baggage, she does not turn out to be nearly as judgmental – or as mixed up – as you might think.

She is also the Goddess of the hunt and nervous deer, she's a great shot with her golden bow, and she packs some seriously cool golden arrows.

In ancient times, Artemis had a retinue of twenty Cloud Nymphs to hang out with. They never showed up for this book – maybe next time.

Athena is the Goddess of wisdom, so if she had gone through the whole growing up and going to school thing, she probably would have got her pigtails pulled a lot. Nobody likes a smartass.

According to legend, though, Athena didn't grow up – she sprang full grown, wearing her armor, from the forehead of Zeus. Zeus always claimed that he just banged his head on a Celestial Cupboard Door, and that Athena was born the "regular way," but since nobody has ever had any idea what the "regular way" might be for Gods to be born, the legends have persisted.

Like Artemis, Athena is a virgin. In addition to being the wisest of all, she is better in a fight than most men, wielding spear, sword, and bow with equal prowess. This, considering how shallow and insecure most men are, may have a lot to do with why she is a virgin.

She is also the Patron Goddess of Athens, which is really a pretty lucky coincidence, given the name of the city and all.

Cronus is the ruler of the Titans, who were in charge of the world before the Olympian Gods came along. He got a memo that one of his offspring was going to overthrow him, so naturally he chose to swallow all his children as soon as they were born. He ate Poseidon, Hades, Hera, and two other of his babies, Hestia and Demeter, who never made it into this book for some reason.

Cronus' wife, Rhea, was not necessarily convinced that this baby-scarfing thing was the best way to go, so she gave Cronus a rock to swallow instead of her youngest son, Zeus. Since Cronus had washed down all those kids with gallons of ouzo, she got away with it.

After Zeus grew up, he released his brothers and sisters, who had grown to adulthood in Cronus' stomach. You don't want to know how he released them – just bear in mind that ouzo kind of sneaks up on you, and it doesn't get along too well with much of anything you eat.

While Hera and the rest cleaned themselves up and got some therapy, Zeus put together an army of Harpies, Cyclopes and Hecatoncheires, then overthrew Cronus and the other Titans, imprisoning them in Tartarus for all eternity.

Hades is the brother of Zeus, and Lord of the Underworld. This is an ancient use of the word, "underworld," meaning that Hades rules over the dead, not New Jersey.

He is also the God of wealth and capital gains. Never known for being real sociable, twenty-first century Hades chose not to hang out with the rest of the Gods in the Delphi. Instead, he opened a funeral home just outside of Olympus.

While his brother Zeus got lightning bolts and his other brother Poseidon got a trident, Hades got the Helm of Darkness, which either makes the wearer invisible or lets him catch a nice nap on a bright subway car.

Hades is not very involved with anything that goes on in this story, so you might as well not worry too much about him until the next book comes along.

Hermes is the God of thieves, literature, poetry, sports, practical jokes, standup comedy, and all forms of commerce. Since he is the prankster of the Gods, it's handy that he's also a good runner.

He is the son of Zeus and a mountain Nymph named Maia, which makes Hera his (as usual) pissed-off stepmother.

In the old days Hermes wore wings on his helmet and sandals, in a sort of general branding effort. He has always served as the messenger of the Gods, especially Zeus, which was a key assignment back in the days before telecommunication, and is still a pretty important job any time Comcast is involved.

Hermes invented the idea of music, along with the "lyre," which is a musical instrument – as opposed to the "liar," which is a politician.

Hera is the wife of Zeus. As a daughter of Cronus, she is also his sister, a situation which is not all that unusual on Mount Olympus or in large parts of Alabama. She is the Goddess of marriage and childbirth. Judging from most of the ancient stories, she is also unofficially the Goddess of PMS.

Hera is known for leading or inspiring revolts against Zeus, for watching over the home and hearth, and for being nasty to just about everyone.

Hephaestus is the God of the forge, the son of Hera and, according to Hera, possibly a turkey baster. He is a master craftsman and has always been the workman of the Gods, making everything from weapons and armor to celestial plumbing. He has a lame leg and walks with a cane, thanks to a little tiff in which Zeus tossed him off of Mount Olympus and he fell on his keys.

Hephaestus is married to Aphrodite, which is strange, considering that he is also the God of back-hair, sweaty tank tops, and being ugly. The fact is, he "won" Aphrodite's hand by making Hera a trick throne, chaining her to it, then demanding Aphrodite as ransom. Zeus, anxious to avoid spending eternity listening to Hera gripe about being chained to a throne, agreed.

Poseidon is the brother of Zeus, God of the sea, and protector of all waters. His weapon is the trident, a huge fork that is obviously handy for skewering enemies and at cocktail parties.

Instead of living in the Delphi Hotel with the rest of the Gods, he decided to open a surfboard store in nearby Sparta and live in an apartment over the workshop. Since anybody (other than, apparently, Poseidon) could predict how well a surfboard store would do in Indiana, it's not surprising that Poseidon also got a job as the Olympus High School swim coach.

Zeus is the God of the sky, ruler of the Olympian Gods, and a fairly crafty old dude. In ancient times, he had a habit of changing himself into various animals in order to seduce mortal women – although why this kind of thing would have even the slightest chance of working is a mystery to pretty much everyone.

His weapon is the thunderbolt, and in his prime he could pick off a Lernaean Hydra from more than 20,000 cubits. Or whatever.

Zeus' squabbles with his wife, Hera, have always been the stuff of legend. But when you think about it, legend is really what this is all about.

About The Author

Mike Ball is an award-winning humorist and author of the *What I've Learned... So Far* series of books, who lives and writes on the shores of Whitmore Lake, Michigan. This is near Ann Arbor, home of the University of Michigan, one of the world's most fertile breeding grounds for aging hippies, folk singers, and Budweiser-soaked football fans.

Mike happens to be one of those folk singers, and the founder of Lost Voices, a Michigan-based non-profit group that puts together therapeutic roots music writing and performing programs for incarcerated and at-risk youth. As the front man of the band Dr. Mike & The Sea Monkeys, he brings his literary world to musical life with such crowd pleasers as "Carlson the Pissed Off Angel," "At Least I've Got Most of My Hair," and "The Colonscopy Song."

Mike has spent most of his adult life writing books, columns, ads, brochures, slogans, songs, menus, and anything else that needed writing, including a eulogy for a dog. During the Internet

Boom of the 1990s he wrote a monthly column for a national information technology-oriented human resources magazine (now there's a combination that just screams humor!) called *Itrecruitermag*. These pieces covered such topics as "What to Do When You Run Into Your Boss at the Career Fair" and "So, You've Been Downsized – Sucks to Be You."

In 2003 Mike won the Erma Bombeck Award, and he was a finalist for the 2011 Robert Benchley Award. For years his weekly column, *What I've Learned... So Far* was internationally syndicated, with readers in eleven countries - that we know of.

Mike also spent some time as a competitive pairs water skier. He and various partners won awards all around the United States, including the 1997 Florida State Show Ski Championship at Cypress Gardens, the 2000 Indoor World Championship, the 2002 Michigan State Expert Division Championship, and the 2002 Division II National Championship. The good-looking member of the pair shown here is the amazing Megan Atkins.

Other Books by Mike Ball:

What I've Learned... So Far Part I
Bikes, Docks & Slush Nuggets

What I've Learned... So Far Part II
Angels, Chimps, & Tater Mitts

What I've Learned... So Far Part III
Banjos, Boats, & Butt Dialing

And keep your eyes peeled for more stories from
Olympus, Indiana

Connect with Mike Ball
learnedsofar.com
Twitter: @tagmike
Facebook.com/MikeBallAuthor

www.ingramcontent.com/pod-product-compliance
Lightning Source LLC
Chambersburg PA
CBHW031426240626
47154CB00001B/224